PRAISE FOR
THE TEDDY LONDON
SUPERNATURAL MYSTERIES

"A great mix of elements . . . a splashy spectacular book with a near-apocalyptic climax!"

—*Locus*

"An expert blend of the hard-boiled detective tale and supernatural horror story . . . Detective Teddy London is bad news for the things that are not there. Robert Morgan is *very good* news for mystery lovers."

—Stefan Dziemianowicz, editor,
Famous Fantastic Mysteries

"In the Teddy London adventures, Robert Morgan sure-handedly combines elements of Hard-boiled Detective with those of Dark Fantasy, and the results are an exciting, entertaining hybrid that should be welcomed by fans of both genres."

—Wayne D. Dundee,
author of ***The Brutal Ballet***

THE THINGS THAT ARE NOT THERE . . . Introduces Teddy London, P.I., on the trail of unearthly winged creatures who stalk a terrified young woman.

SOME THINGS NEVER DIE . . . Teddy London's second supernatural case takes him into the ultimate criminal underground—of vampires.

THE THING THAT DARKNESS HIDES . . . Monsters and vampires are child's play compared to Teddy London's newest foe—the Prince of Darkness.

ALL THINGS UNDER THE MOON

ROBERT MORGAN

BERKLEY PRIME CRIME, NEW YORK

Parts of chapters 28, 29, and 30 appeared under the title
"On All the Snow Around" in greatly altered form in the magazine
Over My Dead Body, copyright © 1993 by C.J. Henderson.

ALL THINGS UNDER THE MOON

A Berkley Prime Crime Book / published by arrangement with
the author

PRINTING HISTORY
Berkley Prime Crime edition / July 1994

ISBN: 0-425-14302-3

Berkley Prime Crime Books are published by
The Berkley Publishing Group,
200 Madison Avenue, New York, NY 10016.
The name BERKLEY PRIME CRIME and the BERKLEY PRIME CRIME
design are trademarks of Berkley Publishing Corporation.

PRINTED IN THE UNITED STATES OF AMERICA

10 9 8 7 6 5 4 3 2 1

There are those to whom we are bound by blood—parents, brothers, sisters, aunts, grandfathers, nephews, cousins . . . you get the idea.

And there are those friendships we make in the backyard and the schoolyard, in boys' clubs and workplaces and church, at camp and so on—the ones that will last forever . . . the people we never write to or call . . . forgotten over the years like favorite songs and toys.

And then there are those special people . . . those rare few who—although they are culled from the above—are the most important to us of all. Dear friends, lovers who become spouses, tightest of buddies . . . the people we count on when the chips are down, our backs are to the wall . . . the protectors whom we protect, and vice versa.

And—if you are lucky—one of those will be that soul mate, that blood brother, that person who . . . you don't know how . . . is just simply your other self, the person you were fated to meet who was destined to be either your best friend or your worst enemy.

This book is dedicated to mine—

Wayne R. Hawkes

No back at mine do I trust better.

"I had most need of blessing, and 'Amen' stuck in my throat."

—Macbeth, *Macbeth*
William Shakespeare

"There can be no stable and balanced development of the mind, apart from the assumption of responsibility."
—John Dewey

"He [criminal man] is the result of man's misunderstanding of his own potentialities—as if a child should see his face in a distorted mirror and assume he has changed into a monster."

—Colin Wilson

ALL THINGS UNDER THE MOON

PROLOGUE

The snow had been falling all night in the fashion people love best—softly, quietly, without either wind or bitter cold to remind any witnesses of its true nature. Most of the children in the Polish village of Srem had been allowed to stay up well past their normal bedtimes to watch it drifting down. For the children of Srem, peering out of candlelit windows at the steadily packing flakes signified all manner of great things.

The first snow of the season was always the happiest. It meant the morning would bring a break from chores—for what parent could ask for wood to be brought in when there were snow people to be rolled? What mother could insist on eggs being gathered, or chickens fed, when there were angels to be created and icicles to be broken? What father could not remember his own first perfect snowfall and then still demand that hay be brought down from the lofts for cows when there were tunnels to be dug and frozen war to be waged?

No, the town elders knew the inevitable when they saw it and like good parents everywhere, had memory enough left to remind them of the times when children simply had to be allowed to be children—wild and reckless and happy to be alive. Throughout the town, the adults puttered through the night's duties quietly, allowing their offspring the simple pleasures of both watching the falling snow and dreaming of the morning to come.

Even in the home of Peter Warhelski, the mayor of Srem, it was the same. Only a few hours earlier, he and his wife Marianna and their four children had returned from Poznan, a city to the north. Having had the duty of delivering certain tax agreements to officials waiting there to courier all the district's agreements back to Warsaw, the mayor had decided to combine business with pleasure, taking his family with him so they might tour the beautiful old city.

Capital of Poland through both the tenth and eleventh centuries, Poznan was filled with fine parks and elegant Renaissance buildings, all of it surrounded by the baroque and classical palaces of the ancient city's former patricians. During their three days there, the leading family of Srem had managed to view the treasures of both Kornik Castle and the Rogalin Palace. The children had walked through mirrored halls, held swords and maces once wielded by the long-since vanquished Teutonic knights, and run their hands over the lacquered and polished covers of books five hundred years old.

And yet, as Marianna watched her children peering through the beveled glass of their home's front window, she knew that everything they had seen was already forgotten. The buildings and weapons, the art and gardens and history of a thousand years—she was certain that not a scrap of it was holding in their brains when compared to the unbroken carpet of white building itself silently across the roofs and streets and yards of their town.

"Peter," she said in quiet voice. As her husband turned, she directed his attention with a movement of her head over toward the window where their two sons and two daughters remained captivated by the falling white. The woman watched her husband's face change abruptly, all thoughts of tax gathering and street repairs put aside instantly as he gazed at his children. Knowing he needed such a break from the pressures of his civil duties, Marianna headed for the kitchen to light the stove. Hot milk for the children, spiced tea for her and her Peter—that would make a perfect end for their day.

Peter Warhelski did not even notice his wife's departure. For him the sight at the window was an arresting moment—a picture in time the like of which every parent prays they will not miss when it happens. The mayor of Srem had come to realize long ago that there was nothing more important to him in the world than his family. Like any loving husband and father, he could not help himself . . . whenever there was a story of a lost child, or a murder of a woman alone, he could only think of his dear Marianna, or of his beautiful children, framed now in the window before him.

If he were ever to lose them, he thought, any of them . . . and then, no more words could come to his mind. Just the slightest imagining of life without his wife or any of his children, from Anna the oldest, down to Max the toddler, left him without words, without speech or sound or the ability to think. The thought left him with a black hole in his mind, one he could not fill with anything but dread and a sense of lost hope and faith—no matter how hard he tried.

But, he told himself, why did he plague his mind with such notions? He did not have to prove he was a good father to himself by worrying over such dark broodings every time he thought about those closest to him. Looking again at his four beloved children staring out at the still falling snow, he stood lost in the moment, enjoying the simple sight of them framed by the clear light of the full moon.

In fact, so caught up in the simple beauty of the scene, he found that he had no idea of how long he had been standing there when his attention was distracted by a noise at the front door of their home. He crossed the room to the mansion's foyer, half looking back at his children, half trying to identify the person outside his door by the sound of the knock.

Not a knock, he thought, more a banging—impatient. Rude, really.

It came again, louder this time . . . more forceful—demanding. Peter Warhelski was surprised—almost angered. Who came banging on the mayor's door at such an hour, with such force and tone? It was not the sound of emergency—there was no entreating ring to it. As his hand touched the door, the rapping came again, so loud and with such violence that for the first time in his life Peter Warhelski was suddenly hesitant to open his own door to whoever was on the other side.

"Who is there?" he called.

The pounding stopped. As the mayor wondered what he should do next, he realized his children had all turned from the window to watch him. As the silence continued, Peter called out through the door again,

"I said, who is there?"

And then, a low growling voice, like that of a man barking his words, came back through the door, saying,

"I am loneliness."

The words shook the mayor, their strangeness making him tremble. What did the speaker mean? Why did he growl like a wounded hound? Why had he pounded on the door? What did he want? Choosing the safest question of those in his head, Peter called out,

"What do you want?"

"To be not lonely."

By now Marianna had come out of the kitchen. She had heard the pounding but not her husband's conversation. She could tell, however, from the poses of her children and their father that something most disturbing had occurred. Before she could act, however, Peter asked,

"How can I help this?"

Silence was the mayor's only answer. He waited at the door, his hand still on its oversized handle, fingers trembling against it. He heard the nails on his hand clicking against its large metal ring and was embarrassed at his show of nerves, shocked that he could be frightened so easily by something he could not see. Pulling his courage together, he called out again,

"I said, how can I help this?"

Again no answer came to his question. As his children began to gather around their mother's skirts, he found the short exchange that had taken place through the thick wood of his door to be unnerving him to the point of panic. Somehow, a knowledge filled him that what he did next would be the most important thing he ever did in his life. Voices of conscience and practicality warred in his ear, trying to sway him to a course of action.

It wasn't like the old days, he told himself. It was 1910. There were all manner of crazy people in the world, anymore. And still, there was something so plaintive about the monstrous voice on the other side of the door . . . was there nothing he could do? Did he have to be afraid of anything he could not explain—of everything he did not understand?

But then, before he could act one way or the other, the tension building in the room focused itself on the mayor's youngest child. The baby of the family, not yet two, suddenly became aware of the mood in the air and grabbed his mother's leg all the more tightly, crying out in fear as he did. That was all Peter Warhelski needed to make up his mind. Frightened for the safety of his family, his hand left the door handle, traveling up to the massive bolting bar above it. With one swift motion he flipped its release chain, dropping it firmly into place. As he did, the howling voice barked again.

"Wrong choice."

And then, the door was struck its most powerful blow, one which shattered it down the middle. As the mayor watched in shock, the shining curve of iron-hard claws forced their way through the break line. Then, they pulled backwards, ripping the center planks of the door away, sending screws and bolts flying into the foyer. All the children started to scream at once as their mother forced them back toward the kitchen. Peter, spurred into action by the sight before him, raced into the next room. There he dragged his father's cavalry sword down from its place on the wall, returning to the foyer as quickly as he could.

And, when he returned, he found himself faced with a sight he could not believe. All of the structure of his door ripped aside, he found the remaining hole acting as a frame for the creature standing inside it. The thing towered nearly seven feet in the air, standing balanced on backward-bent hocks. Long gray and black hair hung from every inch of its canine body. As it took a step forward, the frozen air in its lungs bellowed forth, cold spittle hitting Peter's face.

"Man," it barked cruelly—its voice thick with hate. "Man with nothing but death on his mind. Man come to kill. The never changing attitudes of man . . . man . . . man . . ."

The mayor looked into the large yellow and orange eyes of the thing before him, the hate within them pinning him to the floor. He looked at the power in its flexing arms and thick neck, saw the horrible weight of its gigantic bones. Deep within him, Peter Warhelski knew there was no stopping the monster before him, no way to reason with it, no way to make up for whatever mistake he had made in dealing with it. Despite what he knew to be inevitable, however, he pleaded,

"I, I, I don't, don't want to kill-kill-kill . . . please. Please. I just . . . my family . . . take me . . . kill me but the children oh please oh please oh-oh-oh-ohhhh . . . not my wife, not the children . . . please . . ."

"Too late. Cast me out—now in I come. Kill me if you can, *man*."

Something more than fear opened Peter's sweating hand, releasing his father's sword, dropping it to the floor. As he stood, transfixed by the sight of the beast before him, suddenly the thing moved one shaggy leg forward, stepping closer to the mayor. Then, bending down, it scooped up the fallen sword between two of its heavy claws and returned it to Peter's hand. Guiding the tip of the blade up its chest, the creature moved forward against the point, pinning the sword directly in front of its heart.

One large drop of blood squeezed its way free through flesh; past hair and metal, oozing its way into the sluice cut of the sword. As the long dark stain spread itself thinly down the blade, the monster spoke again.

"Your one chance, man. Do it. Be the one who does it. Kill me, man. Kill me or be killed and be the one who lets your family die and a thousand more until the end of time. I give you the chance—kill me. Kill me! *Kill me! KILL ME!*"

Terrified, blind with fear and the terrible knowledge that he was about to die, Peter Warhelski threw himself onto the hilt of his father's sword. Putting all of his hundred and fifty-nine pounds into the move, he rammed the weapon into the creature's chest with a force that drove it out through the monster's back as well. Then, staggering away from the nightmare before him, he closed his eyes, calling out to the heavens,

"What have I done, oh, Lord? What have I done?"

"Nothing," came his answer in a growl. As Peter opened his eyes, he watched as the beast pulled the sword back out of his body. Resigned to his fate, Peter did nothing save to move his hands helplessly back and forth as the creature twisted the weapon into an awkward knot, the slices on its hands healing as quickly as they were created. Nor did Peter Warhelski do anything but mouth a trembling prayer as the dark thing stalked closer and sunk its claws into his chest, exploding him open with one simple pull as if popping a balloon.

By this time several neighbors had noticed the commotion and headed for the mayor's house to see what was the matter. They found the shattered front door with their chief official's body lying just beyond it. Moving in bravely, they arrived at the smashed kitchen door just in time to see the same monster Peter had. Two of the children were already dead, as was their mother. The third hung in the beast's grip. As the horrified neighbors watched, the thing plucked free the child's eyes like grapes and plopped them into its maw, barking out its cruel laugh as it swallowed them down.

Then it hurled the lifeless body in its paw at the fear-filled spectators, turned, and fled. Throwing itself at the kitchen's only window, it knocked the entire framework out of place, taking sections of the wall with it as it passed through to the outside. And before any could halt its retreat, the terror disappeared into the night, leaving behind only its monstrous paw prints in the fine carpet of snow.

As the shaken neighbors staggered into the charnel pit their mayor's kitchen had become, they all jumped in fear as two screams suddenly split the air at the same moment—one last mournful howl of the fleeing beast, and the lonely, tear-filled cries of the youngest Warhelski.

1

"Just one more to go."

The balding man smiled as he got his hands under the carton in front of him. Lifting it up and then balancing it against his chest, he carried the cardboard box to the back of the small yellow rental truck and then handed it down to the street, announcing happily,

"Hey, send up a cheer. This is the last one."

Standing on the sidewalk, surrounded by tape-sealed boxes, pieces of furniture, and all the other bags and bundles indicative of someone changing residences, the balding man's two helpers responded with whoops and cheers until one of them, a tall, angular man with strong shoulders and dark brown hair reminded his two friends,

"Right, gang—it's the last thing . . . *on the truck*. Now all we have to do is get everything inside."

"Do you know," asked a staggeringly large, heavyset black man, "that at some times you can be a most ungracious fellow, my little brother?"

"Yeah," answered the other. "I've heard tell."

"It is a true thing, this. I swear to you, my friend, sometimes I think you can not allow the simplest of joyous moments to occur without placing some gloomy seal or other upon them."

"Pa'sha," replied the group's obvious leader in friendly tones, "if anyone here thinks they're going to make the party tonight on time without all of us shaking a leg, they've got another thing coming."

"Work, work, work. You are a most terrible slave driver, Theodore London. Not a very correct attitude for a white man to have toward his poor, black brother."

"You and the horse you rode in on, buddy," replied London, hefting two of the heavier boxes, somehow managing to slide one onto each shoulder at the same time. "You kids want to play, I can't stop you. I'm too busy."

"Uuuwww," groaned the man on the truck. "Now I'm just positively burdened by all the guilt."

Knowing when to make a retreat, London headed up the molded concrete front stairway of his brownstone, moving the first of his fiancée's belongings into their home. As he disappeared through the front door, the balding man jumped down from the back of the truck, pulling a flask from his back pocket at the same time. Offering it to the large black man, he said,

"Here, Pa'sha, take the edge off. Know what I mean? Wink wink—nudge nudge."

"Ahhh, I do indeed, friend Morcey." Tilting the flask up, the larger man knocked back a rich three fingers of cognac, exclaiming when he was finished,

"My dear Paul, forgive my rude assumption, but I did not think you a man with such fine tastes. This is an exceedingly good and true ambrosia you have brought amongst us here today."

"Hey," answered Morcey, taking a short pull of his own from the flask, "what's a couple of bucks? I mean, if being a detective for the London Agency has taught me anything, it's that life's too short and money ain't worth it."

"You are a mean philosopher, my friend," answered Pa'sha, grabbing up a large, red, overstuffed chair. "Far ahead of your time."

"Yeah," agreed the balding man. "That's what they all tell me."

"Hey," called London, framed in the doorway at the top of the stairs, already returned from dropping his load on the second floor. "More work, less patting ourselves on the back. That's how we get done."

"Yes, Master London, sir," came Pa'sha's deeply rich island voice. "We leap to do your bidding, sir."

Moving up the stairs, the larger man made to hit his friend with the chair he was carrying, but the detective leapt up onto the stairway's balustraded railing, sliding easily down its concrete surface to the bottom. Pa'sha cursed his friend gleefully, disappearing into the brownstone. As London jumped down to the sidewalk, Morcey said to him,

"You're pretty perky today, boss."

"Hey, Paul, why not?" asked the detective, smiling. "Think about it, partner. One year ago today—*today*, mind you—the bunch of us survived the worst disaster this planet's ever seen. One . . . year . . . ago, remember?"

"Oh, yeah, sorta," answered the balding man, laughing in a

sarcastic tone. "Now that you mention it." Ignoring his friend's tone, London answered,

"You and I were just two regular guys, then. Now, we've both got great girls, we own the most successful investigations shop in town, we're rich, we've kicked vampire ass and touched the mantle of God. Not bad, huh?"

Before Morcey could answer, however, a feminine voice called from behind them,

"Men. Talk, talk, talk." The speaker was a woman in her early twenties—one with long legs, intelligent deep blue eyes, and a luxurious wealth of curly chestnut-colored hair. Walking with her was an older Oriental woman, shorter than her friend and somewhat slighter of figure. Both women were burdened with several bags apiece, all filled with cold drinks, sandwich fixings, and snacks gathered from the local neighborhood deli. Setting one of her bags down, the younger woman continued, saying,

"If there's ever any work to be done, these two sure aren't the ones to do it—right, Lai?"

"This," answered her companion without any evident trace of humor, "I am sad to admit, is most true."

"Oh, sweet bride of the night," said Morcey. "I'm cut to the quick. Dese dames is ridin' us, boss. I say we let them do everything themselves."

Before London could answer, though, Pa'sha's voice sounded from the top of the stairs. Wringing his hands together for comedy effect, he cried out in a mournful voice filled with mock pity,

"Is this not the saddest of pictures? I grieve for you, my little brother. Such disarray in your life. It shatters me to see you with so little control over your destiny."

Knowing his friends well enough to sense where they were headed, London picked up another container, this one an antique railroad worker's rail spike barrel filled with well-wrapped china and glassware, saying,

"Okay, kiddies, a joke's a joke, but really, if we're going to get all this stuff up off the street and have a chance to tear into that lunch I see, we're going to have to get a move on. Lisa, these are your belongings spread all over the sidewalk. What do you say? Shall we get them inside?"

"Ohhhhhh," she drawled, smiling as she teased the detective. "I guess so."

"Swell. Pa'sha, I think you and I can get the rest of this upstairs easily enough. What do you think?"

"As adverse to such arduous exercise as my poor, tired bones are, still I must admit that such a thing would . . . how can I say it . . ."

"Seems to pose no problem, maybe?"

"Perhaps."

"Perhaps, eh?"

"Yes. I am quite positive that we may be able to perhaps do this thing."

"Oh, well good," answered the detective sarcastically. "That being the case, Paul, why don't you get the truck back to the rental agency? Lisa, if you can get that lunch spread out by yourself, Pa'sha and I will do the grunt work while Lai stays down here to watch your stuff. Sound good, everybody?"

Despite the logic of London's plan, everyone still grumbled for a minute longer for the comedy effect but then finally bent to their tasks, as eager as the detective to be finished. Morcey shut down and locked the back of the truck and then assured the others it would take him no more than a half hour to return the truck and get back to the brownstone with his own car, which he had left in the rental agency's neighborhood. Driving away, he looked at his friends grouped on the sidewalk, reflecting on the changes London had mentioned that had occured in his life during the past year.

He had been a janitor before it had all started. Head of Custodial Services, as building management had put it, but a maintenance man none the less. Then fate had drawn him into a daylight nightmare, placing him at London's side during a time when only a tiny handful of people would be given the chance to stop an unspeakable evil from destroying all life throughout the universe. Morcey had jumped at the opportunity to join the detective. Since then the pair had become embroiled with like horrors twice more. Each confrontation had merely made the balding man happier, however—all of it delighting him by giving him a chance to make an actual difference in the world.

Taking Lai Wan's bundles from her so she could remain on the sidewalk, Pa'sha carried the lunch bags she had brought back upstairs along with a heavy braided rug he had swung up onto his shoulder. Despite his earlier protesting to the contrary, the large man actually relished the opportunity to get out of his home and stretch his under-used muscles for once.

Pa'sha Lowe spent most of his hours indoors. He was a weaponeer, an expert dealer in explosives, ammunition, and armaments. He had been at London's side during the fight a year earlier, also. The friendship that existed between the massive arms dealer and the detective went back many years. The two had been as brothers for so long that neither could now easily remember very well any time when such did not seem the case. There was no doubt in Pa'sha's mind that London would give his life for the weaponeer without a second thought. He was sure because he knew he would not hesitate to do the same if circumstances called for such to come to pass.

Ironically, watching Pa'sha ascend the front stairs, Lai Wan's thoughts centered on the relationship between the two men as well. The woman was a psychometrist, meaning she was gifted with the ability to read a person or thing's past through the merest laying on of hands. Although Pa'sha did not know it, the simple act of accepting the lunch bags from Lai Wan had been enough contact for her to skim his thoughts without even having tried to.

Her powers had come to her through an accident which took her life for a short while, then returned her to the world of the living again—forever changed. It was not something she asked for, but something to which she finally became accustomed. The accident gave her much, but took away an equal amount, leaving her a woman finished with life's distractions, intent only on studying the source of her abilities and discovering its meaning.

She had seen a great deal of that meaning since the day Pa'sha had first arranged for her to meet London. She remembered that in the beginning she had hesitated over working with the detective. In appearance far more the supernaturalist than he, she had wished to keep her distance, not wanting to become known as a sideshow attraction. The desperate need of London's situation had pulled her in, however, and when all was said and done, she was actually glad it had.

No one was happier about their relationship with the detective, though, than the woman laying out the lunch upstairs. Born Lisa Hutchinson, she had been the one to first approach London a year earlier, the one who had brought him the problem that set all the wheels in motion. One minute, he had been a man simply trying to make an ordinary living. The next, however, he had been the focal point in a millennium-old struggle between life and death, the rallying point for all the defenders fate could find to throw against that which would have destroyed our world and our galaxy, as well as the entire universe and all that might lie beyond it.

What thrilled Lisa, though—as it would anyone—was the fact

that he had done it all for her. He had taken on a responsibility most men could not have even imagined, but he had not done it for any of the reasons that most men might. As she unwrapped packages of cold cuts and cheese and sliced the poppy seed bagels on the counter before her, Lisa saw in her mind's eye again the man who had championed her—saw him transcend the laws of physical nature through the sheer force of his will—not for wealth or fame or adoration or any of the other normal lures of man, but out of love for her. He had challenged a god for her love and slain it, blackening the sky and rendering the earth barren in the process. It would have sucked away her soul and made her a killer of worlds, but her hero, her knight in shining armor, her lover and partner and friend and everything else they had become—he had saved her from it, and the rest of the world in the bargain as sort of an afterthought.

Make him sandwiches? she thought. Just the way he likes them ... American cheese, sliced sweet gherkins, and mayonnaise? Oh, yes—I'll make you sandwiches, Teddy London—and then I'll walk across hot coals to get your tea.

"Tea's ready?"

Lisa jumped, caught off guard by the detective's quiet entrance. She turned, seeing that he was carrying another pair of the boxes holding her books. She knew he had not snuck up on her on purpose. He just moved ... quietly.

"No," she answered him, shaking her head. "Tea isn't ready. I was just thinking about making some."

"Must have heard you thinking," he joked.

"You do that a lot, you know."

Setting the boxes down there in the kitchen, he grabbed a slice of cheese and folded it over, eating it in a series of small bites, asking her at the same time,

"It doesn't bother you, does it? I mean, after all, you do it to me."

"*I* do ..." Lisa began to protest. She was about to remind him how his brushes with the weird over the last year had left him a far more powerful person than he used to be ... finishing other people's sentences, knowing who was behind doors, what was in letters, et cetera. But then, she realized, he had wanted a cup of tea, and she had heard him through the air as he had unconsciously sensed her preparing to make it.

"I do," she admitted, adding, "*we* do."

"Yes," he agreed, smiling, telling her with the softness in his eyes how much he loved her as he watched her filling the red-lacquered kettle. "I guess we do."

Walking up behind Lisa, not surprising her at all that time, the detective took her in his arms and turned her around gently, staring down into her face, wondering again how a man who had done the things he had done in his life could have possibly been blessed with the love of a woman like her. Knowing his thoughts then, knowing them like she always did, Lisa felt her cheeks coloring and her breath coming faster, thrilled again that a man like Theodore London was hers body and soul.

Their arms wrapping around each other, their faces came together and they kissed for the first time that morning. It was the year anniversary of the day he should have died—horribly, monstrously, in any of a thousand different ways. The year anniversary of the day she should have died as well, that the world and all its peoples should have died. Memories of the hopeless moments from that time came back to them, pushing them into each other, tightening their fingers. The weight of her rememberance moved her against him, the fear of loss reminding them both of how few things actually have any real value.

His eyes closed, London kissed the woman in his arms again—harder. His arms held her in an iron lock, one that could never bruise, only protect. She held onto him just as fiercely, energy from her body flowing out of her and into him and then back again, the two of them trading the force of their love as easily as most couples shook hands.

Behind them, in the hall leading past the kitchen, Pa'sha noted the pair as he passed with another load, boxes packed with shoes, belts, and coats according to the Magic Marker–scrawled block letters on their lids. He made no move to disturb the two—no jokes or teasing comments. He loved his "little brother" far too much. Over the past year, the massive weaponeer had seen far too many bad times cross the detective's path. How, he thought, could he take any moment of happiness away from him?

"No, little brother," he whispered to himself. "Sad as it makes me to think it, I am sure something will come along all too soon enough and do it for me."

2

"Come in, come in," said the tall, bearded man in the doorway. Gently pushing his mixed-breed hound back with his foot, he added, "Hurry along before some of the lunatics running through the streets come crashing in with you."

"There certainly is a little ol' party going on out there tonight, isn't there?" asked the newcomer.

"I prefer the one in here, thank you."

The most recent addition to the indoor party was a man looking perhaps to be somewhere between forty-five and fifty. He was only of average height and perhaps a tiny bit overweight, dressed in a conservative but stylish creme-colored suit, wearing his warm soft white shirt open at the collar. Folding his wire-rimmed glasses and storing them in his inner jacket pocket, he handed the bearded man a cloth bag holding two bottles of well-aged scotch. He then turned away his host's hearty thanks, saying through a wide grin,

"Think nothing of it. Tell me about important things. Like, does my hair look all right?"

"It is impeccable as always, Mr. Barnes."

"You're too kind, Doctor."

"Yes, I know. It's a terrible failing of mine, but I'm trying to have it corrected."

Mr. Barnes was better known to his less formal friends as simply "Wally," and to those of the back door world of stolen property as the best fence in town. His specialties were art and antiques. Barnes maintained a fairly good relationship with the authorities by acting quite often as their go-between, recovering stolen pieces for insurance companies at a fraction of their value from thieves with no other recourse.

His host was Doctor Zachary Goward, a professor of both theology and philosophy, practicing his crafts at the city's famed Columbia University. He was another of the original few who had worked with London a year earlier to save the world. Now, on the anniversary of that meeting, many of the others who had dealt with the bizarre alongside the London Agency over the past year had gathered together to celebrate their successes ... as well as the simple joy of still being alive.

Of course, not everyone knew everyone else—not everyone invited had been present since that first meeting. Some, like Wally, had not learned about London's supernatural dealings until several months later when the Agency had run afoul of a conclave of vampires terrorizing the city's Chinatown. Still others had learned of the detective's hidden sideline only a few weeks previous when he had been hired to go to Hell to reclaim a bartered soul from Satan. The meeting that night, however, was not for any unearthly purpose.

"Doc," Wally began as the two proceeded back through Goward's apartment, "if you don't mind the asking, what the heck kind of dog is this fella here, anyway?"

"Selby," answered the professor, "who I'm sure no more minds the answer than I do the question, is a mutt. And before you ask, I will assure you that he does no tricks, is not a hunter, a tracker, nor much of a watchdog." As Goward spoke, Wally went down on one knee, cradling the old dog's muzzle in one hand while stroking its back with the other. As the grateful beast pressed its head against the fence's chest, the man asked,

"Then why do you keep him?"

"Why, for the reason all men do. Because he is my sanest companion and my oldest friend. Because he is amusing ... and brave and loyal—far more so than most people are capable— loyal with a singular faithfulness of character that, if I were to think on it too long, might break my heart." The older man's eyes growing gentle, his voice, softer than most people had ever heard it, finished his defense, adding simply,

"How could I not keep him, Mr. Barnes? He is my dog."

As Wally continued to stroke Goward's happy hound, the professor walked back toward the main rooms, glad to see Selby had made himself another friend. Pulling his pipe from the pocket of his sweater vest as he walked, he dug his lighter out of his trouser pocket at the same time. Then, as he primed the partially stuffed bowl with a steady series of strong puffs, the flame rising and dipping just inches from his eyes reminded him of why everyone had gathered that night.

On the same date, one year earlier, nearly two million people died in an epic firestorm, which had come to be known as the Conflagration. It had been started when London turned the tide, saving the planet's other six billion residents from the same fate. Which was why that night—throughout New York City—

millions of people had declared their own holidays on the anniversary of the monstrous holocaust—all making observation in their own way, according to their needs.

Some were celebrating animatedly—wildly—dancing in the clubs, in their yards, in the streets—throwing themselves into abandon in simple response to the sheer joy of having survived. Many others were mourning those lives lost, trying to understand why others were taken and they were spared. Many, of course, partied merely to be trendy, to be able to tell their friends and relatives around the country that, yes—certainly—*they* had been part of the choicest celebration of the year.

The majority, however, partied out of terror. They were the ones staggering in the streets, drunk or stoned, screaming and crying, breaking windows, starting fights. As if living a scene from the Bible, they rent their clothes, tore their hair, and reveled themselves into stupors out of simple fear—the fear and guilt of having survived, of having to live on, of never getting an "easy" way out, like those burned to death a year earlier.

The television news teams had reported that hundreds of thousands of people were in the streets throughout the city, drinking and taking drugs openly, having sex and destroying property. Hundreds of blazes had been set in vulgar imitation of the year before, keeping the fire department and the police completely tied up. Those who braved the streets were met by literally thousands of partiers, many dressed in black, many decked out in chains and spikes and heavily studded leather. Many in tears.

A spectator looking for such things would have noted than an unusually high percentage of those in the streets were wearing skull masks—some ornate, some simple, many with just crudely painted faces. Three had come banging on Goward's door earlier, drunkenly demanding payment to keep them from torching his building and himself. Pa'sha had answered the door, shoving the deadly-looking barrel of his Auto-Mag under one of their noses, asking them if they might not be able to bother some other neighborhood. They had left very quietly.

What makes people do such things, wondered the professor as he shoved his lighter back into its usual place. Looking into his living room, just able to see the dining room beyond, he stared at those assembled, the handful that had stood up to the dark things he had seen over the last year. Releasing a cloud of heavily scented smoke into the air, he stopped next to the couch where Morcey and Lai Wan were sitting, lost within his own head for the moment. Noticing Goward's faraway look, the balding man suddenly asked him,

"Ya look pretty deep there, Doc. Whatcha thinkin' about?"

"Paul," answered the professor, "I was looking at everyone here and thinking about all the nonsense going on out there in the streets, and I suppose I was wondering . . . could these people here, could these be all there are—all that fate could find to bear the burden of protecting the rest of humanity from the unknown?"

"If you're judgin' by those nut jobs runnin' around outside," answered the ex-maintenance man, "ya better give up wonderin' who's gonna protect them from the monsters. That bunch needs someone just to protect them from themselves."

Smiling, Goward pulled his pipe from his mouth, saying, "All too true, my lad. Sadly, all too true."

Sitting across the living room on a different couch, which did not match the other in any way, London asked,

"Who was at the door, Doc?"

"Mr. Barnes." When the detective stared, waiting for an explanation as to where Wally was, Goward gave him all the answer he needed.

"Selby."

"I should have known," answered London, pushing himself more comfortably into the section of couch he was sharing with Lisa. She moved closer to him, leaning back; resting the side of her head against his chest.

"Ohhh, and why should you have known, Mr. London, sir?" asked Lisa in a teasing voice. The detective took a deep, clean whiff of the perfumed curls just below his chin and answered,

"Because Wally loves dogs . . . has a pack of his own out in Jersey, somewhere. Cocker spaniels."

"Wally?" asked the young woman, suspiciously.

"Yesssss, Wally," answered London.

" 'Buy low, sell high' . . . 'anything for a dollar' . . . 'a deal here, a job there' . . . that Wally?"

"Yessssss," hissed the detective, jabbing Lisa playfully in the side, catching her off guard and launching her into a laughing fit. "*That* Wally. Yes," he said, jabbing again, "*that* one."

Sliding down the couch, the young woman flipped around as best she could, attacking London back. The pair began practically rolling over each other, alternating between tickling each other and curling into balls for defense. As Lai Wan covered her mouth to hide one of her rare smiles, Morcey shouted across the room to Father Bain, sitting on the same couch as Lisa and London,

"Hey, Father—ya want me to get a bucket of water for those two?"

"No," came Pa'sha's voice from the next room. "I have a much better solution."

And, seconds later, the professor's home began to fill with music—specifically, the light moody jazz of the Rippingtons. Lisa grabbed London's wrist, shouting,

"There we go. At least someone around here knows how to party."

As the detective moved the coffee table out of the center of the room, Lisa added,

"I mean, every goofball in the city is running wild in the streets in skull masks and we're sitting around like we're on some political commentary show or something."

Goward's graduate student secretary, Joylyn Featherstone, stuck her head out of the kitchen, adding her own comments.

"Now there," she said as she pulled off the apron she had been wearing, "is the truth in a nutshell." Tossing it on the counter behind her, she said,

"I've had enough teatime chatter for a while. Get out here, music man. Dance me."

Pa'sha, striding into the large living room with a measured pace, pointed to his massive chest saying,

"A simple island boy such as myself, with a princess such as you. Surely there is some mistake here."

"Yeah, right, big man," answered Joylyn with a chuckle. "And you made it coming here without someone on your arm." As the two began to move to the music, falling in with Lisa and London, Joylyn told Pa'sha,

"I've been waiting to meet you and I'm not going to miss the opportunity—you're the first black ghost hunter I've seen since I started taking care of Dr. Goward's office. You—mister," said the young woman with emphasis as she spun herself around to the music,

"are not getting away."

"Indeed," answered Pa'sha, smiling as he looked down at his shorter, much more compact dance partner, "I was not trying to."

Taking Joylyn's place in the kitchen, Wally retrieved the apron she had thrown behind, asking the two women still there,

"Y'all tell me what she was doing and Selby and me will see to it that it gets done."

Lorna Lattuca, another college student who had gotten involved with the London Agency almost by accident, and Cat, a free-lance surveillance expert who did more than half her work for either Pa'sha or his friends, both turned to Wally at the same time. Cat told him,

"Before Lorna starts to thank you for being so noble, I'll just say that most everything is already done, and if you're anything like I've heard, Mr. Barnes . . . isn't it?"

"Why, yes, Wallace Daniel Barnes . . . at your service. Tell me you like my hair and you can call me Wally."

"It's the hair of a god . . . now look—"

"Why thank you, honey," answered the fence, giving Cat a smile that showed teeth. Filching a spare rib from a platter on the counter, he passed it down to Selby, finishing,

"It's ever so kind of you. Now you just tell ol' W. D. what I can do to give you lovely ladies a break and I'd be ever so happy to oblige."

"We've got it all under control," answered Cat testily. Blowing a lock of hair out of her face, the surveillance woman said,

"We don't need any help."

"Now, now," answered Wally. Picking up a large spoon, he used it to dip a taste up out of a pot of chili simmering on the stove. "This isn't a gift one buys for one's self . . . this is a gift someone buys for you." Looking down to the floor, the fence asked,

"Those ribs ready, boy?" When Selby growled up in appreciation, Wally said,

"Cat, honey, Selby says the ribs are ready to go. Now why don't you aim them in the right direction and take them out to the rest of the party, and take this sweet child along with you." Reaching above the stove for the paprika, the fence had already busied himself stirring the chili as he called over his shoulder,

"Y'all go on and enjoy yourselves. I'll finish this up."

Cat made to protest once more, but Lorna took her arm and guided her hand to the platter of ribs. Then, grabbing up a large bowl of cold pasta salad out of the refrigerator, the younger woman said,

"He's charming and he wants to help. Don't fight it when a man wants to help. It's like winning the lottery . . . it's a wonderful thing when it happens, and taking the money doesn't obligate you to a thing."

"Yeah," answered Cat, still sour over not being able to do

things her way. "And like the lottery it probably only happens once in your lifetime, too."

When she was finally away from the stove and out in the party, however, the short woman abandoned her platter and joined the other dancers, feeling better almost immediately. She had been using the kitchen as a hiding place, not wanting to see the rest of the "freaks," as she had been thinking of those she would meet that night. Cat had had a hard time adjusting to normal life after her brush with the supernatural. Her roommate had even moved out on her, tired of the strawberry blonde's moodiness, of her inability to enjoy simple things anymore once she had seen the true darkness in the night sky. Cat had been afraid for a long time that the normal world held nothing for her anymore—that the only place she could come alive again would be in the face of the unknown.

She was a woman who was used to danger. Working for Pa-'sha had moved her in and out from one tense situation to another over the years. But most people's idea of danger—plain old, everyday ordinary danger, as she called it now—was no longer hers. Fighting alongside the others four stories underground—firing round after round until both her arms ached, hurling fire bombs at vampires, watching their skin burn and finding herself praying it would burn fast enough to kill them—had left her empty of simple terrors like the fear of death. What worried her now was not death, but whatever came after it.

In the meantime, after placing her bowl on the food table, instead of joining the others, Lorna circled back to the kitchen. Coming in behind Wally, she leaned against one of the counters, stretching her legs out at an angle.

"Wally," she said. "Can I ask you a question?"

"One can always ask, honey. What's up?"

"You, you saw the vampires, right?"

"Well, I was involved with that little escapade, all right, but I must admit that I have only actually seen one vampire in my time." Then, still stirring the chili, the fence turned to Lorna, asking,

"Wait a minute, you got mixed up with that Satan stuff—didn't you?" Wally noted the flash of horror that passed through Lorna's eyes as she nodded in agreement. Letting his spoon rest against the inside of the pot, he asked,

"Oh, I get it. You want to play a little 'I'll show you mine if you show me yours.' Right?" When the young woman nodded again shyly, the fence looked at her for a long moment and then finally asked,

"When you saw whatever the hell it was you saw, and you got pulled into all of this, tell me—were you scared?"

"Scared?" answered Lorna as if Wally were joking. "Scared is a word that doesn't even cover how I felt when Mr. London was telling the professor about what he'd seen . . . let alone how I felt when *I* started seeing the same things."

"Yeah, honey-lamb, your uncle Wally understands exactly what you are talking about. You pull up a chair. I'll go first because I know my story's by far the less exciting, but I tell you, I must admit I've kind of been wishing for someone to tell about this—someone other than Teddy, I mean. He's so far into this stuff now, I swear he don't even remember what it's like to be human no more."

And then, a steady stream of tears began to run down Lorna's face. She had done as all had suggested and never said a word—not to her boyfriend, her parents, not to anyone. Automatically, Wally's arms reached out for the woman as hers came toward him. He patted her on the back, remembering his own terror when he had finally realized the true portents of what had been happening around him. His own face growing wet, he hugged Lorna, telling her,

"It's all right, it *is* all right, sweet thing. We made it—we're still alive."

"I know. I know. I know it's bad to think that when you realize how many people have died in all this—the fires and the storms and everything, but I'm, I'm just so glad I'm still *alive*."

"You and me both, honey," answered Wally, knowing exactly what she meant. "You and me both."

3

"Well, well," said Morcey in a cheerful voice, making a short bow at the same time, "if it ain't the guy who killed Hercules."

The ex-maintenance man stood aside to allow the elder martial artist known as Jhong to enter the professor's home. The thin but toughly muscled Oriental stepped over Goward's threshold.

"It is good to see you standing," responded Jhong, referring to the last time the two had seen each other.

"Yeah," answered Morcey, hoisting his beer on high with a motion urging the other man to drink as well. "This beats the intensive care unit any day."

"Besides," said London, stepping into the foyer, shaking Jhong's hand, "who needs to think about that? We've got enough overturned glasses for one party."

As the three walked back toward the inside of the apartment, the older man asked,

"Overturned glasses?"

"Oh, it's just an old custom," explained the detective. "When you have a celebration and someone else should be there, but they can't be for one reason or another, you turn a glass upside down for them. It's symbolic—you know. They aren't there to drink out of their cups, but if somehow they managed to make it . . . then, well, then there'd be one for them."

"I understand. We have no such custom in my country, but it is a good one, nonetheless."

Before anyone could answer, the three came into the living room, all heads turning to see who the new arrival was. Those who knew Jhong greeted him, what they had shared passing back and forth between their eyes. Those who did not know him immediately began to buzz with the others around them, asking—as they had all night—who the new person was, what part had they played, what did they do, and when, and where, et cetera.

Morcey swung Jhong over to the bar, saying,

"Name your poison, pal. The doc stocked in a supply of everything you could want."

The older man looked over the sweeping array of bottles on the professor's sideboard, finally saying,

"Normally I do not take spirits of any kind. But, seeing that the bar is stocked so amply . . . tonight, I will." Pointing to a bottle made of dark green glass with a purple label, the martial artist said, "Pour me the *Hout Mite Gaou*, and I will drink to all the dry cups."

As Morcey unscrewed the cap to the bottle of black rice wine that Jhong had pointed out, he explained to the older man whom each of the glasses represented. As he did, London stared at the seven tumblers lined up on the mantle, one for each person who had died working for the agency during the last year. He saw each of them again in his mind's eye—Michael Coleman—the terrified mathematician who had charted the alignment of the stars for Goward, pinpointing the arrival time of Q'talu—who died of heart failure the night the monster actually appeared right on schedule. But of course, that was only the first tumbler. There were more.

One each for Fathers Wickler and Samuels—friends of Father Bain and dead in the service of their Lord. One for George Collins—the soulless man who hired the agency to recover his immortal essence from the grip of Satan, only to find that there was no one who could rescue his soul but himself. One for Mrs. Xui Zeng Lu—the only woman brave enough to stand against the vampires of Chinatown, and one for Joey Bago'Donuts, the little irritant whose presence had always annoyed London—until he was gone—the first to fall in the battle against the beyond, but not the last.

And then there was the seventh, the one for the Spud. Dr. Timothy Bodenfeld, the detective's oldest friend, dead like the others. Dead but not forgotten. As London stared at the seven tall glasses, Jhong raised his own tumbler of wine, saying,

"I did not know these people save one, and her only briefly. However they died, they all died in the service of a higher purpose than just themselves. It is not good to die, but it is good to die well."

And then he raised his glass to his lips and drank deeply. Morcey followed suit, tilting back his bottle of Rolling Rock until he had drained it. London stood somberly at attention—no glass in his hand, nothing to drink to drown what he was feeling inside. Conscious of a tightness in his throat, he excused himself with a false smile and headed outside for a breath of fresh air, which he did not need—out into the quiet stillness of the night, which he did.

Sitting halfway down the front steps, the detective stared up into the night sky—his mind purposely blank. For the first time that night, nothing was moving in the streets to catch his attention, although it was not likely he would have noticed even if there was. He did not think about anything in particular, nor did the voices that constantly spoke to him have anything of interest to start him thinking. Caught in the melancholy brought on by the moment, he merely wished to empty his mind—escape the world of thought for a moment. Once the moment had stretched for a half an hour, the door opened behind him.

"I assume there is room for one more."

"Sure," said London to Lai Wan—surprised to see her—surprised to see anyone. "It's a big stoop."

The woman flowed gracefully down the steps, her long black dress hiding the movement of her legs. Pulling her shawl a little tighter around her shoulders, she looked over at the detective and asked,

"And you are sad once more?"

"Oh, happens to the best of us."

"You miss the Spud."

"Well, yeah," admitted London. "He died a year ago today and here I am at a party. Some friend, huh?"

Lai Wan did not reply. She could feel his emotions and his pain clearly, just by sitting on the same stair with him. With so few people nearby to give off interference, she could have skimmed his very thoughts out of the air without half trying if she so desired.

Her powers had come to her through an accident that took her all the way to death's door, only to return her to the world of the living forever changed. For reasons of preserving her own sanity, the psychometrist had immediately become a much colder person than the one she had been. Without realizing it, she suddenly found a need for distance—between herself and other people, and everything they ever did or saw or touched. Before long, she became a creature with little variance to her style or routine. It was a comfort for a long time—wearing the same few sets of clothes, walking the same streets, sitting always in the same chair—no new experiences meant no new shocks.

Meeting London had changed all of that. Over the past year, to say she had received a few shocks from her new experiences was an understatement of the highest degree. She had seen things that had driven weaker people mad. She had also learned much about herself, and in so doing, about the world around her. Now, she told the detective,

"If the Spud were here, would you feel better?"

"What do you mean?"

"I am asking you . . . you pulled the trigger that killed your friend. You had to do it. You would have urged him to do the same to you if the situation had been reversed."

"I know all this," he reminded her with a soft growl in his voice. "What's your point?"

"My point, Theodore, is that with that same trigger pull you killed nearly two million people. A year later you still mourn the Spud. Someday you will get past your grief for him and then what will you do—give them each a year of their own?"

"I'm past all the others. Just not the Spud. He was my oldest friend, Lai."

"Yes, he was. And now he is dead and all your other friends are inside and soon your depression will spread and infect them as well. That is not the purpose of a party—despite what you Americans seem to think."

As the woman stood up to return inside, the detective could see that she was not upset—merely concerned. Having said her piece, however, she was leaving him to his own devices. Realizing she was right, he stood up as well, saying,

"You're not going to abandon me now, are you?"

"You were not abandoned, Theodore. You ran away from us. This is merely a lifeline thrown in the hopes you can still pull yourself in."

Smiling despite himself, the detective opened the door for the psychometrist, saying,

"You're tough, lady. I'll give you that."

"Coming from you I know this is a compliment, so I will take it as such."

Closing the door behind them, London said teasingly,

"I thought when a guy pulled a stunt like this at a party that his girlfriend was supposed to come and pull him out of the dumps."

"Who do you think sent me?"

The detective smiled again, instantly understanding why Lisa would do such a thing. His smile growing broad and open, he answered,

"You two. I think I like dealing with modern women better.

Suits and ties, always trying to play the games like men, think like men—they're a lot easier to beat."

"Of course they are, Theodore," answered Lai Wan, walking back into the light of the living room, almost giving London the smile he had been trying to get out of her. "That is why I would never be foolish enough to be one."

Laughing again, the detective headed for the bar. Morcey was there, waiting, knowing Lai Wan would have no trouble fetching his partner inside. He also knew that despite London's usual reservations about such things, he would want a drink when he arrived. Pouring a tall glass of white wine, he handed it over as his friend approached, asking,

"This do ya?"

"Yes, Paul. Thank you," answered London, staring at the empty cups in their line, nodding to each of them in their turn. "This will do fine."

After that, another hour passed without anyone really noticing. Food and drink continued to disappear. Fast dances gave way to slower ones. Partners changed several times over. People broke up into constantly reforming small groups to tell jokes and gossip and just talk. Alcohol was spilled and cleaned up. Dishes piled in the sink and people cleaned them and then dirtied more which they did not clean. The first guest to feel the call of a reality outside the party announced their departure due to their long drive, inspiring another to ask for a ride. It was still early for that particular party, however, and the festivities continued.

Kisses were stolen in private corners. The host's living quarters were examined by the curious. More people left, in the way of that typical, second wave exodus most parties discover somewhere after midnight. The music grew softer after that, people tending to abandon the food and dance in favor of drink and conversation. Then, as the evening went on, and all but the diehards had departed, the subjects people brought up became more and more specific—more and more personal.

"Tell me, Teddy," asked Goward, beginning to feel the effects of his tenth bourbon, "seriously. What's it like?"

"What's what like?" asked London.

Cat sighed loudly, following it with a plaintive, "Oh, please." Bain looked at London with sympathy; Jhong looked at him with curiosity. Acting as his prompt, Lisa said,

"You know what he means."

"Well, yes, sort of. But," continued the detective, groping for an answer, "what does a guy say to that?"

"You just say whatever the truth is," answered Cat. "What's it like to be God's poker partner?"

"That's getting a little beyond what's really happened, isn't it?"

"Is it?" asked Cat. "I thought what I saw was weird enough but, 'wrestling in Hell with the Devil?' What kind of story is that?"

"It wasn't really Hell, and he wasn't really the Devil. It was the dream plane. It was all just a battle of psychic energies—my will against his. Soon as I realized what was going on, it was easy to get around his 'Satan' identity."

"It might have been easy for you," interrupted Goward. "But it wasn't for me."

"You believed he was the Devil?" asked London with a touch of challenge in his voice.

"It was a powerful image he projected, and as we both know he'd practiced it on a great lot of people before us. Good Lord, Theodore, he manifested things before our very eyes—living things. He created life before ... our ... eyes. He spun tissue and hearts and arms and wings and fangs out of thin air, fashioned them into living things, and set them to attack us, and," the professor took another sip of his drink and then said in a calm, measured tone,

"they did."

"But Zachary ..."

"No, no—you don't understand because you're the one fate prepared for all this—taught its secrets to so you would know what you were up against—well," the professor took another sip from his drink, saying,

"I'll tell you this ... I didn't know who he was or even *what* he was, but I *was* afraid of him. When we were in his presence, the evil—the pure *evil* came off him to the point where it didn't matter if he was *the* Asmodeus or not. He was Satan enough to do for me until the real thing comes along."

"You're turning into Batman and you don't even know it," said Cat. "You've seen so much of this stuff now that it's getting to be second nature to you. I don't even like spiders in my bathtub, okay? You go into psychos' heads—into their *dreams* and kick their asses on their own turf." The short, strawberry blonde turned and stared at the detective.

"How?" she asked loudly. "How do you do it? How can you beat someone at their own game? How the ... how do you go to a place where someone else makes up all the rules—changing them whenever they want . . . and still win?"

"They don't make up all the rules," answered London, beginning to feel uncomfortable. "The dream plane is a big place. Nobody makes up all the rules for it. Anybody who can reach it can do whatever they want."

"Easier said than done," interrupted Goward.

"He's right, Teddy," said Lisa. "I've been to the dream plane. I can't perform miracles."

"I've been there more times than her," added the professor, almost absently, "and I've barely been able to do more than walk around and gawk at the sights."

"Miracles aren't so hard," offered Father Bain, softly. "Once you get the hang of it. You just have to believe that whatever you want to happen will happen."

"But, Father," said Cat, "I mean, it just isn't that easy. If that was the case—then anyone could perform miracles, anytime they wanted to."

"My dear young woman," answered the priest, "when I was a cardinal I had faith in everything a man could want—money and limousines and fine brandies—in everything except my own self. After meeting Theodore, my faith in things temporal came crashing down and all I was left with was my self—a feeble, dying frame of flesh and blood with no spirit, no purpose beyond feeding itself better and better tidbits without returning anything to the general pool of being." The priest brushed a wisp of his thin white hair away from his forehead and then continued, saying,

"To make up for such a life I began living in the streets, preaching the real word of God. Not the sanitized word of the cathedral pulpit, but the real, true words of God Almighty, the prevailing wind, the growing oak, the grazing sheep, the hunting wolf, the rising sun and all its fellow stars—the one and only God, which is all of us and everything else." Taking a sip from the glass of water in his hand, Bain added,

"They tell me that as I preached my new gospel in the streets miracles happened all around me. I believe them, but I have no proof. Those who have been healed in my presence, my thought is that they came to be healed by me and that their faith that such a miracle was going to occur . . . *made* it occur. Faith is such a precious thing. To believe in something—I mean, to really *believe* in it . . . I have no words to explain how important the having of faith in one's own self is. The loss of it is everything lost, the finding of it everything restored."

"The father has it right," added London, struggling to pull into conscious thought the explanation for that which he did so often, but could not explain. "It's not like I think about what I'm doing. I just react, and things happen. I'm afraid to actually analyze it too much because, well, I think if I understand what it is I'm doing, I won't be able to do it anymore."

"You know," added Goward suddenly, stuffing his pipe as he spoke, "I'm reminded of what happened to many of the astronauts after they returned to earth. There was great speculation at the time that they—having actually flown through the heavens themselves—would lose their faith in God entirely ... that they would become completely secular beings, rational and scientific and cold to the frivolous notions this world has to offer. But," said the professor as he lifted his lighter to the bowl of his pipe,

"actually, quite the opposite happened."

Taking several long pulls on his pipe, Goward continued, telling the others,

"From all the reports I've found, for the most part the faith in a larger universe has become a stronger part of each of these men. I mean, let us look at who we're talking about here. These were all young air force men, warrior pilots—the best of the best. Do you know what happened to them when they returned to the earth? They became poets, artists—painters. Their belief in God seems to have increased exponentially—in every one of them. What was it the one said ... what was his name now, ah ... Russell, Russell Schweickart—I remember it because I was so impressed with it when I first heard it. You see," the professor took another deep drag from his pipe and continued, saying,

"his work had taken him outside the ship on a space walk. Now, these people were always incredibly busy when they were on the outside, and so he didn't really get a chance to look about until something went wrong inside—nothing serious—just a delay which forced him to have to wait for, oh, maybe five minutes. Anyway, after a moment he realized that he was *alone* ... alone and traveling through the heavens at seventeen thousand miles an hour, suspended in the air halfway between the earth and the moon, and he looked about him and suddenly the overwhelming enormity of it all just struck him. And he said to himself, 'What have I ever done to deserve this experience?' And yet, fate had been preparing him and paving the way for him for that experience his entire life."

Goward took in another deep pull of smoke and then released it, saying,

"Just as it did for our Theodore, here. Indeed, just as it did for all of us."

4

The party broke up fairly soon after its philosophical high point. Father Bain left on foot, as did Jhong—the elder warrior telling London that he would meet with him at his offices the next day. Cat offered Lisa and the detective a ride to their home, which they gratefully accepted. On the way they viewed the aftermath of the evening's citywide party. Litter of every type filled the streets, from cigarette butts to the carcasses of burned out cars. The remains of broken bottles lay everywhere—paper flew through the air, the wind pushing all manner of trash up and down the still-full streets. Police cars and ambulances forced their way through the crowds, dashing along ignoring traffic signs, their lights and sirens adding to the almost surreal carnival atmosphere.

In the buildings they passed, they glimpsed other parties still going full tilt, the music of them so loud it reached the street. The trio ignored the partiers and their carrying-on, ultimately just too tired to be very interested. When they arrived near the section of Greenwich Village where London's building lay, the couple told Cat they could walk from there.

When the electronics expert asked if they weren't worried about all the crazies running around, the detective just smiled, assuring the woman that they would both be all right. Cat conceded,

"Yeah, I guess you've got a point. Okay, you two, don't get your throats cut for a dollar."

As Cat pulled away from the curb, the pair waved at the retreating car and then walked toward their home, hand in hand. Pressing up against London, the night having grown quite unseasonably cold, Lisa said,

"They kind of put you on the spot back there, didn't they?"

"They had help, if I remember correctly," answered the detective with a scowl meant to tease.

"I had to say something to keep things moving. I couldn't let you look like some big goof, now could I?"

"Oh, in that case, thanks," answered London with a thin trace of sarcasm. Lisa, feeling the warmth from the detective flow into her, replied,

"You're welcome. It is my duty to take care of you now, you know. Now that I'm all moved into your place and all."

"*Our* place," corrected the detective. "I think now that I own the whole building it's a big enough place to think of as 'ours.' "

"Yeah," answered Lisa with a laugh. "*Our* giant mess of boxes and crates and junk that's going to have to be straightened out into one life."

"Well," said London, "I figure you should stay home from the office tomorrow and start making some of the place yours. There's a lot of empty rooms now. You can start mapping out where you want your computer room—you know—so you can double store everything from the office at home."

"Ummm-hummm."

"So then you won't have to go in every day, if you don't want to. I mean, we could certainly afford to get a secretary to take over a lot of the stuff you do—let you concentrate on the computers. You've been turning into a pretty good little skip-chaser. But anyway, about the apartment . . ."

"Oh yes," answered Lisa with mock seriousness. "The apartment."

"Right," said London, a bit puzzled but willing to play the game. "Anyway . . . like I said, you could pick out a computer room, or, well . . . anything else you wanted to do, I suppose. I mean, I'm like most guys. I don't care which room is the living room and which one the dining room or where the bedroom is. You've probably got a much better sense of all that than I do, so, really—anything you want to do, anything you want to change, or to . . ." And then suddenly London caught the look in Lisa's eye. As she started to laugh softly, he said,

"Something tells me that you don't have to *start* thinking about what changes you're going to make."

"Well, I might have had a little time recently to think up a few changes."

"Yeah. You've probably already had the blueprints drawn up and started interviewing contractors."

"I haven't called a single contractor."

"Unnn-hhuhh," said the detective. "Well, I just hope your design scheme leaves me enough room for my fossil collection. That's all I ask."

"Oh, you poor dear," responded the young woman, tossing her head to throw all her chestnut curls over her shoulder. "Just to put your poor mind at ease, I'll tell you that I was thinking of turning that studio apartment on the first floor into a den for you. Then you could surround yourself with all your treasures and whenever you needed to get away and think, you'd have all those little bits and pieces and all to cut you off from the rest of the world."

"Translation for males: in other words, all of my crap gets shoved into one room and you take over everything else."

"That isn't what I meant," said Lisa without offense, knowing better than to think that London was serious. Giving her hand a light squeeze, the detective said,

"Oh, I know, sweetheart." As they turned the corner onto their street, he repeated, "I know."

The massive trees on their block—some of the only ones left in Manhattan outside of Central Park—cut off much of the illumination from the street lamps. Walking from one pool of light to the next, Lisa asked,

"So, am I going to be doing all the wash from now on?"

"If you like."

"Oh, thank you. And can I do all the dishes, and cook all the meals, and do the vacuuming too, oh, especially the vacuuming—please?"

"Anything to make you happy, sweetheart."

"Oh, you're just so good to me."

The detective chuckled while Lisa pretended to scowl. Then, as they neared the bottom of their stoop, he told her,

"Actually, I was thinking that another thing you could do tomorrow would be to start looking for some kind of maid service for us. Outside of the meals, I think that as two of the three partners of the London Agency, we bring home enough between us to be able to afford some kind of luxuries. Besides, four stories is a lot of vacuuming."

"Are you sure?" asked Lisa, her inborn practicality rushing to the surface. "I was teasing, you know. Those kinds of services can cost an awful lot in Manhattan. And besides, we're not going to be using all of the space all of the time. How many floors are we . . ."

"Sweetheart," said London, cutting Lisa off softly, "I didn't ask you to move in here because of your wicked ability with a bucket and mop. Granted, if we were poorer we'd have to work some things like that out, but . . . we're not, so we don't."

Not letting go of her one hand, the detective stepped around from the young woman's side, taking up her other hand as well as they came face-to-face. Lifting her hands upward, he raised them to his mouth and gently kissed them both. Then, looking into her eyes, he told her,

"I love you, Lisa. You. You get caught up in a frenzy someday and you just have to iron some shirts or something—that's all right—I'll understand. But I didn't carry all those boxes inside today to get myself someone who could fetch me beers while I watch the fights. You're the only thing that's kept me going this last year. After the Conflagration, I didn't have any reason to live except for you. The months it took me to heal, I was afraid to see you, afraid to let you see what had become of me. But you didn't care. You stayed beside me while I relearned how to be a human being, and as each thing has happened you've been right there, keeping me anchored, keeping me human."

Pausing for just a moment, London took in an unconscious breath, studying Lisa's face as he did so. Lost in the piercing pale blueness of her eyes, unable to see anything else but them, he told her,

"You're the shore I swim back to when these things try to pull me away—you're everything I need to stay whole, to remain whole—to be ... me. If I were to lose you someday, somehow, there wouldn't be any more Teddy London. There'd just be this guy like me, with a big hole in his heart who didn't know how to smile anymore ... who didn't have a reason to do anything. I love you, sweetheart, with all the power that's in me."

And then, the detective swept the young woman up off her feet. Throwing her arms around his neck, Lisa pulled herself close to London, whispering in his ear,

"And I love you, too."

"Good," replied the detective, carrying his beloved up the stairs to the front door. "Glad to hear it. Now let's go in and find that vacuum cleaner, eh?"

Lisa thought about hitting London, but did not, figuring that making him unlock and then open the door and then the next all while still holding her was punishment enough. He managed both with relative ease, not bumping her head or feet on any railings or door frames or walls. Then, when they were on the other side of the wood and metal and glass that separated them from the rest of the world, London held her closer to himself, saying,

"Well, Ms. Hutchinson, you're home."

"I know," she told him, smiling. "I've been there since the first day we met."

And then, he sat down on the stairs in the darkness, cradling Lisa on his thighs. She pushed against him as he came forward, their lips meeting in a long kiss, or perhaps it was two, that lasted until morning.

5

"Oh, my." Morcey laughed. "Look what the cat dragged in."
London, yawning as he came through the door, did not laugh in
turn. Instead, he made his way to his office past his partner, who
was manning the front desk in Lisa's absence. Sharpening a pen-
cil just for the comic effect of looking efficient in the face of the
detective's lack thereof, Morcey said,

"Now if you were a good boy who went home on time on
school nights—like some guys I know—and didn't hang out until the wee hours at wild parties . . . gee, then maybe you
wouldn't look such a wreck in the mornings."

London turned in the doorway to his office to make some
comment, but stopped for a moment and then turned back, too
tired to bother. He and Lisa had needed the time to themselves.
What difference, he asked himself, would it make to the London
Agency's day? As he parked himself behind his desk, he pushed
his back into the leather of his desk chair, feeling its buttons
against his shoulders. Morcey stuck his head in through the door,
saying,

"Seriously, boss, you want me to head on down to the Cosmic
to get you a tea or somethin'? You do look a little bit burnt, if
you know what I mean."

"I know, but how hectic a day is it going to be?"

"Well, we've got that character who contacted us from Europe
last month comin' in today."

"Which one?"

"The one who wanted us to hunt werewolves."

London craned his neck around to stretch it out, barely paying
his partner any attention. Stretching his arms out as well, he said,

"This guy is serious, I take it?" When the ex-maintenance man
answered with a firm nod, the detective asked, "Any idea how he
got hold of our name? Obviously it's not going to be good for us
if too many people start thinking of us as 'Ghostbusters Head-
quarters.' "

"Not sure, boss," answered Morcey. "No mention in either of
his letters. First he just said that if what he had planned didn't

stop the werewolf then he'd be back in touch. Then two weeks later we got another one saying that things hadn't worked out and that he'd like to see us. I faxed him an 'okay' in Brussels, and he faxed one back saying today would be fine. He's supposed to be here in around an hour."

"Damn," the detective said softly, urging himself awake. Sending orders throughout his body, he communicated with his muscles, pumping additional blood through them. Taking several deep breaths in a row, he directed the extra oxygen straight to his head, telling his partner,

"This is not a good thing. We can't have these crackpots coming to us all the time."

"But we invited him, boss."

"We responded to his letter—yes. But, it's not like we've got an ad in the Yellow Pages promising an end to your spectral problems. I mean, how far are we supposed to stretch things here?" When the balding man said nothing, London stopped his stretching and said,

"Werewolves, for Christ's sake? Werewolves?"

"Yeah," answered Morcey, agreement in his voice, "I know how you feel, but don't forget . . . you didn't buy vampires before Mrs. Lu came to us."

"I know," said the detective, torn between what seemed like reality and what did not. "I know. But where are the limits? What next? Do we head for Egypt and hunt for mummies? Do we start sweeping the Amazon basin for that particular black lagoon that the creature came from?"

The ex-maintenance man came into the room, pulling one of the leather client chairs closer to London's desk. Sitting down on the edge, he intertwined his fingers, resting them on the edge of the detective's desk. Then, banging his thumbs against each other, he said,

"I think I know why you're upset here." As London stared, waiting for an answer, Morcey said, "You and Lisa just got moved in and all and, probably, I think you're sorta wantin' things ta be normal for a while." The balding man bit his lower lip, not wanting to add any pressure to that which the situation was already exerting. Choosing his words as carefully as he could, he continued, saying,

"Hey, boss, believe me—I understand. Not that I haven't liked some of this head-buttin' we've done, but we've had some awful close calls. You and me's both come back from the dead already, you know? I mean . . . how many go-arounds does a guy get in one lifetime, anyway? But, as I was sayin', I mean, I don't want to make you nuts or nuthin' ..." The ex-maintenance man pushed himself away from London's desk as he spoke, his spine grinding the back of his chair. Arching his head back, he looked at the ceiling for a moment as he finished.

"I don't know ... I don't want you to think I'm crazy or anything but, I sorta think the doc is right about all this. Fate just keeps movin' us in the path of stuff. What's gonna happen's gonna happen, whether we try to avoid it or not. So, why don't I go and get you that tea—okay? If this guy is a nut job, we get rid of him and that's that. But, if he's for real ..."

Morcey let his statement hang as he got up and headed for the door connecting London's office to the waiting room. Once he crossed the threshold, he turned and said,

"After all, it's not like you won't be able to tell the difference after five minutes—right?"

"Just go get the tea. And get me one of those jumbo chocolate chip cookies."

"You lookin' for a cheap sugar fix?" asked the ex-maintenance man.

"Something like that—why?" asked the detective.

"They just stocked in these new brownies. They make 'em with a whole Snickers bar melted inside each one." While London looked at his partner, waiting for a value judgment on the treat's merits, the balding man rolled his eyes and poked the end of his tongue out, running it along half his upper lip, adding,

"They're awful good."

"Yeah, they sound good. All right, go on—go," said London, laughing. "Get whatever you want. Hell, I guess I'll try anything once."

"Great," answered Morcey, happy to see the detective getting back to his normal mood. "And so like this time maybe we'll try werewolves."

The ex-maintenance man laughed while London frowned at his partner's joke. Heading toward the door to the hall, Morcey did a waddling victory dance, pointing his hand in the air in "We're number one" fashion, shaking his near foot-long ponytail behind him as he did so. His hand on the knob, he was surprised as the door gave outward a split second before he began to push. Catching himself, he backed up, not knowing what to expect. A moment later, however, he said,

"Hey, Jhong. Long time no see. I was just headin' out ta get some supplies. You want anythin'—somethin' ta drink, somethin' ta eat?" When the elder warrior responded in the negative, Morcey extended another greeting and then said he would be right back, shutting the door behind him. Jhong crossed to London's office and entered, saying,

"He is a man filled with a great human energy."

"That he is," agreed the detective. "That he is. So tell me, how'd you like the party last night?"

"It was a good gathering. I was pleased to see so many ready to launch themselves into the fray once more."

"Well," replied London good-naturedly, missing the elder's point, "everybody was certainly willing to have themselves a good time. I don't know about 'launching themselves into the fray,' though."

"Why else then were they gathered?"

The detective stared at the elder warrior for a moment, trying to see where they had crossed purposes. Although he did not know why, he was sure the two of them were suddenly not talking about the same thing. Following the suggestion of a small voice that had been nagging him with a question since the night before, London said,

"Jhong, I meant to run this by you last night. When we decided to have our little anniversary celebration, no one knew how to get in touch with you." All the different facets of his brain wondering as to the answer to his question, each paid particular attention as the detective asked,

"Who was it that finally got through to you?"

"No one contacted me from your agency, if that is what you mean."

"Then, how did you know when and where to show up last night?"

"I was following that which had to be answered. I did not arrive at the doctor's expecting a party. I only went to his home because I was seeking you."

"Why?" asked London.

"Because," responded Jhong with puzzlement in his voice, wondering how the detective could not know the answer to his own question. Without drama, he said simply, "There is the threat of great danger in the air. It is coming to the fore, stronger every day. I have beheld many sights in my dreams of recent— scenes of blood and death. Among them I have seen the vision of a particular face in my dreams. And, I have known that when this man I have dreamed of finally crosses your path that monstrous events will be set into motion."

As London's eyes narrowed, the elder warrior moved closer to the detective's desk, his arms outstretched . . . almost pleading.

"Can you not feel it?" he asked. "Can you not smell it on the air . . . thick and heavy, dripping with the moist, deep odor of . . ."

And then, suddenly, Jhong went quiet. From the way he turned his head, the detective could tell he was listening to something in the hallway. London could feel something—something moving toward his office. The presence moved unseen through the hallway, stopping before the outer door. Then, as the two men watched from the back office, the knob of the outer door began turning. A moment later it was pushed open, revealing an old man on the other side.

He stood framed by the door, a large, stiff leather case hanging from one arm. London and Jhong were confronted by a tall, rangy figure, one with thinning white hair and a gaunt look. Deep wrinkles cut into his face, mourning lines that expressed nothing but unhappiness. The man with the sorrowful expression stepped into the office, moving slowly, almost dragging himself forward through strength of will alone.

The detective looked from the figure moving toward them up into the face of the elder warrior near his desk. Jhong nodded, understanding the question in London's eyes, saying aloud,

"Yes. This is the face from my dreams." Sitting down in the chair Morcey had used earlier, the warrior crossed his legs beneath him, and then added,

"It has begun."

6

"Good mornin'-tide to you both," said the man with the mournful eyes. His voice, not sounding nearly as tired as the rest of him looked, was heavily accented—an accent the detective could not quite place. The man continued speaking, introducing himself. "I am called Maxim Warhelski. I believe you are to have been expecting me."

"Yes," answered London. "I guess we have. Won't you come in and have a seat?"

The man moved his gaunt frame across the room with a slow but steady measure to his gait. He set his case down with a solid thud on the floor next to one of the two remaining client chairs. As he bent over to do so, Jhong and London both noticed that his left hand was missing and that, whatever mishap had taken it, the man before them had chosen not to have it replaced with an artificial limb. Maxim Warhelski had instead had his wrist capped off with a hard, rough-looking piece of metal. As the one-handed man seated himself, both London and Jhong introduced themselves in turn. The man with the mournful eyes told them,

"I have come a quite long way to see you gentlemen. I hope it will not have been in vain."

"That would depend mainly," replied the detective, "on whatever it is you came to see us about, Mr. Warhelski."

"You, Mr. London. I have come to see you. There are tremendous tales of your adventures circulating throughout the—what could one call it—the *underworld* of our civilization. They say you are a man afraid of nothing. That you will seek the answer to any problem . . . for a price. By which, it seems it is meant that the problem must be interesting and the price suited to it. I have come with hopefully such a problem. I wish to enlist your aid, Mr. London . . . in tracking down and killing the monster that murdered my family."

"I'm a private investigator, Mr. Warhelski—not an assassin. I don't contract out to kill people. Most of the P.I.'s in this town won't—"

"Please," interrupted Walhelski in a stern voice. "Do not treat me as a child. I did not come here to ask you to kill a person. I said a 'monster,' Mr. London. And that is what I meant. I believe my English is correct in this usage. I am not making reference to some person who has acted monstrously. I am speaking about a monster. A true monster. As evil a thing as ever walked God's earth."

And then, at that moment, Morcey returned, slightly burdened with a deli bag in each hand. Shifting them both to one hand, he set the pair on London's desk while the detective introduced him to Warhelski. The man with the mournful eyes refused the various offers from London and Morcey for either food or drink, telling them to please go ahead. The pair put their snack treats away for a more appropriate time, only keeping their cups of tea out as the conversation continued. Taking the lead, London asked,

"This evil thing . . . I assume this is the werewolf you wrote to us about."

"Yes. Your tone tells me you do not believe."

"Let's just say I'm a little skeptical about things that so far I've only seen in old Universal movies."

"That is a valid point. But you see . . . I *have* seen." London stared at the one-handed man, waiting for him to continue. Warhelski told him,

"It was 1910 . . . Poland, the village of Srem—a mother, father, and three of their four children were savagely torn to pieces—those few witnesses on the scene recounted the story of a giant wolf standing on its hindquarters, plucking the children's eyes out one by one, swallowing them like grapes." The one-handed man fixed London with his gaze and then said,

"I know. I was one of those present. Witness and victim both. It was my family that was attacked. My family destroyed by the thing the others saw. My memories of it are not so old, however. I cannot claim true memory of the monster until ten years later." Warhelski cleared his throat, undaunted by his audience's skepticism. Beginning again, he said,

"I was twelve. Because of the war, my uncle had taken me along with his own family to Czechoslovakia, to the town of Hrinova. One night two soldiers cornered a suspected looter. One of them was torn apart, the other shot through the head with his own pistol. I saw it that time."

The mournful man stopped for a moment, resting his voice. London sipped at his tea, Morcey sat spellbound by the tale. Jhong sat without refreshment, waiting calmly, seeming neither bored nor interested. Having caught his breath, Warhelski continued.

"From the window of our hotel room I saw the thing kill the first man with an ease I cannot begin to describe. Then, this gigantic wolf-thing, it took the other's pistol from his belt side, put it to its owner's head and pulled the trigger. And then it turned. Even though we were separated by forty, fifty yards, it spotted me. It stared into my eyes and the resulting connection made it feel as if we were as close as I am to any of you. And I tell you, the thing recognized me, and it laughed. And then, as I stared transfixed, it bounded toward the hotel, covering the distance between us, crossing the street and scaling the wall, before I could turn away. Without pause, the thing snapped at me, taking my hand. Then, it disappeared down the street into the darkness. None saw it but me."

Pushing himself back in his chair, the one-handed man gave them more dates and places and events, rattling them off from memory.

"I followed news of it ever after, tracking its movements as best I could. 1923 . . . Hungary, Hajduhadhaz—fifteen farmers tracked a wolf pack to its lair, an abandoned coal mine. All were later found dead in the mine. Only one set of tracks is found leading away from the bodies . . .wolf tracks. 1937 . . . the Soviet Union, Karaganda—an entire neighborhood is found dead—seventy-nine people ripped apart one at a time in a single night—the first night of the new moon. 1949 . . . Afghanistan, the Khyber Pass—more of the same. 1953 . . . India, Warangal—more of the same. 1962 . . . Nepal, Darjeeling—more of the same. 1969 . . . China, Jiggitai—" The mournful man's tone dropped sharply, as if the life had suddenly drained out of him as he finished, repeating slowly,

"More of the same."

London set his paper tea cup down, wondering what to make of the one-handed man and his story. The detective knew he believed Warhelski—at least to the point where he knew the mournful man believed what he was saying.

Why wouldn't he, asked one of the voices in the back of London's head. After all, he ought to know whatever it was that bit his hand off.

Other voices rushed in to argue with the first, though, reminded it that people can disguise all manner of facts from themselves, believe all manner of things if they need to cover some unbearable truth from themselves. Yes—but, asked one, to track something across continents for decades, and now come to London, if it weren't true? Wasn't that an awful lot of denial?

The detective asked the mournful man,

"Sir, maybe I'm missing something here, but why recite these tales now? You've found these stories from across Europe and Asia and kept your records . . ."

"No!" spat Warhelski furiously, slamming his metal-capped wrist against the detective's desk. "You do not understand. I was there—every time. I was in each place—looking for *it*. In 1923, I organized the farmers of Hajduhadhaz. In 1937, it was I who convinced an entire neighborhood in Karaganda that the thing was coming for them. There and in every place I have ever found anyone interested in the thing—always the same. It comes and kills. Over the years, I have seen a pattern. At first I began to think that I was the cause . . . that it delighted in tormenting me, that it waited for me to find some new ally only to prove its power to me. But that, that was ego.

"In India, in Warangal, there was a man who had been studying the monster's movements from afar. He was the focus of that attack, as was a supposed monster hunter in Nepal." As those in the room stared at the one-handed man, he exclaimed,

"Do you not see? I had only been able to make my way to the spots where the thing was going. It has been looking for those that could confront it—those who might be able to destroy it. The monster is eliminating all who might believe in it, who might possibly stand against it."

"All but you," added Morcey in an edgy voice. As London looked to his partner, the ex-maintenance man shot his eyes toward Warhelski and then made a long face, spinning his head slightly at the same time, trying to imply through gesture that perhaps if there was indeed a werewolf on the loose that it might be one with a missing paw. The detective had to admit in a glance of his own that the idea held merit.

The mournful man, however, looked over at Morcey and, for one short moment, the heavy depression that seemed an eternal part of him lifted, allowing him the briefest of smiles. His eyes softening, he said,

"Yes, Mr. Morcey, sir . . . all but me. Why the beast permits me to live . . . I do not know. At first I thought it was a game it enjoyed—thwarting my attempts to put an end to it. But as I said, such is not the case. The thing has moved across the landscape, seeking out those who believe in it, looking for those who might have the power to kill it. One by one the creature has destroyed them all, laughing at me on those occasions when I was able to be there."

Warhelski stopped talking then, his brief smile fading. He folded his wrists across each other in his lap, his shoulders sagging as much of the life seemed to drain out of him. Lifting his head, he looked from side to side, staring at Jhong and Morcey to his left, then at London to his right. As he studied their faces, he finally said,

"I see. You still do not understand why I have come to here."

"We thought," answered London, "it was to enlist us in your, ah, quest to kill this werewolf."

"That is, of course, of interest to me, but do you not yet comprehend? You will be forced to try and kill the monster soon enough . . . whether you have heeded what I have told you or not."

"Why's that, Mr. Warhelski?" asked Morcey.

"Because, as I have learned of your agency and its doings . . . so has it. The beast is come to America, to this city to match itself against you." Warhelski's tone struck through to the detective's core, convincing him of the one-handed man's sincerity. As that chilling realization crept over London, the mournful man looked into the detective's eyes, then said,

"Ah—now you understand."

7

"And I say that it *is* that simple."

The voice of Professor Zachary Goward carried through the hallway, echoing all the way to the elevators. As London and the others began to move toward the professor's office, his voice came to them again, saying,

"You must understand, that the chronicles of the Christian religion are indeed a history, but they are a false history. Its regulators over the centuries have tried to turn it into a collection of historical dates as if the day the rabbi Jeshrua—who the Greeks lazily translated as Jesus—died was anywhere near as important as what it was he was trying to get across to everyone."

"Damn it, Zachary," came another voice, one with which none in the hall were familiar. "The lessons of the Bible are not balderdash—they are valid."

"Valid—yes, but not history. Not fact."

"How dare you, Zachary Goward—"

"How dare I what?" came the professor's voice again, overpowering his opponent's. "How dare I teach that the story of humanity's placement in the Garden is really just a metaphor for our own births into innocence? That Genesis was written as a sort of self-help guide for people to get through their lives? It was, you know, you stubborn ox."

"Genesis is the story of Creation . . . pure and simple. And I'll hear no more of your pychobabbling nonsense."

And then suddenly a short, portly bearded man, apparently in his middle fifties, stormed out of the professor's office, slamming his way blindly through London and the trio approaching with him. Right behind him came Goward, stopping just outside his doorway. Shaking his finger after the departing figure, the professor roared, his words spewing from him at an incredibly accelerated rate.

"*Yes*, indeed, it *is* the story of creation—each individual's creation. The eating from the Tree of Knowledge is accepting *self*-knowledge, development of the ego—and *that* is why man is cast out of the Garden, you great jackass—it is because we are cast out of the innocence of the Godhead ... each child's oneness with the universe lost in his desire to understand himself as a focalized event—the guardian at the gate with his flaming sword to keep man from the Tree of Immortal Life is just that—the ego protecting itself for ..." Goward took a great ragged deep breath, and then bellowed,

"it damn well realizes that to accept the notion of any sort of universality is to deny God *except that to say we are all part of the great fabric of the cosmos*!"

And then came the sound of the elevator landing on their floor, to which Goward shouted even louder,

"Just accept it, Webler—'Jesus went to the Cross as the bridegroom to the bride.' Sacrifice of the corporeal to attain oneness with the Godhead. Even Augustine got it right, for God's sake. . . ."

As the elevator doors clanged shut, the professor sucked in one last quick breath and then shouted,

"And he died *fifteen hundred years ago.*"

"Havin' fun, Professor?"

"Just a little spirited debate with a colleague, Paul."

"Webler," said London. "Isn't that the name of your department head?"

"Yes," said Goward, mopping at his brow. "Isn't the concept of tenure just a wonderful thing?" Without waiting for an answer, the professor wiped his hand on the pants of his suit. Extending a then dry palm to the mournful man, he said,

"And you must be Maxim Warhelski. Won't you please come in, sir? I think that it will be most interesting to compare notes with you."

As Jhong, Morcey, and Warhelski filed into the office, the detective caught Goward's shoulder. Holding him back for a moment, he asked,

"Is that why you were so interested when I told you we wanted to talk to you about Warhelski and werewolves? Have you heard of this guy before?"

"Oh, yes. He's circulated some interesting things—proofs, as it were—in his time. I've never known what to make of his claims . . . never had the time to investigate, really. This is a marvelous opportunity."

"But do you buy what he's selling, Zack?"

The professor regarded the detective for a short moment, then told him, "There is never any harm in seeking out what knowledge you can. It costs us nothing to listen. . . ."

"But," said London uneasily. "Werewolves?"

"Tut-tut, Theodore. As Augustine said, '*Audi partem alteram.*'" One of the detective's ancestral voices flashed a translation for the Latin through his head, causing him to ask,

"Hear the other side?"

"Exactly. Let's go do that, shall we?"

Stepping into his foyer, Goward crossed through his office, telling his secretary,

"Ms. Featherstone, be so good as to reschedule any students who come looking for me for, oh, at least the next two hours." Then, just as the professor started through the door to his inner office where Morcey had herded the others, he turned back to his secretary, telling her,

"Oh, yes—and do order up a bundle of those spider mums Mrs. Webler fancies and have them sent to the head's apartment . . . preferably before he gets home. I'm sure you'll find some way to make me sound witty and attentive on the card."

"I'll think of something," answered the young woman.

"Oh, and sincere," added Goward, a look of mischief in his eye. "Do try for sincere."

The woman frowned at the professor, letting him know his joke had hit home as she reached for both the phone and her Rolodex. In the meantime, in his own office, Goward moved behind his desk, trying to find a place to put his hands on its surface amid the overwhelming stacks of books and papers everywhere atop it. Giving up and just putting his elbows atop two nearly even stacks, he asked,

"Well, well, so what exactly are we about here today, anyway?" Staring from face to face, Goward dug his hand down into the pocket of his jacket, fishing out his pipe. As he searched in the same deep pocket for his tobacco pouch as well, he said,

"Let's not waste too much time, shall we? I can guess at most of this. I've heard of you, sir, Mr. Warhelski. Most people in the field have heard of your chasings about. And I know everyone else here. You went to them for help with your werewolf, am I correct?"

"I, I went to enlist their aid, yes. But also to warn them that the monster is aware of them, as well."

The professor's eyes closed with those of the mournful man, scrutinizing them carefully as he asked,

"Do tell. And how is it that you are privy to what the beast is thinking?"

"He tells me."

"Messages through the air, perhaps? Special signals only you can interpret?"

"No," answered Warhelski, digging in his large leather bag. "Through the post house." Pulling forth a small handful of letters, bound together with several rubber bands, the one-handed man gave them to the professor, saying,

"About fifteen years ago, the thing began to write to me. These are all his messages."

Everyone in the room, even Jhong, leaned forward in interest, staring at the thin bundle of envelopes as if there might be some clue to be garnered merely by looking at their outside. Goward undid the rubber bands.

"And why do you think it has sent you these letters over the years?" asked the professor as he began sliding one of the letters out of its envelope with only the barest edges of his fingertips. Warhelski told him,

"I do not know. Sometimes I think it is merely laughing at my attempts to kill it. At other times I think it wants me to succeed." As the others waited for him to explain, the one-handed man continued,

"The way it tells me for where it is bound . . . after whom it is going next. I don't know . . . is it taunting me, or urging me on?" Warhelski reached forward suddenly, pushing the top few letters aside as he searched for one in particular. Pulling it up, he handed it to Goward, saying,

"Read this one first. Then, you tell me."

As the professor unfolded the aging, semi-yellowed paper from the envelope, he asked,

"Are they all this long?"

"No. Most are very terse. This one letter is longer than all his other words to me put together."

"You read fast," said London. "Why don't you just skim it and then just give us the important stuff?"

The professor did as the detective suggested, flipping through the pages at a brisk pace, lighting his pipe at the same time. Surprisingly, to London anyway, as soon as he finished reading the letter the first time he began once more. Indeed, so intent was he on his reading that he let his pipe go out, forgotten in his ashtray. Finally, the detective asked,

"Doc? I take it you found something?"

"Yes," answered the professor in an absent voice. "Oh, yes." Then, before reading any of what he had been looking at, Goward asked the one-handed man,

"This isn't the original copy . . . is it?"

"No. I was forced to have many sections of it translated. The beast wrote it in tongues. One sentence in German, another in Czechoslovakian, Carpathian dialects . . . many others. As if the words were not all his own, as if he were writing down bits and pieces of conversation he was hearing in a crowded room."

"Yes," agreed the professor. "A room filled with manic depressives. Here. Listen to this." Goward flipped back to the first page of the letter and began to read,

" 'Dear Maxim,' note the salutation . . . I don't think it's meant facetiously, either—listen. 'Another loss I gift to us both by eluding you once more. Are you as tired as I am, old friend? Are you as weary of this as I?' Fascinating. And I truly do believe he means his 'old friend.' Just from the tone of what I've been reading, I get the feeling the irony of the phrase is totally eluding the author." The professor began flipping pages again, reading a passage from the third.

" 'Today I tried to count the number of souls whose blood is on my hands. I started back as far as I could remember and I added them up, month after month, moon after moon—each set of victims bound together by the year of their occurrence. I counted the years and then the decades and soon I was counting not even centuries, but the millenniums, themselves."

Goward lowered the letter, looking at those assembled. Looking at London in particular, he said,

"I don't want to sound like some leftist psychiatric apologist, especially since such work is a bit out of my field, but in my opinion this is the writing of a man who is deeply concerned about himself and what he has done with his life. Listen to this further . . . 'I spend my clear days each month doing whatever I can to make amends for my dark side, for the curse I wear as you do your skin. Forgive the pain I have caused you, forgive me—I know what I'm doing . . . I simply cannot help it.' " The professor lowered the letter again, adding,

"And you think he is coming here?"

"I am sure of it." Reaching to the desk again, the mournful man pulled one envelope free—one distinctly fresher-looking than most of the others. Turning toward his left, he handed it to the detective, saying,

"Please—open it, Mr. London."

The detective slid open the envelope, pulling out the small folded piece of paper inside. Within its folds he found one of the London Agency's business cards. That was not nearly as important as the paper itself, however. On the slip he found his own name and address, along with those of Morcey, Lai Wan, and Lisa. London found it particularly disturbing that despite the fact the envelope was postmarked several weeks earlier, the letter correctly listed Lisa's address as the detective's brownstone. A fact which had not been concrete for even twenty-four hours.

Liquid cold dripped through London's spine, forcing him to shiver involuntarily for a moment before he could again control himself. Looking at the one-handed man, he threatened,

"If this is a joke, it's one played in very bad taste, Mr. Warhelski."

"When I was two years old, Mr. London, I saw my sister's eyes pulled from her head and swallowed as this monster's idea of a prank. I have not much been one for humor since then."

8

"May I ask a question?"

Everyone turned toward Jhong, everyone except for London, who rose even as the elder warrior spoke, abruptly leaving the room. As the others stared, Jhong said,

"Perhaps it is only because I was a businessman for so long before my life changed to that which it is now, but I am curious of one thing. You have pursued this monster across the faces of Europe and Asia, sir. How have you been able to afford your ventures?"

"I am a shoemaker, sir."

"A shoemaker?" answered Jhong, his eyebrows going up unconsciously. Without any further show of surprise, he asked, "And how does a shoemaker run the expense of mounting this kind of operation?"

Goward made to apologize for the elder warrior's curiosity, but Warhelski put him off. Taking a long slow breath, like a weary runner readying himself to cover a familiar track, the one-handed man said,

"My uncle took me in when the rest of my family was taken from me. I learned the trade of his fathers instead of mine own. My uncle was a good man. He provided for his wife, her brother, his father while he lived, and both his wife's parents while they lived. They never had any children of their own. In time, I inherited his business—which was not a great thing, but it was all he had to leave to me." The mournful man's expression closed in on itself, like the field of vision left to a horse with blinders. Falling back through the years, Warhelski said,

"I have continued as best I could. What moneys I have made I have put into tracking my enemy. Because of my efforts, a network of the monster's victims have come together. Some have helped finance my efforts. Some have lent what they could of strong backs and brave hearts. Some have had nothing more than their support to give. And I have taken all offered to me wherever it has been found. Money, weapons . . . a kind word of hope from another widow or orphan or parent left without child . . . it has all helped to sustain me over the years, and to bring me to this spot now."

London reentered the room then. Slipping back into his seat, he said,

"I apologize for the interruption. Whether I want to believe what Mr. Warhelski has to say or not, I couldn't not tell Lisa. I just wanted to call her and let her know to ... well, to just be careful until I could tell her more."

"A wise precaution, Theodore," said Goward. Then, addressing his words to the detective but focusing his attention on the entire crowd, he said,

"And, with the permission of the unusually healthy skepticism you seem to have brought to this event, I would like to proceed with the operating assumption that we are indeed confronted at this point with some agency that has operated for some time with great impunity ... one possessed of enormous physical strength and other abilities which we shall catalogue as we go along."

"Fine by me, Zack," answered London.

"Very good," responded the professor. Reaching again for his pipe, Goward depressed the button on his intercom which connected him to his secretary. "Ms. Featherstone, could you come in and watch over the recorders?"

London stood up out of his chair as they waited. He seemed uncomfortable—almost nervous—like a man being bothered unconsciously by the heat in a stuffy room. Then, as the young woman entered, bringing a fresh carton of tapes for the office recorder, Goward worked at relighting his pipe. Once the young woman had set up their machine, the professor asked,

"All right then, Mr. Warhelski, your claim is that the attack which took your family happened over eighty years ago. Has your network been able to trace the creature's movements to any time earlier than that?"

"Yes," responded the mournful man. Reaching into his heavy case, Warhelski pulled forth a slightly worn manila folder, saying, "This is a genealogy chart worked out by our people. If we are correct, the monster's crimes stretched back some four hundred years before I began to track it."

Goward flipped through the chart while the others waited in silence. Conscious of the running tape, he put the file aside for the moment, asking,

"And you, sir, do you believe the creature to be some five hundred years old?"

"The night I saw it in the window, the night it snapped off my hand, I looked into its eyes and it into mine. As a child the view meant nothing to me but horror. Over the years, however, like any man I have come to know what certain things mean. Yes—from looking into the soul of the monster, if that is what it can be called—yes, I think it is over five hundred years old. I think it is as old as time itself."

"Do you have any more concrete proofs?"

Reaching into his bag once more, the mournful man struggled for a moment and then pulled forth a great bundle of papers. The stack he put on Goward's desk measured at least seven inches in thickness. He told the professor,

"These are testimonials of other witnesses. Reports from the authorities in all the areas detailing their findings—their official reports and their own, more personal comments. There are newspaper clippings of sightings of the monster . . . everything that has been written about it that any of us has ever been able to uncover."

While he was still speaking, Warhelski had gone into his bag once more, pulling forth a much thinner file folder. Before Goward could ask if he had anything more substantive, the one-handed man gave him the file saying,

"And this is a set of copies of all the known photographs of the monster."

The professor's hand moved with startling speed, his fingers closing around the folder like those of a child grabbing a lollipop from out of a doctor's grasp. As he began to pull the manila leaves open, he said,

"I've heard about these prints. You know that most of your work has never reached any of the serious researchers here in the States."

"I am not surprised," answered Warhelski. "We—myself and the others involved—have become most insular. How can I explain it? We are the cranks, the fanatics, the lunatics. And how can I blame people? Stories of werewolves . . . who would believe? Who could?" The old man's face went calm. Closing his eyes, he raised his hand and rubbed at them both at the same time. Speaking in a voice suddenly very tired, he told both those assembled and the quietly whirling tapes,

"No—no one has believed us until tragedy strikes again and suddenly they have become one of us—and then they believe with a passion. But then, of course, they are fanatics also. And why should anyone believe them, either? It becomes a very convenient circle."

Goward did not comment, too caught up in his study of the photos before them. There were twenty-seven in number, many of them—although now all reproduced at the same size on similiar paper—originally taken with different cameras. One series of eleven shots, obviously a set due to the consistency of their backgrounds, caught the professor's eye. As he passed the other shots around for the rest of the room to view, he retained those for himself for the moment, looking at them from different angles, studying them intently. As he did, he spoke aloud for the recorder, saying,

"I am observing a somewhat disturbing montage of eleven photographs—rather dark and toward the end somewhat erratic—which show a definite humanoid figure with striking lupine characteristics running down what appears to be a forest trail. The direction of the figure is pointed toward the camera. The figure grows larger in each frame, although not necessarily clearer, until the final shot showing only mostly chest and snout. The nipple formation of the left breast seems clearly human, but the snout tip bent low into the picture is most assuredly canine in nature."

Finally getting his hands on a few of the other pictures being passed around the room, Morcey let out a sharp, high-pitched whistle, unintentionally interrupting the professor's monologue as he exclaimed,

"Man, oh man—sweet bride of the night. This might not definitely be a see-the-moon-and-need-a-haircut kinda guy, but I mean, Christ Almighty ... these is not pictures of yer Aunt Mabel. What are you thinkin', Doc?"

"I'm thinking that this is more than I'd ever dreamed of when I'd first heard of Mr. Warhelski." Turning to the one-handed man, he said,

"I'm thinking you may have been treated very badly in the press, my friend. Who took this series of photos?"

As Goward flashed several of the eleven pictures in question at the mournful man, Warhelski answered,

"A very dedicated young man by the name of Vincent Bragonier."

"Bragonier?" asked the professor. "His reputation was beyond reproach. When did he take these?"

"Several years ago."

"When, specifically? Bragonier was killed several years ago—skiing in Austria."

"That was the story released. He was on winter holiday, but,"
continued the mournful man, "he was not skiing when he took
those pictures—nor when he died."

And then, suddenly, London walked over to look at the set
of photos in the professor's hand. Pulling them from Goward's
fingers, he studied them in order, watching the approach of the
monster captured within them as he shuffled them one behind
the other. Moving his hands faster and faster, he made the
eleven frames of the short, horrible film pass more and more
rapidly, moving the photos again and again, watching the mo-
mentary play a score of times until he abruptly stopped.

With all eyes on him, the detective slapped the pictures of the
thing against a by then standing Goward's chest. Releasing his
hold on them, London gave no attention to whether they scattered in the air or not, turning to Warhelski instead, moving toward him and demanding,

"There's a thousand shows on television that would have paid
a mint for a one-handed smoothie like you—with your fucking
charts and documents and photographs and dedicated staff of
moon watchers. You and your network need money to stop your
boogeyman? Well, why haven't you gone to them? Why hasn't
your whole sad story about being made an orphan and a cripple
by the big bad wolf been on TV and flashed around the world
with all the ghosts and sea serpents and UFOs?" Closing on
Warhelski, the detective grabbed up the front of his jacket,
screaming,

"Tell me that!"

Without rancor, beyond feeling anger at other men's fears, the
mournful man answered,

"It was. We have been on the BBC. The Japanese, the Italians,
the Germans . . . they have all produced shows. Three different
productions have been completed in your country alone." Looking into London's eyes, Warhelski said,

"Did you think anyone ever listens?"

The detective's rage passed for a moment, but then boiled up
within him again. Releasing the one-handed man with a shove,
London moved toward the door, saying,

"I'm not doing this. This is nuts. This is a fucking wild animal! I'm the Destroyer, not some damn exterminator, and I don't
care what anyone says—I'm not the world's watchdog. I don't
have to take care of every lousy thing that goes bump in the
night." Swinging his hand across the room, pointing at each of

the people there he had known before that day, London said in a suddenly lowered, even flat voice,

"You people don't know what you're in for." Then the detective turned and pointed at Warhelski, bouncing his finger off the old man's chest.

"But you . . . you do. You're going to get people killed. You've done it before and you've come here to do it again."

Backing away from the mournful man, London moved toward the door, telling the others in turn,

"Jhong, I hope you know what you're doing. Professor, try to remember you almost didn't live through the last time we did this. Ms. Featherstone—I suggest you leave town. Right now. Don't come back until the full moon is over. Paul . . . don't use any of the company's money or resources on this. I won't allow it. Anyone who messes with this does it without my blessing." Stepping back, completely through into Ms. Featherstone's office, the detective stopped for one last moment, saying,

"People are going to die here—and for once, I'm not going to be the cause of it."

Then, London looked at Warhelski, telling him,

"And you—my friends start dying, you'd better be with them."

And with that, the detective turned on his heel and disappeared. None made to move after him. All within the room were too stunned, too taken by surprise to react—except, ironically, for the mournful man who had been the focal target of London's wrath. After some long moments, Goward set his pipe in his ashtray, saying,

"I'm sorry, I . . . I . . ." But Warhelski stopped the professor, telling him,

"Please. Do not apologize."

"But," piped in Morcey, "Doc Goward is right. I mean, this ain't like the boss at all."

"Oh," corrected the one-handed man, "but I think it is. He is a very decent sort of man and he is worried over what he has seen coming ahead." Suddenly feeling very tired, Warhelski sat back down, speaking to the room absently as he did so. Telling himself the truth loud enough for everyone present to hear it, the mournful man looked down at the eleven photographs piled on the desk and said,

"There is much pain within him, maybe too much for any one man. He has looked into the face of the monster and seen the future, and he is correct." Taking a deep breath, Warhelski continued softly,

"People here *are* going to die."

Then he closed his eyes and finished,

"And I *shall* be with them."

9

The group remaining within Goward's office took some few minutes to recompose themselves. The detective's incredibly uncharacteristic outburst—on top of the unusual attitude he had been displaying all day—had knocked some of the eagerness to delve into Warhelski's mystery out of them. They sat without speaking for so long that eventually Ms. Featherstone turned off the tape recorder, embarrassed they had allowed it to run so long, recording their silence.

"I must admit," ventured the professor finally, "that this does change things somewhat."

"How so, Doctor Goward?" asked the one-handed man.

"I'll tell ya how so, Mr. Warhelski," offered Morcey, his voice strained and agitated. "Mr. London is the boss, that's how so. He's the one that knows what gives with this stuff—I mean what really gives. He's stood up to some pretty mean odds . . . you, you can't even begin to understand. Hell, I was there, and I don't even understand it."

As the mournful man watched the listened, Morcey grew more and more animated, waving both his arms in the air as he made his points. Catching hold of what he felt growing inside of him, a nameless bundle of anxiety trying to mushroom into actual fear, he forced himself to calm down somewhat, putting his hands to rest on the arms of his chair. Then, finally a bit more under control, he continued, saying,

"Lemme put it this way. You've had to deal with a lotta people over this werewolf thing, right?" When Warhelski nodded, the ex-maintenance man said,

"Okay, over the what—decades—you've seen this thing and chased it, you've tried to tell people about it and all but, you've probably met a lotta folks who didn't understand . . . who got themselves killed, just 'cause of things that you knew and they didn't—things you even tried to tell 'em that they wouldn't listen to or couldn't understand. Right?"

"Yes," agreed the one-handed man. "This is all true, but what does it—"

"Have to do with this?" interrupted Morcey, finishing the old man's sentence. "What I'm tryin' to tell you is that as far advanced as you are over ordinary folks about this kinda stuff . . . that's how far the boss is past everyone here. Even the doc and, no offense, Mr. Warhelski, but even you."

The mournful man sat back in his chair—defeated. Crippled. All of his years crashed against his face then, etching it with a score of new lines, all deeper and longer than any he already had. The strength rushed out of him with his breath, leaving him so weak a part of his mind wondered for a split second if he actually had the energy to fill his lungs again. His eyelids drooping, he said weakly,

"Then there is nothing more to do. It is over this time. Finally, truly, over."

"Not necessarily," added Goward. "There is no doubt that Theodore is the guiding light of this little troupe. Although he has not the martial skills of Mr. Jhong here, or my own background in the world of the arcane, he is the Destroyer. And, there is little doubt that if he says someone is going to die, then someone probably is going to die. But," continued the professor, reaching for his lighter yet again,

"as you have pointed out, sir, someone is going to die whether we act or not." With his pipe going, Goward took a long, satisfying pull and then exhaled, asking,

"Jhong, I have been told on more than one occasion of your exceeding abilities as a member of the warrior class, but these tales seem to all be of martial skills. May I assume correctly that the use of firearms and the such does not fall within your general range of expertise?"

"Although I have some small skills with the use of armaments, I must confess that such does not make up a major part of my talents."

"Huummmm, yes. Very well, Paul—can I get you to run a small errand here?"

"Whatd'ya mean, Doc?"

"I'd like you to go to visit Pa'sha. Tell him what we are going to be up against and see whether or not he wishes to join in. His abilities will be in sore need."

Morcey looked at the professor without responding . . . hesitant. Goward was moving too fast for the ex-maintenance man. He had not considered actually proceeding without London. When the detective had left the room, it had only been the shocking abruptness of his departure that had kept the balding man from going with him. Now, Morcey wondered what he should do next. Recognizing his hesitation as such, Goward said,

"Paul . . . think. If Mr. Warhelski is correct . . . if this thing really has come to New York to stalk the London Agency—for whatever reason—then it is coming after you and Lisa and Theodore . . . and perhaps even everyone else who has ever helped in your investigations . . . including Lai Wan."

"I'm sorry, Doc, I mean . . ."

"Paul, look at it this way. If we prepare a welcome for this thing and nothing shows . . . then no harm's been done. But if it is coming, don't you think we'd best be ready for it?" Goward sat back in his chair, quietly taking in a thick lungful of smoke. After a long pause, Morcey took a deep breath and then let it out slowly, saying,

"Yeah, okay—I guess ya got a point."

"Who," interrupted Warhelski, "is this Pa'sha?"

"He's a friend of the boss's," answered the balding man. "He makes weapons. He's the best."

"Many things have been tried," cautioned the mournful man. "I have seen the monster's flesh turn bullets, absorb them. It is not frightened of fire or explosives. Please, tell this Pa'sha he will have to engineer his most ingenious weapons if they are to succeed."

"Any suggestions?" asked Morcey, rising from his chair.

"Sadly, no," answered Warhelski, his sad eyes staring deeply into the ex-maintenance man. "I have made many in the past, and they have all failed. Please to understand me, sir. I made my journey to America more to warn you than anything else. I have tried everything I could think of over the years—the decades—to destroy the monster. But, in the end, I have been proven to be nothing more than a one-handed shoemaker with a bag filled with proofs that, sadly, no one wishes to look at."

"Cheer up, Mr. Warhelski," said Morcey as he moved for the door. "After all, you must have somethin' on the ball. It can't be that easy to actually make shoes with just one hand." The balding man moved himself into the doorway to Ms. Featherstone's office, then said,

"I'll call ya from Pa'sha's, Doc."

And then, after a few words from Goward, Morcey disappeared out into the hall. Not wasting time, the professor turned back to Jhong, asking him,

"Well, that was simple enough. Now then, may I enlist your

aid for a different errand, Mr. Jhong?" When the elder warrior agreed, Goward told him,

"I'd like to send you to the home of another of our associates—the psychometrist Lai Wan—to ask her to join us in preparing for this ... 'expedition' shall we call it, as well. I could simply ring her on the telephone, but I think that procuring her assistance in the face of Mr. London's somewhat strenuous objections is going to take a personalized approach."

"Of course, Professor," answered the elder, rising from his chair. "Interesting how you sent her lover on another assignment first before sending me to her."

"Are you insinuating something, sir?" asked Goward evenly, lifting his pipe to his mouth.

"I do not waste time with insinuations. I said that I find your methods 'interesting.' If I had meant more than that, I would have said so. Now, if you would provide me with the young lady's address, I will be on my way ... Doc."

And then, after both Morcey and Jhong had left to complete their errands for Goward, the professor turned his attention back to his secretary. The young woman had been staring unpleasantly at Goward for a number of minutes. Not certain of the reason for her displeasure, he asked,

"What seems to be the matter, Ms. Featherstone?"

"I'm not sure I should say anything, Professor."

"Please, Joylyn," said Goward, somewhat taken aback by his secretary's sudden shift in attitude. "We have had no secrets between us in the past ... none that I know of, anyway. But, I have obviously done something to earn your enmity and I am simply wondering what that thing could be. If you are adamant in your refusal, however, I shall not waste time with guessing." Turning from the young woman, the professor asked the mournful man,

"How much time do we have remaining until the next full moon, Mr. Warhelski?"

"Tomorrow evening will be the first night of the new full moon," answered the one-handed man.

"There, you see? We have little time for soap opera. So, if you have something to say, please speak up and let us clear the air, shall we?"

Joylyn Featherstone came from a rare mix of bloods—Native American, island black, and African-American. The women of her family had always been tremendous helpmates—fiercely supportive of their men when they were correct, but willing to defy them when they were wrong. And, despite her proud loyalty to

Professor Goward, for the first time Joylyn suddenly felt she could not condone something which he was doing.

"All right, Professor. You want it, you got it. I think you're doing these people wrong."

"Wrong?" repeated Goward, questioningly. "And in what way 'wrong?' "

"Mr. London is right. Something *is* coming. Something bad. People are going to get hurt. He's thinking to barricade himself in and weather out the storm. You're thinking of going on the hunt. And he knows it. And he knows what's going to happen when you do it, too."

"Oh." The single word, coldly uttered, was all the professor had in the way of an immediate response. He had valued the young woman's help over the past few years. In many ways he had come to see her as more than a teaching assistant, more than a secretary—more than even a woman. He had come to know that her blood pounded to a like pulse as his. He knew she believed in his work, that she felt the same need he did to experience the supernatural . . . to know the unknown. But, suddenly he was faced with the knowledge that although she shared his vision, she did not share his methodology.

Finally, after several long moments of harsh silence, he was able to add, quietly,

"I'm sorry to hear that you feel this way. I find it most painful to discover at this point in our relationship that you do not trust my judgment."

"Professor Goward," answered the young woman in a plaintive voice, "I've always trusted you. You must know that. But this . . . this is—please . . ." With the feeling of tears welling behind her eyes, she told him,

"Mr. London knows about these things. He *knows*. Just last month, you almost died. You almost *died*. Doesn't that mean anything to you?"

"Not in the face of knowledge, Joylyn. No. I'm afraid that I believe our poor detective has, simply speaking, lost his nerve. I will give Theodore his due. He has withstood an amazing assortment of horrors. He has looked into the face of things that only a handful of men have since the beginning of time—out of the countless millions, the billions of beings who have trod this world . . . he is the only one man who has seen the things he has and still retained his sanity." In a whisper filled with honest admiration, the professor admitted,

"My appreciation for his accomplishments, Joylyn—let alone my gratitude—knows no limits."

"Then . . ."

"But they are accomplishments past. This danger Mr. Warhelski has brought us is of the future—and soon to be of the present. I cannot allow my feelings for what was to interfere in what is. Do you understand?" Nodding her head slowly, sadly, the young woman answered,

"Yes, Professor Goward, I understand." Feeling something warm deep within her suddenly harden over, ice filled her blood as she told him,

"I had feelings for something, too. But it's passed. Just like yours. And I won't let it interfere with what is, either."

"We're not talking about the same thing, are we?" asked Goward.

"We are," answered Joylyn, rising from her chair. Placing her pad and pen on the professor's desk, leaving them behind her like the last of a chocolate bar one had simply eaten too much of, she explained, "We're just looking at the same thing from different angles." Walking into the office outside of Goward's, she gathered up her purse, saying,

"You're the one who taught me that we all create our own realities, Professor." Taking her jacket from its hanger, she slipped it on while she said,

"It looks like I'm just going to have to work a little harder to have mine the way I want it."

And then, she walked through the door leading to the hallway. Watching her disappear off toward the elevators, the mournful man told Goward,

"Her tone. Sir, it is not my business, but I do not believe she means to return."

"No," answered the professor, sad for a moment, "no, neither do I." Then, he turned away from the empty space both he and Warhelski had been staring at and said,

"So. Let's get down to business. Shall we?"

10

London walked about the grounds of the Columbia campus, trying to find an outlet for his emotions, for his reason, for any part of him that would allow him to function in some rational direction. He knew that Warhelski spoke the truth. Having looked into the mournful man's eyes left little doubt that he believed every word he had said. Besides, the detective had been wrestling with darker portents than one man's ability to tell the truth or not.

"What?" he wondered aloud to himself. "What am I going to do?"

"About what?" came a voice to one side.

Turning, London found an overweight young man, both much younger and taller than himself, with a wild crop of long hair which lashed at both sides of his head. The detective looked up into the student's face and said,

"Excuse me. I didn't mean to bother you. I was just talking to myself."

"Ahh, yeah. No offense, but like the lady said in the cartoon, I figured that one out on my own. People talking to themselves is right up my alley, though. Hey, liking a good conversation as much as the next guy, I do it all the time myself. So, what is it you don't know how to handle?"

Studying the young man briefly, London sensed only an honest desire to be helpful within him. Not wishing to be rude to such a samaritan, London answered,

"Well, if I can say this without seeming too patronizing, I'm honestly grateful that someone might want to be on my side in this thing I'm dealing with, but what I have to deal with here really might just be a little out of your league." Not losing his smile, the young man replied,

"Buddy, to be just as honest in return . . . I didn't say I was on your side. I simply offered to listen to your problem and offer you whatever I thought you needed. Maybe that might be some of my worldly experience or just a shoulder to cry on, but it's a solid offer, and you do seem like a guy who needs one or the other."

The detective turned and stared at the young man, searching him with his inner eye for any trace of deception. One voice within him scoffed at the possibility, but it was shouted down by a number of others—from those simply advising caution to those shouting outright warnings or dire consequence. Seeing nothing in the student he felt he need caution himself over, though, London allowed himself a small smile and then said,

"Without going into things, I am intrigued enough to ask you a question."

"Sure, it's a start."

"I hear Columbia's undergraduate program is a pretty tough one. What is it that gives you the time to go around befriending every wild-eyed lunatic crisscrossing the campus muttering to himself?"

"One makes time, buddy. Classes are one thing, but to be level with you, something inside just told me to do the reach-out thing—you know?" Suddenly growing more serious, the massive student told the detective,

"I've been sitting here for a while. And even though I wouldn't exactly call you wild-eyed, or a lunatic, I must confess that I couldn't help notice you doing the crisscross bit. You've walked in and out of the gardens about twenty times. That something I mentioned . . . it just sort of pointed out that maybe you needed a friend and pushed me over here." Breaking contact with London's eyes, the hefty young man admitted,

"I understand what's going on. I mean, I've done it myself a few times. It's a good place for working out problems. Maybe better for some of us than others. Anyway, I didn't want you going off and giving our gardens a bad name, telling people they weren't any good anymore for getting yourself straight so . . . I guess I just thought I'd give it a shot and see if I could give you a hand."

And then, suddenly, a wave of calm settled through the detective, helping him to see through the conflicting emotions tearing at him. Putting out his hand, he said,

"Well, thank you . . ."

"Vinn," answered the younger man, taking the detective's hand, shaking it solidly.

"Thank you, Vinn. My name's Ted. It's nice to see a member of the so-called younger generation taking time out to help an outsider."

"Ahh, you know. My Oriental studies class says we're supposed to venerate our elders, and all. Besides, cast your bread upon the waters and it'll come back threefold and like that kind of stuff. You know what I mean . . . right?"

"Yes," answered London simply, trying not to wince at the word 'elders.' "I think so. Anyway, let me put your mind at ease that the recuperative reputation of the Columbia University gardens is intact. I may not know exactly what's going to happen next, but at least I know what I'm going to do next. Is that good enough?"

"Yeah, sure." Then, looking down at the detective, Vinn asked him,

"You sure you're going to be all right? I mean, you're dressed okay and all, but you wouldn't need, like, a couple of bucks or something, —would you?"

"No," answered the millionaire many times over. "That's all right."

London was astounded that he could be projecting such a negative force that he could make a complete stranger worry about him so. A casual study of the young man showed the detective nothing to mistrust. He simply seemed like a person honestly interested in helping.

"I'll be fine," continued London, wishing his problem could be handled so easily, but grateful to his companion for trying. "But let me say 'thank you' once again. I doubt I'll ever be able to explain how, but you actually have been a big help."

As Vinn extended his hand toward the detective, London sent his senses out over the large student. Doing so, he found no trace of deceit or ulterior motives, only an inner calm and balance unusually high for one so young. He sensibly made nothing of it, though, realizing that after the legion of bizarre people he had met over the last year, the talkative student before him was nothing to worry about.

"Hey," said the hefty young man, closing his eyes in a moment of self-congratulatory pride, "that's me. Always glad to be of service. It's like I always say . . ."

And then, Vinn opened his eyes again, his moment of internal back-patting over, only to discover that London had vanished. The young man looked rapidly in all directions around him, but he could find no trace of the detective. Finally, admitting that London was no longer to be found, he placed his customary smile back on his face and headed back to his favorite spot within the gardens, saying out loud,

"Ahh, well . . . another victory. It's so easy."

•   •   •

Far above the Columbia campus gardens, Professor Zachary Goward sat in his office with the one-handed man, looking over several objects on his desk. In his hands he held a twisted length of metal. Although there had been obvious attempts to keep it polished over the years, the shaft had been knotted so savagely that rust and tarnish had been able to build within its harshly tight bends and folds. As the professor turned the ruined hunk of steel over and over in his hands, he said,

"And you say this was a sword once?"

"Yes," answered Warhelski in a shaking voice. "My father's. We saw him run the monster through with it before the beast killed him. I remember it pulling the sword from its chest and twisting the blade up into the ribbon you have in your hands. Our mother removed us from the room then. We, the other children and I, we did not see our father die. We only heard it. As you might imagine, however . . . it was enough."

"Fascinating." Goward set the one-time weapon back down on the piece of purple fabric in which it had been wrapped, reaching for the tightly sealed plastic container next to it. As he lifted the container into the light to examine its contents, he asked,

"And what have we here?"

"A patch of the beast's fur . . . held together by a crisped layer of its skin."

" 'Crisped?' " repeated the professor absently. "As in burned?"

"Yes," answered the mournful man. "Last year, last fall, actually, in Romania."

"What happened?" asked Goward, turning the container upside down to get a better look at the charred skin remains. "You set the creature on fire somehow?"

"Not myself, actually. NATO soldiers."

The professor set the container back on the desk, his attention returning to Warhelski. Warning voices going off in his head, he asked,

"The beast has had a run-in with modern soldiers?"

"Yes. He has had many such encounters. The one last year in Romania, however, was by far the worst. My people and I, we had managed to convince a French major of the monster's existence. Not daring to try and convince NATO of the same, he instead scheduled night maneuvers for a valley in the neighboring country. The surrounding countryside had been plagued by wolves for some time. We knew it had become the lair of our foe. It was an inaccessible place—no good for anything except a brute's hideaway. The major proposed shelling the valley and then sending his men in afterwards to kill anything that moved. The farmers for miles in every direction were overjoyed. So were we. After so long, it looked as if an end would come to the beast at last. Such, however," said the mournful man with a low laugh cracking his voice, "was not the case."

Goward sat in his chair unmoving—his legs and arms and head motionless as if carved in stone. Even the hairs of his moustache stood perfectly still—as if his very breath had ceased to move within him. Remembering the events of the year before, Warhelski told him,

"They pounded the valley with artillery fire. A solid hour of shelling lashed the hillsides, leveling the trees, flaming the brush—destroying everything. What had been cliffs covered with dense briar and pine thickets became nothing but burning holes. The soldiers went in joking. Singing. They were looking for wolves—expecting to find nothing. They had a right to, after all. Nothing in their experience could have lived through such a nightmare of destruction. Their meager collective experience was about to be challenged, however."

Warhelski's voice lowered, pain soaking his words as he grieved for the dead anew merely by telling their tale.

"There was a horrible cry. The blistering howl of a lone wolf—long and cold and terrible. Instantly all the men went on the alert. Suddenly they knew something was ahead of them, stalking them. Fear cut through their ranks. What could have lived through the shelling? What kind of thing could have made the noise they heard—noise so loud, so angry? Their nerves at that instant pulling taut under their skin, they trod forward quietly, spreading out over the land, searching the smoke and holes before them in earnest—their weapons ready, their hearts in their throats. They marched for several more long minutes and then, suddenly, the thing howled again. But this time, the noise had moved behind them."

The mournful man motioned with the fingers of his one hand, drawing a circle on Goward's desk. Sketching the movements of the beast slowly, he said,

"It played the game with them for nearly twenty minutes, moving around them again and again—letting them think they knew where it was, and then howling from behind. Over and over, tearing at their resolve until many of them were crying— weeping amongst the craters and the burning pine stumps . . . praying in the smoking night to a God that did not hear them. Finally, the monster started his carnage, herding them into each

other, delighting in watching them kill each other out of stupidity
and fear. Of course, he killed many as well. By the time the night
was finished, over two hundred men were dead. You may remember a story of an explosion at a routine staging site . . . a terrible tragedy which had been judged an unavoidable accident by
NATO officials."

The professor nodded his head. He remembered the stories.
Just as he had remembered the stories of Vincent Bragonier's
skiing accident. Just as he remembered the stories released by the
American government a year earlier to explain the destruction of
the Conflagration. Determined not to allow his own resolve to
dissipate, he picked up the plastic container on his desk again,
asking,

"And how did this come into your possession?"

"One of the survivors, a lucky man fortuitously buried under
the bodies of several of his slain fellows, brought it to the major
and I, telling the tale of it. Stunned from his own wound, he
watched from his hiding place under the dead as the monster
came up behind three of his fellows. One had been armed with
a flamethrower—incredibly efficient. The beast grabbed up the
man so armed and two of his fellows in its massive grasp and
squeezed them together. So powerful was the pressure that the
men's ribs burst through their skin, impaling themselves to each
other on their own shattered bones. As he died, the man wearing
the flamethrower released the trigger. The tanks containing its
fuel ruptured as it was set off, igniting all its flaming power in
one gigantic fireball. We could see the effect from the top of the
hill, of course. Saw the flames burst skyward, saw the flaming
form of the monster running across the fields."

Warhelski's voice grew tired. Clearing his throat, straining to
find some saliva to send down to ease his dryness, he said in a
whisper,

"Every man still standing fired at the retreating flames. Hundreds, maybe thousands of rounds of ammunition were ex-
pended. It did no good. None of it. None of it did any good at
all."

"Guess we're going to have to find something that will, then."

Both men turned violently in their seats, startled by the abrupt
new voice in the outer office. Goward dropped the plastic container of hair and skin. He fumbled after it, but was unable to
catch it as it rolled off the edge of his desk. Although Warhelski
did not recognize the figure in the doorway, the professor did,
shouting,

"Good Lord, Benson. You damn near gave me a heart attack. How long have you been standing there?"

"Long enough, Zack." The man, tall and blond, with thin shoulders and a hairline crawling back toward his ears, moved into the office, grabbing at one of the chairs near the professor's desk. Turning it around, he slid his long legs on either side of it, resting his chest against its back as he said,

"So, monsters from Hell again, is it?"

"Possibly," admitted Goward.

"Well," answered Benson glibly, pulling the plastic container up from the floor. "Let's check it out and make certain, shall we?"

11

London left his cab at the corner, approaching Lai Wan's home on foot. Knowing she could sense his approach, he wanted to introduce his presence to her slowly, hoping to shed some of the anxiety propelling him toward the psychometrist. He understood some of what he wanted to ask her, of course, but some of it was still unclear in his mind. In truth, the only thing that he was sure of was that he needed a plan of action—fast—and that Lai Wan was probably the only person left who could help him.

Looking up at the large white blocks that made up the front of her building, he knew instinctively that she was home. Pushing open the unlocked front door, he walked into the lobby, his finger poised to press the bell to her apartment when suddenly the buzzer over the detective's head sounded, letting him know the security door's electronic seal had been broken for him.

"Well," he said to himself, "so much for taking her by surprise, eh?"

London passed through the lobby unnoticed by the doorman. Ever since he had left the Columbia University gardens, he had begun to take Warhelski's warning to heart. Realizing that there was a werewolf headed for New York—searching for him—he had unconsciously begun pulling in upon himself. Folding down the energy field surrounding his body, moving silently, keeping his attention focused on only what he was doing and nothing else, the detective had become virtually invisible. Already, those not actively looking for him did not notice him.

Lai Wan, however, being the center of his attention, could not help but notice his approach. She had been his only thought for close to a half an hour. For someone with her abilities, he could not have made her more aware of his presence if he had shone a flashlight into her eyes. An open elevator waited for him in the foyer. He pressed for the sixth floor, stepping to the back. As its doors slid shut, the doorman turned and stared at the departing car, wondering who had called it from above—certain that no one was in it.

The psychometrist lived in an unusual building. Every floor

had been designed as a maze, both to vary the size of the apartments and to give them a less sterile, more baroque feel. The floors were also broken up by sets of swinging fire doors positioned at odd junctures . . . placed for the standard safety reasons, of course, but also to enhance the building's unique, confusing mood.

London, of course, had no trouble in immediately finding his way to apartment D. Lai Wan, dressed almost completely in black, was waiting for him in her doorway. As he approached, the psychometrist took in the tilt of his head, the tension in his shoulders—the tightness in his hips, his stride, the way his arms were moving . . . the way his eyes were not. Pushing her door open for him, she said,

"Won't you come in?"

"Good idea."

The detective entered the apartment without losing his faraway look, passing his hostess almost without seeing her. Moving past Lai Wan's massive print of Jules Basttien-Lepage's *Joan of Arc*, he threw himself onto her floor couch, sinking into its spongy cushions.

"Make yourself comfortable, Mr. London."

"Thanks," answered the detective sarcastically. Pushing his back down into the couch, he moved the surface of its pillows this way and that, looking for the perfect spot to center himself on as he added, "Don't mind if I do."

Her door locked once more, the psychometrist swept into her living room, the lengthy skirts of her dress and robe flowing behind her. Standing over London, she asked,

"Something to drink? Could I make you lunch, perhaps? Or maybe you just came for some quick sex."

"Very funny," answered the detective through tight-pressed lips.

"You may make note of the fact that I am not smiling."

"Yeah," agreed London. "That is one of your problems."

"If we are about to make catalogues of each other's faults, I beg your forgiveness. Here I was thinking you had something in mind I was not going to enjoy."

"Hey," snarled the detective, his confusion over what to do next making him tenser—bitter, "can the attitude, all right?"

"Not on your life," answered Lai Wan. Glancing at the clock hanging between her bookshelves and the door to her study, she answered,

"For the past . . . thirty-seven minutes—hhoooh, I would have thought it ten times as long—I have had to endure the buzz in the air letting me know that you were bringing your self-righteous presence in my direction. Meditation, Advil, two glasses of wine, and Andreas Vollenweider's *Caverna Magica* were not enough to drown it out and I am growing increasingly tired of it." Planting her palms on her hips, she took a deep breath and then snapped,

"Very well, you have proved your point—I am on your mind. Now, could you please get something else on it and leave me alone?"

London shuddered, feeling his fingers curling into fists, his leg muscles hardening into steel. Fighting his nerves, pulling himself inward, his mind shuddered at the notion of shifting subjects. It had focused on the psychometrist and nothing else, avoiding that which it knew was coming. Now, suddenly, the detective felt his psychic energies extending outward from his body, flooding into the very floor. Moving at the speed of light, the fear which London had been hiding from himself burst open throughout his consciousness, filling his perceptions and his aura.

For a brief moment Lai Wan could see the energy flashing out of the detective's body. Before she could react, however, before she could turn away, move forward, or even think about what she was seeing, the psychic current seared up out of the floor and into her body, connecting the two of them as solidly as if they were handcuffed together. Suddenly, the fears that had been plaguing London, the terror he could not interpret, cut its way brutally through the psychometrist. The woman screamed as she felt the pain to come—screamed again as her apartment disappeared from her view, replaced by a blinding burst of pink and violet light.

Unable to stand against the electrical forces blasting her body, Lai Wan toppled, falling toward the floor leadenly, only so much deadweight. She was stopped less than a foot from the polished wood by London, however. He managed to catch her at the last second, only by throwing himself across the room to stop what he had inadvertently started. Unconscious of his hold on her, the psychometrist clutched herself, shaking from head to foot.

Getting both arms under the woman, the detective made to stand. Before he could reach his feet, however, he found he had to stop and catch himself, ending on one knee—gasping for breath, still shaking. Redoubling his efforts, he forced himself erect, lifting Lai Wan upward along with himself. Holding her close, allowing her access to anything she might need, London felt his chakras warming. Vital energy flowed from the detective into Lai Wan, stimulating her once more. Finally, London noted her eyelids fluttering. In a whisper, he asked,

"Are you all right?"

"Yes—yes, I believe so."

"Ah, where should I . . . put you?"

"If you would not mind, the gray couch would be fine."

The detective placed the woman gently on the softer of her two couches, then sat down at an angle from her in the next one, waiting for her recovery to be completed. After several minutes, when he could sense she was ready for conversation, he said quietly,

"I'm sorry about all that. I've, I don't know . . . I've been carrying this, this *feeling* around with me for days now. At first it was just in the background, just something disturbing I couldn't put my finger on. Then, at the party, I started to fixate on death."

"I know," answered the psychometrist in a voice stronger than London expected. "I was there."

"Yes. It was all right most of today—I got flashes of it here and there, but I didn't know what it meant. But we had a meeting today with a man who wanted us to help him destroy a werewolf. . . ."

The detective noted Lai Wan's lack of curiosity at his statement. Understanding his hesitation, she told him,

"I know this, also. Everything that has transpired today . . . I now have a picture of it as clearly in my head as you have in yours. You have been fighting a vision. A moment of the future has been struggling to reveal itself to you, but you have been resisting it."

"Then, what I·just saw in my head," he asked, his voice cold, afraid, "you saw it, too?"

"Yes. All of it."

"Well," implored the detective, "what can we do about it?"

"Nothing, Theodore," answered Lai Wan, her voice filled with pity. "It was a vision. One does not do anything about them. One merely waits for them."

"But, but . . ."

"I know," she answered, tears pooling in her eyes as she spoke, her normally dull voice softer, almost frightened. "And now, you do as well." Staring into London's eyes, the psychometrist told him,

"Yes, they are going to die. All of them. And there is nothing we can do about it."

Morcey had not been able to manage to return with Pa'sha before Goward and the others had left the professor's office. The professor had left a note telling him where he and Warhelski were going, however. The ex-maintenance man followed the few paragraphs worth of instructions, leading himself and Pa'sha to the subbasement level of another building. Once the pair had caught up with Goward, the professor introduced the man he and Warhelski had left with.

"Paul, Pa'sha, I'd like you to meet Dr. Joseph Benson."

"Hey, Joe, whatd'ya know?"

"That time is wasting, my fellows. I have been dragged, dragged I tell you—kicking and screaming, no less—away from my beloved petri dishes and spectral analyzers by this philosophical charlatan with promises of monsters from Hell. He's made this promise before, you know."

"Yes?" asked Pa'sha in a mild voice, interested in what the tall blond man had to say. "And what happened when you followed him into the breech?"

"We saw monsters from Hell. Doesn't everybody?"

"Everybody we know does," answered Morcey.

"These are not men to be overly impressed with your boogeyman tales, Joseph," warned Goward.

"Another batch of skeptics to deal with—eh, Zack?"

Goward smiled widely, reaching for his pipe. As he stuffed his bowl, he answered his colleague, shaking his head while saying,

"Hooho, hoohoohoo—oh, oh, oh my, hardly. These two gentlemen have witnessed events and phenomenon I'd give your left arm to have seen."

"*My* left arm, huh?"

"Yes, gladly," answered the professor, lighting his pipe. "In a heartbeat."

"Anything for science," said the doctor, turning back to his table for a moment. "Right, Zack?"

"Oh, but of course."

The tall blond turned back to the others, bringing with him the skin sample the one-handed man had brought with him. Passing it over to Pa'sha and Paul to inspect, he reached for a stack of computer printouts while he told them,

"Let's take a look at what we've got here, shall we?" Flipping through his printouts, he started to throw facts and figures at the others, saying,

"First off, I haven't got the slightest clue as to what kind of beastie that furry tissue sample came from. Trying to tab a coding on that thing's DNA ... oh my—I'm going to need a few weeks. ..." The doctor paused suddenly, reflecting on what he had just said. Starting again after the second's pause, he corrected himself, saying,

"Weeks? Well, if I'm the genius I keep telling people I am it might only take a few weeks. But, since I'm told I have to give up whatever information I can now for people to prepare to meet this thing head-on tomorrow night ... let's see what I can tell you right now." Pulling the twisted sword forward, holding it in one hand and the plastic container with the crisped tissue sample in the other, Benson told those assembled,

"There was a sufficient sampling of dried blood bonded to the metal—deep inside the bend points—to allow me to do a blood test. I am willing to say that whatever it was that left its blood on this blade is most likely the same thing that this chunk of skin came from."

"So, the thing really is at least, at the very least, over eighty years old," exclaimed Goward, believing completely for the first time.

"I take it," asked Benson of Warhelski, "that if the story I overhead you telling earlier about how you got this sample is true, then old age is not slowing this thing down much?"

"It is not an easy beast to kill—no," admitted the one-handed man. "That is very true."

"Perhaps then," interjected Pa'sha quietly, "you have been attempting to kill this thing with the wrong armaments." As everyone's attention focused on the large weaponeer, he continued, asking the assembly,

"So far, it has been bullets and fire ... no?" As the mournful man nodded his head, Pa'sha said,

"Then other methods must be tried. I have seen living beings regrow the flesh blown away by bullets—sometimes in mere seconds—since I have begun joining Theodore and the good doctor on these little excursions. If we know bullets are not going to be of much help, then we must think of something else."

"What better'n bullets?" asked Morcey.

" 'Better' may not be the word we want here, my friend. Death is an orchard which produces many fruits. One can die from a vast number of methods—a great fall, electrical shock, drowning, poisons, from being crushed, or . . ."

"Of course. Poison!" interrupted Benson, suddenly wildly excited. "If this truly is some kind of regenerative beast—one that can replace lost blood cells, muscle, hair, tissue, et cetera, with the speed of thought—we have to ask ourselves, how? How does it do it?" Picking up a slide he had been examining earlier, the doctor held it up to the light, studying it absently as he said,

"My guess would be that its adrenal glands—or something quite similar—must work overtime, pumping fantastic amounts of adrenaline into its system. It must release massive quantities of white blood cells to the damaged areas. There has to be a radical inflow of all coagulants, from . . ."

"Joseph," asked Goward sharply, "before you get carried too far away from the original problem, allow me to inquire . . . what does all this have to do with poisons?"

"This thing's ability to replace its lost body parts has to be slowed. That's why it has to be poisoned. Slow down its system's response time . . . give it something to concentrate on besides superficial, or well, shall we say, external problems. It has always, in the past, I assume, only been attacked on one front. People shooting at it, trying to boil it in oil, or fill it with arrows, or whatever. Am I right?"

"To the best of my knowledge," answered Warhelski, his eyes beginning to glow, just slightly, as he began to get caught up in the doctor's enthusiasm, "this is truth. I know of very few times when the monster has been confronted by any real show of force whatsoever, let alone with different . . . what would you say . . . means of attack, from different directions at the same time." Turning to Goward, to everyone, the mournful man said,

"This could work. This, this idea—to fill it with poisons, and then crush it—electrify it—then burn it and shoot it and blow it into pieces into the highest heavens . . . this could be the answer. This could do it!"

"If you can come up with a way to do it," answered Benson. As everyone looked at him, he said,

"I'm, I'm, well, a little surprised at myself here—getting so caught up in all this. I've wanted to see one of your juicy monsters for so long, Zack, that I guess I'm turning into something of a little kid, here. I mean, getting a, a . . ." His eyes glanced over toward the table next to him, seeing the stack of Warhelski's photographs. As his eyes focused on the running shape in the largest picture, he said,

"A werewolf."

Benson's pale blue eyes widened as it dawned on him exactly what it was he was talking about. Catching hold of his nerves before his hands could actually begin to shake as severely as they wanted to, he continued, talking in a less powerful voice, saying,

"God . . . I'm actually talking as if there were, I mean, I don't want to insult anyone, but well . . . even if this is all real—in fact, *especially* if this is all real . . . how would you plan . . . er, I, well—any of it? The poison. There, there's a good one. How would you get massive doses of poison into this thing?"

"Doctor," came Pa'sha's even tone, one that told Benson that there probably were werewolves in the world, "I will make a deal with you, sir. You supply the poison . . . I will worry about getting our beastie to swallow it."

12

London and Lai Wan had each just started their second cup of tea when her door buzzer caught them both off guard. Usually the psychometrist had no trouble anticipating even accidental pressings of her bell, but then was not a usual moment. She had been greatly unnerved by the vision she had shared with the detective, upset to the point where she could barely get enough water from the warmer in her kitchen to make the tea they were drinking.

Collecting herself, though, she moved across the room to the door panel, asked who it was, and discovered that it was Jhong. When she asked London what she should do, he answered simply,

"It is your home."

Given command of the situation, she pulled in on herself to deepen her composure. Then she reached up and buzzed the elder warrior in, unlocking the door so he could enter when he arrived. She did not feel like standing at the door and waiting for him, or returning to it when he got there. In fact, the only thing she felt like doing was returning to her large, overstuffed chair, crawling under her quilt, and warming her nervous hands with her teacup.

"What do you think he wants?" asked the detective.

Closing her eyes, the psychometrist extended her mental touch down into her chair, down into the floorboards, across them, through them—out into the hall, into the elevator shafts, into the cars. Coming into the car carrying Jhong, she pierced the soles of his shoes, his feet, her consciousness racing into his nervous system, up his spine, into his skull, into his brain. Skimming his surface thoughts, she said aloud,

"He is here to bring me to Professor Goward." Lifting her cup up to her lips, she took a short sip of the steaming, bitter green tea within, then added,

"He wishes to escort me to the massacre."

"Yeah? You going?" asked London, taking a sip from his own cup.

"I do not know," she answered seriously. "Let us see if he brought roses."

The detective did a short spit-take, dribbling his tea ungraciously back into his cup. Wiping at his chin with his sleeve, he said,

"Ho ho. Very funny."

"Thank you," answered Lai Wan, her lips drawn into a straight line, but her eyes smiling. "Perhaps I should consider a career in stand-up comedy."

"Yeah," complained London. "That or a lobotomy."

"Why, Theodore," replied the psychometrist. "If you stop to consider the scale and scope of the witticism the cosmos is playing on us at the moment, what is one more little joke?"

Jhong's knock came at the door before the detective could answer. Calmly, Lai Wan called out, bidding him to enter. He came in without undue hurry, noting London's presence. Nodding to the detective, he said,

"Good to see you again."

"Is it?"

"Please—Mr. London. The professor is most eager to match his wits against the power of the beast. Who am I to say him no?"

"I thought you told me you showed up because you sensed trouble? When you saw Warhelski, you said he was it. Well, what the hell kind of 'it' were you talking about? Have you seen the vision, too? Have you?"

Jhong stepped over to the table standing in between Lai Wan and the detective. Sitting down cross-legged, he filled the empty third cup sitting next to the pot, nodding to his hostess as he said,

"It is so pleasant to be expected." The psychometrist nodded back to the elder warrior, noting to herself that she had set a third cup on her tray without realizing it. Taking a sip of the still hot tea, Jhong set his cup back down, and then returned his attention to London.

"Allow me to explain my part in the events unfolding around us. As best I understand them myself, that is. For some months I have been feeling most uneasy about . . . things. Over the past few weeks, I have been filled with the desire, the need to be at your side. I have known that horrible danger was coming your way and that I had to be there."

"Baloney. Last month we had the psychic ceiling drop in on us. Where were you then?" The elder shrugged his shoulders, telling the detective,

"What can I say? Perhaps you did not need my presence then but do now. Perhaps this is all a coincidence and you don't need me now any more than you did then. You tell me. All I can say is that the closer I came to New York, the more positive I was that something quite disastrous was headed here with me. When I saw you at the party last night, I was sure."

"Sure? Why?" asked London. "Sure of what?"

"That something terrible was stalking you. When I saw Mr. Warhelski, it was almost as if I could see a connection in the air between the two of you." The elder sipped his tea again, replaced his cup on the table, and then asked,

"And, I know that if I can almost see it that the lady must. Would you care to comment, madame?" Lai Wan glared at Jhong darkly for a moment. Then, taking a deep breath, she resigned herself to the following, and looked at London, saying,

"I had hoped to ignore this, but I see I cannot. He is correct, Theodore. There is a deep black haloing force circling about your head. Death is thick in all the air around you. I have seen this before. It is not come to claim you, however. As in the vision . . . it has come for those around you."

"Your talk of visions, the two of you . . . it is most intriguing. Can I induce you to comment further?"

"Yeah," answered the detective. "I'll comment up a storm for you." Draining the last of the tea from his cup, London stood up and began pacing the room behind Jhong as he explained the picture that had been growing in his mind for weeks—that he and the psychometrist had seen earlier.

"I'll cut right to the chase. We both saw me—at some point in the future. My feeling is that it was tomorrow night." Turning to Lai Wan, the detective asked,

"What did you think?"

"That was my impression, as well."

"All right—we agree—we saw me, tomorrow night. And I think it's fairly safe to conclude that the time is after moonrise. Now you might ask, 'Why is it so safe to conclude that the time is after moonrise?' Well, I'll tell you why." Growing more agitated by the second, London tried to catch hold of himself—calm himself down—but failed. Unable to control his growing tension, he balled his fists unconsciously, flailing them about himself as he continued to walk about the apartment, his voice growing louder with each word.

"Because," he shouted, "what we saw was me, crying and screaming. We couldn't see what I could see—whatever it was that I was seeing, the thing that was causing all the crying and screaming . . . but we knew—I know, anyway—what it was . . . what it is. What it will be. It's the bodies of my friends, torn to shreds. Arms and legs scattered across the scenery, scenery flooded with gallons of blood." Turning to Lai Wan, the detective ordered,

"Tell him. Tell him what you felt."

"As much as I wish it different, I am certain Mr. London is correct. Those who attempt to stop this creature of the night are in great danger. They will not succeed. Many of them will die. Period."

Sipping again at his tea, the elder warrior held his cup in one hand while he used the other to pull at his beardless chin. Turning from the one to the other, he finally let his gaze settle on Lai Wan, asking her,

"This is an absolute thing? There is no going around it in any way?"

"None whatsoever. There is no question that the thing will not be killed or captured. There is no question that those making the attempt will fail. There is no question either that some of them will die."

"The only question," interrupted the detective, "is how many."

Jhong looked into London's eyes. The despair that greeted him shocked the elder warrior, chilling him as few things ever had. Controlling his emotions, however, he poured himself another cup of tea, took a short sip, and then announced,

"I believe you."

"Then," asked the detective, "what are you going to do?"

"That depends on the lady." London merely looked at the older man, waiting for him to explain himself. Jhong took another sip from his cup, then said,

"The professor has asked me to fetch her to his offices. I have come to do that. If she decides to go with me, then I shall return with her. If she decides against going with me, then I shall return without her."

As both men looked on, the psychometrist rose from her chair and left the room. She returned a moment later, drawing a large black lace shawl around her head and shoulders. Walking up to London, she placed her hand on his wrist, telling him,

"Paul is with the professor, is he not?" When the detective confirmed her fear, she continued, saying,

"Then I must go. I cannot allow him to be destroyed in such

a fashion without even attempting to stop him. What will you do next?"

The detective placed the fingers of his other hand over Lai Wan's. Pressing her hand in between his hand and wrist, he felt her determination and the strength behind it flowing into him. And, as he did, a great relief flooded through him. Giving her a small smile, he said,

"I think I'll go home. I've been getting a little too excited here and that's probably the worst thing I could be doing, right?"

"It is, as you might say, 'up there.' "

"Yeah. Well, anyway, I've got to tell Lisa what's going on and take some time to relax and see just what I'm going to be doing tomorrow night. I know from all the facts we have that this thing means to confront me. But, trying to capture it or kill it . . . I just have this gnawing feeling that it's a mistake. Or something . . . I don't know."

"Maybe you do not at this time," offered the psychometrist, "but, I am sure you will when the time is right." As they disengaged hands, she added,

"It is your way."

And then, suddenly, the detective swept Lai Wan up in an embrace, hugging her to himself, fear and pain and torment flooding out of him, disappearing into the air and beyond. Feeling his need, the psychometrist did not resist, giving him what strength she could. Then, surprisingly, she felt her energies returning to her, doubled in force. Releasing his hold on her, London smiled, telling her,

"Thanks."

Flustered, awed at the ease with which the detective had taken part of her life force to cleanse his system, only to then return it seconds later doubled in power, she smiled weakly back, saying to him,

"You are a fascinating man, Mr. London. You have learned so much in such a short period of time. If you do not get all of us and yourself killed, it will be interesting to see how far you go."

"Right now," he answered, "I'm just going home." Then, turning to Jhong, he asked,

"What about you?"

"I assume you ask as to where I will be tomorrow night. To answer you truthfully, I must admit that I do not know at this time. I have seen some of what the professor has to offer and I have heard what the two of you have to say. Now I shall return and see what else the professor has to offer. As I told you, a strong force has guided me to this place at this time. I know I am to be here. *Here* is a very large place, however. At present I simply do not know exactly where in all this here I am meant to be when the moon is full tomorrow."

London looked at the elder warrior, wanting more, knowing he could not ask for it. Sensing his need, Jhong reminded him simply,

"It is my way also, remember?"

The detective acknowledged that he did. Then the trio moved out into the hall together, all three of them wondering where their feet were going to lead them.

"Oh, oh God, Teddy," said Lisa, the pain in her heart bleeding out into her voice, tearing at the detective. She stood in the kitchen, utensils in hand—clutched but forgotten. "Why us? Why now? Why does it have to be now?"

"I don't know, sweetheart," answered London quietly, honestly. "I don't know."

She had been working on dinner when he had come in. He had started talking while still in another room, almost unable to look at her as he spoke. The detective had, of course, told her everything that had happened. From the time Jhong had first entered their offices that morning to his own parting from the elder warrior and Lai Wan to return to home—return to her. And, she had known from the first sight of his face that something was wrong. Actually, she had been receiving disturbing signals all day. London's arrival only confirmed her worst fears—that something had happened, something monstrous . . . that something from the other side had come to challenge her man—to try and take him from her side once more.

London stared at the young woman, her chestnut curls framing her face, the luster of them in the bright afternoon light almost enough to distract him from the tears starting to well in the corners of both her eyes. Almost. Tenderly, he held out his arms to her. Gratefully, she abandoned the strainer and the ladle she was still holding in her hands and then fell into the strength he offered, desperate to understand why fate had decided to use the two of them so cruelly.

Holding her to himself, the detective wondered silently at the same things as she—why now? For that matter, why did anything have to happen ever again? Yes, he admitted to himself, sure—he had been waiting for something new to happen, almost impatient for it even.

But now? he asked himself. *Damn it all . . . Now? Did it have to be . . . now?*

"I'm sorry, sweetheart. I wish I had something I could say that would make it all different, but the things I told you—those are the facts." And then, in a dazzling brief moment, Lisa reheard all that London had said to her over in her mind, suddenly realizing the most important thing he had told her. Not understanding, she asked,

"Teddy, I just realized. You said you weren't going to go after this ... this *werewolf* thing. Why? I mean, I thought you were the Destroyer—that there was no getting around these things for us ... for you."

Pushing Lisa away slightly, breaking their contact just enough so he could see her eyes, he told her,

"Warhelski said that thing was coming for the London Agency. Not just me—Paul and me ... and you."

"But, Teddy, how can we fight it? Shouldn't we get together with the others? Maybe—" The detective cut her off, saying,

"No. I don't know why I feel this way. I can't explain it. The vision ... I've seen the future." His voice cracking slightly, his arms and shoulders beginning to tremble, he started to half-move toward the couch, half-allow Lisa to move him toward the couch, as he said,

"I'm not there. Or at least, I'm not supposed to be there. Other people are supposed to meet it. Other people are supposed to die before I go after it."

"But, but, but," stammered the young woman as they sat each other down on the couch. Torn between wanting her lover safe and wanting to understand what was happening around them, she asked the question neither of them wanted spoken aloud. "Who is it? Who is it that's going to die? Who has to die so that ... so that you don't?"

"I don't know," answered London, his words tinged with a cold terror of what was to come. "The vision only showed me myself—staring at the dead. I just know I'll be seeing friends— people I love, their bodies covering the ground—dead there in front of me. I know they're all dead, I ... I just don't know who they are!"

And then the detective stood up, walking away from Lisa as he raged,

"*I don't know!!* I should, but I don't! I thought I was the Destroyer, that there was always going to be an answer. But now when I need one the most ... I don't have one! I've tried—" he said, his voice pulsing with agony. Not knowing where he was going, he stopped in his tracks and turned toward Lisa. Bending over, his arms shaking in front of him, he shouted,

"I've looked at this from every angle ... and there's just noth-

ing I can do. From everything I can feel ... *inside* ... there's
nothing I can do ...." And then, his voice cracked, breaking
under the strain of his battered nerves into a wrenching sob that
broke open the floodgate of Lisa's tears. She rose to her feet,
crossing the room toward the detective as he cried in a low and
pitiful voice,

"There's nothing that I'm even *supposed* to do."

Sinking to his knees, London sobbed openly and loudly, wailing in pain. Holding on to the detective, Lisa gave him her
strength, her love—letting every ounce of courage and hope and
faith she had flow into him. She said nothing as she clutched at
his shaking form, simply moving her head up and down reassur-
ingly against his chest and shoulder. His arms circled her as well,
the deadweight of them dragging at the young woman, threatening to pull her down to the floor.

Holding her close, as if she were the only thing solid in a
maddened ocean, he whispered through his despair,

"I don't know what to do. When my father died, saving my
mother and me, I was just a baby. There was nothing I could do.
My brothers died then and there was nothing I could do for
them, either. My mother raised me by herself, and she died right
in front of me—in my arms—and there was nothing I could do
for her ... just like my brothers and my father." Wiping at his
face, he tried to pull himself together, sputtering,

"Just like all those hundreds of thousands who died in the
Conflagration. Like Father Wickler and Joey Bago'Donuts. And
Mrs. Lu and George Collins. Just like the Spud." Then, his voice
lowered again as he added,

"Just like Jenny."

Confused by his last reference, Lisa asked,

"Who?"

"Jenny," repeated London, knowing what he was doing as he
added, "my first wife." He had avoided the subject for a long
time, not knowing how to broach it, not knowing why he should.
A part of him realizing that Lisa would need more information
than he had given her, though, he continued, telling her,

"I'm sorry. I never mentioned her before. She died ... a very
long time ago. A car wreck. We were married all of eighteen
weeks when a woman hurrying her kids to, to ...." And then he
stopped, his voice puzzled, unsure. Finally, he said in a faraway
voice,

"Funny. It's been so long I don't even remember what was so
important anymore ... so important to that other driver that she

had to kill herself and her children . . . and Jenny. I just remember that she did . . . and that I couldn't do anything about that, either. Not that I knew anything about it until I was told later. There was no flash in my mind when she died—no message of love that I pulled out of the airways. I was just sitting at home studying when the sheriff's men came to the door." He remembered the horrible moment, his shock, and his guilt over being shocked, over not somehow already knowing. Aloud, however, he said simply,

"They took me to the hospital for the identification and the whole way there I still didn't believe them, still just couldn't reach through the ether and just *feel* that she was no longer a . . . a part of things."

Looking into Lisa's eyes, suddenly sobering, he told her in a once more even voice,

"I went crazy then—for a long time. I was in law school, but . . . I don't know. I just walked away from our apartment, from school and what little was left of my life—just left it behind me and took a train north. I became a cop first, and then I left the force as soon as I had enough years in to get my private license."

Testing his legs, feeling secure in their ability to hold him, he pushed off from the floor gently, taking Lisa upward with him. Standing again, holding on to the young woman's hands with both of his, he told her,

"I've had some small feelings for a few women over the years since then, but I couldn't let anyone mean anything to me . . . I tried. More than once. But it didn't work." Then he drew her close, telling her,

"Until there was you."

And then the detective kissed the woman in his arms. Their lips met again as if for the first time, timidly but hungry, desperate. Their arms encircling each other anew, they pulled into one another, their kiss long and deep and needed by each of them like nothing else, more important than oxygen or bread or the sun itself. Neither of them had the slightest idea of how long their embrace lasted—neither of them cared.

When finally they pulled away from each other for a moment's rest, London said softly,

"And that's why I've been so upset—so panicked by all of this. What if it's you, Lisa? What if it's your body I'm seeing in those eyes in my vision? What am I supposed to do if we don't even get eighteen weeks?"

"I don't know, Teddy," answered the young woman, feeling

strangely calmer than she felt she had any right to be. "You know, I've never really thought about dying . . . through all of this, I mean. No matter what's happened, I've never felt like I was ever really in any danger."

The detective's senses flashed through Lisa automatically, assuring him of what he assumed—that she was telling the truth. He smiled weakly, no longer unsure, simply drained by the day and its assault on his emotions. Then, knowing the answer she would give, but needing to hear it just for its healing properties, he asked,

"Why?"

"Because," she answered in the voice of a mother telling her firstborn the answer to one-plus-one, "I knew you'd never let anything happen to me." And then his smile blossomed, filling his face, exposing teeth, causing Lisa to flush while she asked playfully,

"What? What's that stupid grin for?"

But then, before London could answer, he suddenly straightened, his head jerking toward the front of the building as he said,

"Paul."

And then the doorbell rang, followed by the noise of a key turning in the lock and Morcey's voice calling,

"Hello? Boss—you home?"

"Upstairs, Paul."

Lisa stepped quickly over into the kitchen. Grabbing up a dish towel, she threw it to the detective so he could wipe his face down before their partner reached the second floor. He threw it back to her, blowing her a kiss at the same time as the ex-maintenance man reached the landing. As he entered the living room of their main apartment, Morcey asked,

"Hey, boss. Hey, Lisa. I'm not interrupting anything, am I?" When they assured him he wasn't, the balding man said,

"Look, ah, Lai Wan came over ta the doc's and all, and, like, he's got things hummin' along pretty good. I just came down because . . . umm, some of us are a little concerned about how ya was feelin' about all this . . . and . . ."

"Paul." London cut his partner off before he could say any more. Waving him in toward the main couch, he said,

"Listen. Maybe I'm getting too high-strung for this work or something, but I'm feeling better now."

"Uhh, yeah," answered Morcey, still obviously agitated. Summoning up his courage, he continued, saying,

"Lai Wan told me about that, like, vision you two had. Where you saw people dyin' outta this."

"Yes," admitted the detective. "That's right. I wish I knew more than that, but I don't. It's a bad deal we've got here. If Warhelski's right—and it sure looks as if he is—this thing is coming to match itself against us and there isn't much we can do to prevent it. We're going to have to stand up to it—there's no way around it, but . . ."

"Yeah, *but*. Don't I know it. I mean, it's not like we haven't been ready to die a couple of times this last year and all, but . . ."

"Like you said . . . 'yeah, *but*.' We only knew there was a chance of dying before. Now we know someone's going to die for sure."

"Boss," said Morcey, his voice low and steady, "let's face it, people have been gettin' stacked up like cordwood ever since we took this show on the road. Okay, yeah—it's a little nerve-wrackin' and all, I mean, *knowin'* someone's going to get it when we do this tomorrow night but, like everyone keeps sayin', we ain't got much choice. We sorta have to do it. And, ah, sweet bride of the night, let's face it—this shit gets started, someone always dies, anyway."

"Well, another little point," added London with a fatalistic tone, "is that there's no one saying that my little insight into the future doesn't come a stroke before I get it myself. There's no guarantees that I'm going to get out of this, either. But," said the detective, grabbing up his jacket from where he had dropped it earlier,

"like George Washington said, 'I die hard. But I am not afraid to go.' "

"Well," added Lisa, "if we're going to get literary . . . I've always liked Emily Dickinson's thought, that 'Dying is a wild night and a new road.' "

"Oh, murrr-derr. Ain't the two of you quiz kids just ever so droll?" said Morcey, sending an artificial shiver through his body for comic effect. "Me, if I've gotta throw a quote in the ring on the subject, I'll take Mark Twain and hope for the best."

"What did he say about dying?" asked Lisa.

"What I hope to be saying day after tomorrow . . . 'The reports of my death are greatly exaggerated.' "

Shrugging his jacket on, London turned to Lisa and asked her, "Think you can bear waiting here for us?"

"Thinking of your stomach?"

"Yeah, actually. I hate to admit it, but I am getting a little between meals. I'll call you and let you know who all might be coming back. Think you can bear up under a little traditional role-playing here?"

"I knew that's why you wanted me to move in," teased the young woman, hands on her hips. Throwing the left one over her head with a haughty gesture, she said, "Now I'm just supposed to sit here and wait to see how many people I have to stretch dinner for. Right?"

"Yeah," answered the detective, joking back at her, "that would be perfectly swell, honey-bunchikins."

The two drew together for one last time before parting, kissing briefly, exchanging warnings and assurances. After that, London simply pointed toward the door, telling Morcey,

"After you, partner."

"I'm wit'cha, boss."

Then, as the two men descended the stairs down toward the street, the ex-maintenance man turned toward the detective and told him,

"Like I was saying . . . greatly exaggerated. Know what I mean? Greatly. G-R-E-A-T-L . . ."

"Yes, Paul," answered London, half-laughing, half-wondering if his partner's joke would still be one after the next night had passed.

"I get the idea."

14

For the obvious reason of much needed privacy, all of those involved shifted their meeting to the detective's midtown offices. A call from Morcey's car phone brought those still at Columbia down to the far more tightly secured suite of the London Agency. Once everyone necessary had been gathered, however, the size of the crew assembled had grown to almost ridiculous proportions. Finding seats for everyone had been accomplished only by the moving of nearly every available chair into London's office. And even then one of the chairs had to be placed in the doorway between the office and the reception area.

Seated behind his desk, the detective looked out over the assembly as they got themselves arranged. Goward had chosen the leather chair next to London's desk, both to situate himself near the natural front of the crowd and also to be able to reach the room's only ashtray. Jhong had taken the wooden armchair on the other side of the desk mainly because he preferred simple, hard seats above all others.

Warhelski had been given the chair from behind Lisa's desk which he had moved forward until it was next to that of the elder warrior. Lai Wan had taken the remaining leather chair on the other side of the room from Jhong, Morcey sitting on her right in the chair he had brought in from behind the desk in his own office. Benson and Cat had taken the two simulated leather-covered chairs from the ex-maintenance man's office, positioning them in between the detective's desk and the doorway to reception—the doorway being filled by Pa'sha in the oversized, stuffed chair he had dragged around from the back wall of the reception area.

Looking out over the assembly while those gathered continued to settle in, London braced himself for the meeting to come. He had agreed that the monster had to be met—realized that there seemed to be no way around the confrontation. The monster was following a set pattern—notify someone that it is coming, then do exactly what it announced it would do ... arrive ... and kill them. The detective steeled his nerves, silencing the etching tingle they were pulsing throughout his system with a single but terse command. He had faced death many times in his lifetime, especially during the last twelve months.

But this—this time was different.

Sure, said one of the voices in his head, lots of the other cases you've handled have been dangerous. And, sure again, it isn't as if every other time you've butted heads with the supernatural people haven't died. Somebody's always dying. That's what people do . . . they die all the time. So, what's got you so wound up this time?

And, of course, the answer was simple. Every other time there had been a chance that no one would die. There had at least been a *chance*. But on the next night, there was no escaping the reaper. The detective knew—*knew* beyond a shadow of a doubt—that the next night, at least one of the people in the room with him was going to die. At least one. Maybe more. Maybe everyone he could see before him. Maybe himself as well.

There was also no doubt in London's mind that Warhelski was telling the truth about everything. It had been a year since the world had lost the ability to lie to the detective. He had looked into the one-handed man's eyes and all had been made obvious. Yes . . . it was true . . . the werewolf was real. Its methods were fact. It had sent the letter, and it would stalk the London Agency the next night . . . as soon as the light of the full moon bathed the landscape.

A werewolf, thought the detective. Jesus Christ, Lord Almighty . . . a werewolf. Werewolves. Is every stupid thing we've ever seen in the movies real? Hiding out there somewhere? Waiting to throw itself against me?

Leaning over to the right, London asked Goward,

"Doc, if you don't mind, I've got to play the skeptic for us one last time here and ask about all this." Spreading his hands wide before himself, opening his aura to the professor, the detective asked,

"I mean . . . werewolves? Have I missed something here? When the hell did the world become infested with goddamned werewolves for crying out loud?"

"Do you want a lecture or just the short of it?" asked Goward. London told him,

"Go for the whole nine yards. I'll let you know if you're getting too long-winded."

"Fair enough. I'm glad for a bit of extra time with this one." Pulling at his tie, the professor said,

"Once again I suppose I must confess to being both extremely excited, and then again, somewhat confused at the same time." The professor leaned his head over to one side, scratching distractedly at his neck as he explained,

"Werewolves are a bigger part of modern fiction and filmmaking than they are folklore, but they are strongly represented in the legends of the past. Of course, a lot of it just goes back to the first hunting societies—hunting magic, tribal sorcerers dressed in skins . . . you know, become the animal, feel its pain, beg its forgiveness, thank it for sacrificing itself for the tribe. A lot of dancing and chanting, a little drinking of inebriants and perhaps chewing some narcotic fungus or leaves or whatever, and suddenly people are seeing all manner of things." As the room quieted, most everyone's attention shifted to Goward as he continued to tell the detective,

"Now the Vikings are perhaps the best example of another way things could have been confused over the years—their berserkers, men who wore the pelts of bears, not only for warmth and the addition to their already menacing appearances, but more because wearing the shirt was thought to being akin to eating an animal's or an enemy's heart . . . sympathetic magic . . . keep a part of the bear with you and gain its strength, its courage— become the bear. Then there are the secret cults, skin wearers . . . Africa's leopard-man cult again. But, of course, these are not transformers." Beginning to warm to his story-telling, Goward's hand unconsciously slid into his pocket, searching out his pipe and pouch as he said,

"True werewolf legends do exist, and by that I mean legends of true werewolves, not necessarily true legends . . ."

"I get the idea, Doc," said London.

"Oh, yes. Anyway, the Romans had werewolf stories . . . the old saw—man-sees-friend-turn-into-wolf, later wounds-a-wolf, later finds-his-friend-dead-of-the-same-type-of-wound story. But it was widely believed, and it didn't stop there. The Middle Ages were full of werewolf tales, and a lot of people were executed for being werewolves. It was the time for it, blasted Christian theology with its neverending paranoia about such things. To the Church, of course, medieval werewolves weren't just people turning into wolves, or wolfmen, or whatever, they were demon slaves of Satan. Lots of idiot ideas there. . . ." Goward stared off absently for a moment, shaking his head sadly as he said,

"Things like Satan giving his most trusted witches magic wolf skins to wear, or wolf ointment to rub on their bodies . . . or even the drinking of water from cups fashioned from the skulls of wolves ... even that was supposed to work. Finally it got to the point where all you had to do was simply just eat roasted wolf flesh." Tapping the last bit of loose tobacco down into the bowl of his pipe, the professor added,

"Right out of the Bible, you know, 'Beware of false prophets, who come to you in the clothing of sheep, but inwardly they are ravening wolves ...' Stuff like that goes a long way rattling around in an empty skull. And the Christian theologians had a ball with it. You see, there are several passages in the Bible about avoiding wolves and men who act like wolves and all, but it makes no actual mention of werewolves themselves. So, the bright lights of Middle Age thinking postulated all sorts of theories ... they weren't wolves, but demons shaped like wolves ... the witch didn't change into a wolf but had been given the power to project the illusion of changing into a wolf ... no one changed into a werewolf, they simply left their bodies and let their spirits take over the bodies of real wolves."

"But," asked London, slightly agitated as the professor played his lighter over the bowl of his pipe, "is there any what you could call hard evidence of actual werewolves ... anywhere at all in history? And, you know what I mean ... not necessarily conclusive evidence, but just something that we can accept that no one else has to."

"Not really, Theodore. The sad truth is that all the evidence we have points to the werewolves of the Middle Ages simply being men with elongated index fingers, hairy palms, and solid eyebrows. And, there is the other problem that from the Romans on up, werewolves were people who transformed into *wolves*, not hairy human beings. That aspect is strictly a Hollywood touch, along with silver bullets and the bite of the werewolf transforming others into werewolves as well. Although ..."

The professor stopped long enough to touch a flame to the bowl of his pipe, then said,

"there is a fairly well-documented case from south central France in the 1760s. Many folks shot at the beast, but the hunter who actually slew it gave the credit to silver bu—"

"My brother," interrupted Pa'sha, anxious to get down to the meat of what they had gathered to do, "my purpose is not to distract us, but of what importance is it if these things have crawled the land for a million years or ten? Is not our only concern how we shall kill the one coming for some number of us on the morrow?"

"Well, yes," agreed London, "in the short run, anyway. Sorry—you're right. Guess I was curious. And, now that we have what few facts there are, I'm even more curious. How about it, Doc? What's your guess on how we add up everything you had to say with Warhelski's photos?"

"To be perfectly honest, Theodore, I'd be hard put to draw any conclusion from such mathematics other than to say that all the myths about wolfmen and women are just that . . . legends, tales to frighten children. And that Mr. Warhelski's bits of evidence are something new entirely being introduced into the world consciousness."

"What do you think of that, Mr. Warhelski?" asked the detective. "I mean, you say that your people have traced back the doings of your werewolf for hundreds of years . . . and yet the professor here says that before the movies there was no concept of a bipedal werewolf. What's your explanation for that?"

The mournful man looked at London, the pain in his eyes flooding the room. With a tremor in his voice, he answered,

"I cannot say. I only know what I have told you. I have shared all that I know. I have no more."

"Yes, I know," answered the detective, his voice finally touched by a note of sympathy. "Hopefully we do." Turning his attention to the large weaponeer sitting in the doorway, London asked,

"You asked a question before, my brother, about killing our werewolf."

"Indeed I did, little brother."

"Have you come up with a way for doing that?"

"In all modesty," answered the massive weaponeer through a large smile, his teeth shining against the backdrop of his coal-black skin, "I think it is safe to say that I have."

"Well, then," answered the detective, sharing none of his friend's enthusiasm, seeing nothing as he looked out over all the assembled except the shapes of coffins hanging in the air over their heads, "let's hear it."

15

"First off," started Pa'sha as all heads turned in his direction, "let me just cheer this sadly depressed meeting by saying that not only have I found something that I think will kill our monster, but that will do it quite simply."

"Well," admitted London, "that's certainly good news. You know the usual boom boom won't work on this thing."

"Supposedly, yes?"

"Supposedly, very goddamned big yes," answered the detective with deadly seriousness. "You have been paying attention all day—right? I assume you've been given all the bloody details of just how tough it is to kill this damn thing—yes?"

"Of course, yes, little brother. Dr. Benson here made quite a great number of things clear about our new breed of monster when we met in his laboratory."

"Dr. Benson," said London, stretching out over his desk to offer his hand, "I'm sorry, but I guess we haven't actually been introduced yet. I'm Ted London."

"Quite, quite," answered the scientist, shaking the detective's hand. As both men sat back in their seats, the tall blond continued, saying,

"And I'm Joseph Benson. Joseph, Joe, either is fine. I would like to avoid Joey, however."

"Easy enough," said London in a reassuring voice. "Tell me about our werewolf, Joseph."

"Certainly. We were working under a rather short time constraint, but with what Mr. Warhelski provided us, I was able to do a study of the beast—rough—but enough to determine that the thing is human. Quick and dirty—I admit . . . assuredly, though I've already sent a healthy portion of the tissue sample off for thorough DNA sampling . . . we'll know soon enough for certain, ah, actually, not soon enough, I mean, not by tomorrow night. An accurate physical mapping of this creature's DNA— anything's DNA for that matter—takes at least ten days, at best. Two weeks, really. You see, it's a series of tests which must be run. They can't be run simultaneously. The results of the second test depend on those of the first and so on down the line, but . . ."

"Joe," interrupted London in a whispered but sharp tone, "this isn't your doctoral dissertation. We're all friends here—all right? Friends under the gun, I might add. You don't have to prove each and everything you tell us. *Comprende?* If Zack says you're good. . . ." The detective turned his head to the right and asked the professor,

"You did say that he was good somewhere along the line, didn't you, Zack?"

"Oh, yes."

"Then, that's all it takes. We trust you, Joe. If we didn't, do you think we'd be including you so openly in our plans to murder a man?" The scientist jerked in his seat, caught off guard by London's words. He stared at the detective, blinking hard, unsure of what he had just heard, unsure of what to say or do next—suddenly unsure of everything. Understanding what had happened, feeling sympathy for the doctor actually, London continued, telling the man,

"I hate for these things to be such surprises. You did realize that was what we were doing? Didn't you?"

"Actually, I hadn't given it . . . I mean, the pictures and all, and with what . . . er, to be sure . . . ah . . ."

"Listen, Joe," said London, his voice even, commanding. Focusing all of his attention on the doctor, hoping to stem the tide of nervous panic he could see streaking its way through the tall blond, he told the man, "I want you to keep calm. Don't let your mind run away with you here—that's not going to help anyone. Just stop and think for a moment. This thing we're up against . . . twenty-six, twenty-eight days out of the month, it's not a killing machine. For all we know, most of the time it's a human being. Just like you and me. That means that it's possible that after we're done slaughtering it like we're hoping to, if the movies are correct, we're going to be left with a human corpse. Now, things like that can be handled easily enough, but it is best one goes into them knowing what's going on from the beginning."

The detective stretched his arms over his head while taking a long breath, giving Benson a moment to catch his own. Not wanting him to start asking useless questions, however, he made it a very short moment, saying,

"We're playing cop, judge, and jury here. And, of course, it might help to remember that the only reason we're getting a shot at this thing is because it's coming here to kill us. But . . . are you getting the idea?"

The scientist craned his neck around, using the motion to gain a few seconds before answering. Finally, however, he turned back to London, saying,

"It's not like the old 'Chiller Theater,' is it? I mean, it's all sort of hitting me—I got so caught up and all—but you are right. That's what we're doing. We're talking about killing someone. Oh, I've heard Mr. Warhelski's effective little story about what it did to all those soldiers, and I've seen the photos and everything. But . . . killing . . . actually *killing* . . ." As everyone listened quietly, the fingers of Benson's hands rolled over each other as he continued to talk. In a voice growing shallower and more frightened with every new sentence, he told those around him,

"You know, I'm one of those men . . . those men? Most men, I would imagine . . . who feels the hero when a woman hands him a rolled-up magazine and sends him forth into the bathroom to kill a spider. This time we live in, no more dragons . . . just spiders trying to escape a porcelain valley." The scientist shuddered, the look on his face telling those around him how much of what he was saying had never occurred to him before that moment.

"And," he blurted, his words tumbling out of him, "I, I'll tell you all something else, as well. On those rare occasions when I've been blessed with the opportunity to prove my modern manhood to the world by squashing the bugs in the bathroom . . . I never realized it before, but it dawns on me now that I've never actually picked one of them up with my hands. You know, claim my meager trophy. No. It's always been a Kleenex or piece of toilet paper . . ."

"As it should be," interrupted Pa'sha, knowing the scientist had been allowed to say enough. Continuing in a voice heavy with guilt, the massive weaponeer admitted,

"I have taken many lives in my time—men and animals and insects as well. I have never touched a dead bug with my hands either. The old saying, 'Death be not proud,' yes? I tell you this, it be not hanging off the end of my fingers in the form of dangling legs and spider intestines, either."

Morcey and Cat laughed out loud. Jhong smiled politely, as did Lai Wan and Goward. London, hoping to head off a large changing of the subject, said quickly,

"Well, this is all fascinating, but . . ."

"I use my hand," interrupted Cat.

"What?" questioned the detective.

"I said, I use my hand," repeated Cat. "You know. To kill bugs."

"I prefer Roach Motels myself," added Morcey, barely able to keep from laughing as he did so.

"Oh, thank you for sharing that with us," said London, narrowing his eyes in impatience.

"Hey, that's all right—just remember their motto . . . 'Bugs check in, but they don't check out.' "

"We'll try," answered the detective drolly. "In the meantime, however, unless the plan is to lure our hairy friend into a large cardboard box filled with glue . . . if we could return to the problem at hand?" The room quieted in response to London's request. As it did, he extended his hand toward Benson, palm up, telling him,

"It's your stage again, Joseph." Straightening the front of his jacket without rising from his seat, the scientist resumed his talk, telling the assembly,

"Running what tests I could in the time I've had so far, I have determined two things about the beast. First off, although I can't be absolutely positive yet, but even from the brief look I've had I'm betting this thing's DNA contains twenty-three pairs of chromosomes. Now, that is important because only human DNA is built from twenty-three pairs. That means that no matter what that thing in the pictures looks like, it's human."

No one said anything. Benson looked around the room for a moment before he realized no one would until he told them his second bit of information. Steeling his nerves, he averted his eyes from all the other faces around him, suddenly only able to speak if he could pretend he were talking aloud to himself in an empty room.

"The second thing," he said, praying his voice would not crack on him, "goes back to something Zack and I did earlier this month. He brought me a scraping from what he told me was an antler. He said it had been broken off the head of a man who had transformed himself into a devil. Anyway, it was definitely composed of the kind of skin tissue that calcifies into antlers in deer and the such. But, this stuff was comprised of twenty-three pairings, as well. Fascinating stuff . . . at the very least it signified a human being out there somewhere who was growing antlers. Fascinating." Then, focusing his eyes again, he moved them from face to face, swinging around in his chair to face each person in the room in their turn as he said,

"But that was nothing. This DNA was also sheathed in a type of radioactive agent. I wondered if it might be the catalytic agent, as well. You know . . . the force whose presence allowed the transformations. Going with that, I began to study it. Who wouldn't, in my place, I mean? Regardless, though, let me get to the point. The skin sample I was given earlier today . . . of the werewolf, I mean . . . its DNA was sheathed in the same radioactive agent I found in the antler."

"Oh, yeah?" said London, with a start, sharply interested. "Imagine that."

A month earlier, the detective had entered the dream plane, a state of being that despite his several visits he still did not understand, to do battle with a creature purporting to be the biblical Satan. During their skirmish, London had broken one of the monster's antlers free from its head. That action had ended their combat, propelling the detective back to his own reality. When he regained consciousness, however, he had found that he had brought the antler back with him from the dream plane, something he had never done before. Indeed, it was something he had never even thought to try to accomplish before the accidental retrieval. Turning to Goward, the detective asked,

"Is this another lunatic's game? Have we got some nut job running around on the full moon, using the energy of the dream plane to play werewolf?"

"Or perhaps," offered the professor, "it is some creature that has designed to escape the dream plane . . . now working here?"

As the two men stared at each other, Morcey interrupted, asking them,

"What's the difference, boss?"

"The Morcey-man is correct," added Pa'sha. "No matter what this thing is or where it is from—our main concern is only in stopping the beating of its heart. Is yes or no, my little brother?"

"Is yes, big brother," answered London. "And with time wasting, let's get down to it. Pa'sha . . ."

"Yes, Theodore?"

"Have you got a plan for putting this thing on ice or not?"

"On most thin ice, my brother. Ice so clear it will not see it . . . ice so cold it will not smell it . . . ice so cleverly spun that it will be too dazzled by its beauty to notice the intellect behind its pale blue eyes. Until it is too late, of course. Much like the best women, eh, my friend?"

"You think you might be able to give me a clearer notion of what you're talking about?"

"My brother, you drain the poetry from a man's soul."

"Well, it's a talent." A smile played across the detective's lips—one so long in coming it almost hurt the muscles of his face. Enjoying the feeling, London allowed himself to chuckle quietly, despite the seriousness of what they were trying to plan.

"Very funny," said Pa'sha, his huge mouth breaking into a smile of its own. While the others in the office looked at the two men, not exactly sure what they found so funny, the large weaponeer stretched his arms out in front of him, saying,

"But, I am glad to bring a bit of amusement to my little brother. You have of late been far too serious."

"Oh, and I thank you for the laugh," said London.

"It is but the duty of every good believer. As the Koran teaches us, 'He deserves paradise who makes his companions laugh.' "

"Hey," answered London, "makes sense to me. But, if we could get back to the problem at hand . . . ?"

"That is my brother the pragmatist speaking."

"It's another talent," said the detective, pushing his back into the leather padding of his chair. Propping his elbows on the desk before him, London extended his palms outward toward Pa'sha and asked,

"Anyway . . . your plan?" The massive weaponeer stood up out of his seat, pulling a large roll of paper from the bag lying next to his chair. Then, moving forward through the office, dodging around the seats in his way, he asked,

"Theodore, have you ever heard of . . . Hell Gate?"

16

Pa'sha unrolled the County of Queens Sector Survey Map in his hands across the detective's desk. He held down one end while London pulled a stapler and a dictionary from his top left-hand drawer to weight down the other. As the detective looked for more things to hold the other two corners, the weaponeer began his explanation.

"Near the upper reaches of Manhattan, the Harlem and East rivers converge, forming the boundary between Manhattan and Queens. At this point the two become one, the Harlem River disappearing and the East River remaining. Also, at this point, they meet another, much smaller body of land known as Wards Island." Pa'sha pointed out the island on the map with his meaty index finger, adding,

"Some of you may already know it."

"Yeah, sure," added Morcey. "Ain't that where they keep the loonies locked up?"

"It is the home of the Manhattan Psychiatric Center," said Goward in a correcting tone.

"Hey," interrupted Cat, her voice cut with a sarcastic edge, "you can see that place from the Triborough Bridge. It passes right in front of it. And, Doc, from the amount of bars and mesh they've got on those windows, that 'home' of yours looks an awful lot like a lockup to me."

"Be all this as it may," said Pa'sha, steering the conversation back to its former heading, "yes, the psychiatric center is there, as well as Downing Stadium and one of the city's larger sewage treatment plants. But, none of those are what we are interested in."

"No," agreed London. "So, where's this Hell Gate?"

Moving his finger from Wards Island to a spot over the water between it and Queens, the weaponeer pronounced,

"Here."

Looking at the map, the detective saw a circle drawn with a broken line. Looking up from the map, London's eyes narrowed as he stared into Pa'sha's face. The large man smiled as he nodded his head up and down, saying,

"Yes, my brother, Hell Gate. The most powerful whirlpool I have ever seen. So constant in the violence of its motion that its waters have never frozen, so powerful, so irresistible that no boat can escape its pull—so monstrous in its appetite that no scientific measurements of it have ever been made. How deep is it, how far do its currents run, how crushing its force—no one knows, for no instruments have yet been made that can withstand its awesome powers."

By this time others in the room had begun to move forward, curious to look at the spot on a piece of paper that had excited Pa'sha so. As they did, Morcey added,

"Didn't I read about that place? Isn't that where, like, the mobsters like to ditch bodies, 'cause anythin' that gets thrown in there just, like, never gets seen again?"

"This is the place."

"So," asked London, a thin smile on his face, "do we just ask the werewolf to jump in, or do we jump in first and hope it will follow?"

"Why, Theodore, I am perfectly willing to let you try either, of course," answered the weaponeer. "You are so good at this monster hunting game that I will always bend to your expertise. But . . ."

"Yes," said the detective sarcastically, "*but . . .*"

"I did have something somewhat different than either of those ideas in mind. I could even tell it to you now. . . ."

"Oh, you could, huh?"

"Yes, and I would be happy to do so."

"Well, and I do so want you to be happy."

"You are certain it would not vex you terribly to hear it? No?"

"No," answered London, actually managing to laugh again. "I think my ego can bear up under the pressure of someone coming up with a better plan."

"Yours were very silly."

"Best I could do off the top of my head."

"Painfully amateurish. Only a dolt could be so clumsy in his work."

"I'm going to kill you."

"One of these days," agreed Pa'sha, "I am sure one of your escapades will. It is what my mama has told me."

"Don't remind me," said London. "Anyway . . . your plan?"

"Yes. Very well, all amusement aside . . . as our Dr. Benson said, we will first have to slow this beast down. That will be accomplished on one of the three following fronts. First, the good doctor has supplied me with a healthy batch of very nasty biologicals."

"We going into the germ warfare business?"

"Ahh, yes, in a manner of speaking. Our first line of attack will be tranquilizers, both airborne and rifle-directed. Our attempt, of course, is to slow our beast down to make it more vulnerable to more conventional machines of the killing field. Dr. Benson . . ."

"Yes, Mr. Lowe?"

"If you could explain the marvelous toxicity of your chemicals for—"

"Pa'sha," said London, "just give me the battle sequence, will you? How do you expect to find this thing? What are you going to do to get it out to Wards Island? I know you have a plan." The detective looked up into the weaponeer's broad face, telling him with a soft voice,

"If I don't know that you know what you're doing by now, well, I never will, will I, my brother?"

"This is most true—indeed. Immodest as it might sound, I must agree with you."

"Yeah." London narrowed his yes, smiling at the weaponeer. "Well, now that we're all agreed as to what a genius you are, if you could just run through the step-by-step . . . all right?"

"But, of course." Moving his hand over to point toward the lower right corner of the drawing of Wards Island on the map, Pa'sha said, "And I will start by being horribly blunt. We know the beast is coming. It has thrown its gauntlet—"

"Sporting of it," added Goward, thick smoke filtering out of his mouth and up through his moustache.

"I must agree. In fact," said Jhong, one of the only people in the room still sitting, "I think we are faced with an enemy who actually wants to die."

"What makes you say that?" asked London.

"I have been trying to make sense of his 'gauntlet,' as Pa'sha called it. If this thing had some reason to kill any of us . . . why would it not just do it? The only answer seems to me that this beast does not want the London Agency destroyed. Our monster is the one seeking destruction. The only reason for it to alert the world's elite monster-killers to its presence would be because it wishes to die."

"Yeah?" asked Morcey. "Hope he remembers that tomorrow night."

"Anyway," said the weaponeer, reclaiming the floor, "since we know he is looking to confront you—you will be on Wards Island waiting for him."

"By 'you' I figure you mean the agency ... the whole agency." London's voice darkened as he continued,

"Meaning Lisa, too."

"Yes, my brother," admitted Pa'sha. He gave his friend a moment, then added, "Remember, I do have a plan."

The detective crossed his fingers before his eyes, blocking his vision for a moment. Speaking from the self-created darkness, he said,

"Don't worry. I know it has to be this way. If we were to leave Lisa somewhere else, there's no doubt that that's exactly where this thing would go. If Jhong is correct—and it sure sounds like he is—killing her would be just what this thing would do, just to keep us after him."

"My God," said Warhelski, in a voice so sharp and cold that everyone turned to stare at him. "Is that what I have been for him? The one tracker allowed? The only hound given the scent?" The mournful man stopped for a second, then asked,

"Has it always realized I am not up to the job it wants done? Have I always been used simply to spread the news of its existence—to ready fresh opponents for it?" Staring back at the assembly, his eyes traveling from face to face, he asked,

"And, am I even the first to be so used?"

"Who cares?" said Cat in a voice as chilled as the elderly monster hunter's. "What difference does it make if you were the first, the second, the third ... whatever—what would it count for? We're going to be last. Why don't we chuck all the philosophy and get down to what matters? Snagging a wolf hide to nail to the barn door?"

"Ahhh, my little kitten," said Pa'sha with agreement. "When you are right, you are right. Theodore, with no more interruptions ... our plan. Yes, Lisa must be present, but my Murder Dogs are already at the island, covering it with sensors. We will know when our monster arrives. I have already made arrangements for a team of helicopters to work with us. One will be in the air at all times—silent rotors, unheard even by canine ears—ready to take noncombatants out of the area. Instantly, I assure you. Knowing the speed and power of this thing—we will be taking no chances. It will be spotted with infrared—tagged as soon as it is on the island. From that point on we shall use a few simple steps to bring it to both the Hell Gate and its destruction."

"My poisons first," said Benson, giving Pa'sha a moment to catch his breath. "I believe your friend has started its transfer into gas form for bombs as well as having the liquid capsulized for tranquilizer dart use."

"It will be slowed by the time it sees us," added the weaponeer. "Or, more importantly, by the time it sees what we have in store for it."

"The Murder Dogs are planting more than scanners," added Cat. "They're also laying a field of pattern mines."

"Mines?" asked London, not shocked, but certainly wondering what the answer to his next question might be. "In a public park?"

"Electronically activated. Until they are switched on, you can jump up and down on them, run cars over them—nothing," answered Pa'sha. "Nice toys. They will be planted in a conic formation, one which forces our beast toward the Hell Gate. As will select members of the Murder Dogs, all of whom will be outfitted with flamethrowers. We know it can heal from fire, but we also know it can be hurt by it and that it does not like it. A good shepherd's tool it will make."

"At the same time," added Cat, the short electronics expert wanting to let London see that their funnel should be unescapable, "we'll be using something else to keep it inside the mouth of the cone—white noise." As London stared, waiting for an explanation, the blonde told him,

"I'll be setting up a high-range frequency overlay, one pitched to be as painful as possible for canines. If it tries to go back the way it came, go for the Murder Dogs, go anywhere except down to the river . . . I'll boil its brains with white sound. Trust me, London," said Cat with a mean smirk plastered on her face,

"that sucker's gonna head for the water."

"And how do we get him in?" asked the detective.

"Nets and grapples," answered Pa'sha. "Our helicopter crews will have animal nets which have been used to snare and unfoot rhinoceros. As soon as it is at the edge, we will burn it, bomb it, blast it with sound and shells, all just to get it to pose for the nets. Then"—the weaponeer demonstrated the ease of their next moves with his hands—

"it will simply be grab . . . lift . . . and drop. And then we only have to wave bye-bye."

"Bye-bye, huh?"

"Oh, yes. The merest bye-bye." Pa'sha continued to stand near the detective's desk even as some of the others headed back for their seats. As London looked at the map spread out on his desk, Morcey asked,

"Jeez, whatd'ya think, boss? Is it an okay enough plan, or what?"

The detective continued to stare at the map, his eyes not seeing it, his desk, the room, its walls, or any of the people gathered within them. The reality of the scene had been replaced again by the vision he had seen earlier, or more specifically, the memory of it. He saw his face again, twisted in horror, filled with hate, covered in tears and blood, the two blended by sweat running down and dripping away below his field of vision. He stared into his own eyes, wondering again, asking all the voices within his head . . . whose death was he seeing? What was the sight tearing him apart?

Who was dead? An old friend? A new one? Was it Lisa, he asked himself again—for the thousandth time—*was it*? Had the nightmare world he had never suspected existed, the one he had been drawn into one year earlier . . . the one that had given him the woman of his dreams . . . now spun up a new horror to take her away?

Turning from the pain of what was coming, he weighed what was, and then finally answered,

"No, it's a fine plan, Paul . . . Pa'sha. I can't imagine what could stop this thing if this doesn't. What about you, Mr. Warhelski? What do you think?"

The mournful man sat forward in his chair, his frame animated with more spirit than he had showed since the detective had first seen him. Nodding vigorously up and down, he answered with fire in his voice,

"Oh, yes. I have watched Mr. Lowe engineer this throughout the day . . . advising him some little bit, even. This plan, Mr. London, yes—it is a fine thing. I would think that this would have to be the end of the beast." And then, he sat back in his chair, saying the words again in a holy whisper . . .

"The end of the beast."

Yeah, thought the detective. The end of the beast. And who the hell else?

Looking out the window, seeing the lateness of the day, London knew he would have his answer in less than twenty-four hours.

17

"Teddy, that's you—right?"

"Nobody else, sweetheart," answered the detective as he climbed the stairs to the second level of their home. He had called her from the office before coming home, letting her know that it would only be him for dinner. The sound of his voice let her know many other things as well.

On some subconscious level, she had heard Morcey's car pulling up outside. Her brain had registered the fact that it had pulled away again, not with the slow sound of a vehicle whose owner was looking for parking, but of one leaving the area with another destination in mind. The same unconscious fact-gathering part of her brain had recognized London's footsteps on the outside stoop, had known the sound of his hand turning the key—one sharp flip to the left, opening the dead bolt and pulling back the lock with another half turn—had felt the hesitation in his entrance. The door had been held open for a long moment, letting the back of her mind know that something had held the detective on the stoop, making him pause before entering.

"Is everything okay?" she called out, wishing she had not used those words the second they were out of her mouth, unable to think of any to replace them. London reached the landing, his eyes making contact with hers in the doorway.

"Did you want the truth?" he asked her, his mouth twisted in a wry smile, his eyes cold and worried. "Or maybe just something comfortable?"

Lisa wrapped her arms around the detective, kissing him without answering. He kissed her back, his hands sliding into their unconsciously accustomed places—the left on the side of her head, capturing it, cradling it, the other in the small of her back, giving her support, drawing her into him. Her arms pressed down along his shoulders and back, the muscles in them working as she pulled herself up into him, her feet almost leaving the ground as she drifted into the feeling of unburdening the weight of her soul into the man who made all her pain vanish.

They broke for air and then kissed again, time and again, eyes closed, lips moist, their need for each other transcending the explanations for that desire. Why they needed each other did not matter—only the need was important. Both of them took strength from comforting the other, like any true pair of lovers. Then, finally, when both again felt the ability to face the world around them, their eyes opened at the same moment, staring directly into each other's.

"Hi, stranger. New in town?"

"Why, yes, ma'am. I am. And might I say you've got a real friendly community here."

"Thinking of staying?"

"Depends on how the food is."

"Oh, right," answered Lisa with a laugh, twisting the fingers of one hand into London's side, "now there's a man's answer if I've ever heard one."

"Ah, yeah?" asked the detective in his best John Wayne imitation, retreating from her attack, raising his hand to threaten one of his own. "And just how many men's answers have you got down cold, little lady?"

"All of yours," she teased, slipping out of his grasp, drawing him into their apartment, "that's for sure."

"Well," he admitted as he followed her inside, leaving the door open behind him, "I guess I can't argue with that." Throwing his jacket onto the coatrack near the door, he sniffed at the air, then said,

"Oh, man, I thought I caught a whiff of that coming up the stairs. Smells good, sweetheart."

"Thank you, kind sir," said Lisa, disappearing into the kitchen. "Go get washed up. I can have this on the table in two minutes. We'll eat . . . you'll tell me how good it is . . . I'll agree . . . and then you can give me your bad news."

Almost laughing—almost—London did feel some of the heaviness dragging at him disappear in response to Lisa's positive attitude. As he headed for the bathroom he called out,

"That obvious, huh?"

"Hey, I'm a partner in the London Agency. We're all supposed to be clairvoyant or something—aren't we?"

"Yeah," he agreed, lathering up his hands, "I guess so."

The detective did a fast rinse then splashed hot water on his face once, then again, then again. Rubbing the heat into his eyes, he felt some of the tired ache clawing at them disappear. He repeated the process just for good measure, then did the same for the back of his neck. Feeling much better by the time he had toweled himself off, he went into the dining room with something like an honest smile on his face. It grew the rest of the way into one when he saw the table.

Lisa had arranged a score of variously sized candles around the table in small groups of twos and threes to set off the different dishes, the four parts of their meal circling a centerpiece of deeply purple heather and yellow lilies. She had made her own soup and baked her own bread to go with the meal, one that consisted of a simple green salad and large stuffed Italian shells. As London slid into his place at their table, he eyed everything in front of him, saying,

"I'm impressed."

"Thank you. I worked hard enough."

"It sure looks like it." As she filled his soup bowl, he asked, "But, how does a girl from Vermont learn to cook Italian?"

"Anyone can boil noodles. I just stuffed them with the same mix my mother used for meat loaf . . . of course, with a lot more bread crumbs and cheese and a lot less meat."

"Of course," agreed London, "and, thank you, dear."

"You're quite welcome. And the sauce is out of a jar with my own doctoring which you can sample after you've had your soup."

"Pass it over. Trust me, sweetheart, I'm ready for a good meal."

"Ready to tell me the story, too? In between bites, that is?"

"Yeah, I guess."

"Teddy," said Lisa, the sound of the one word making the detective stop to stare into her eyes, "you know you never have to tell me anything. It's just that you seem, so . . . so much, can I say . . . so much like you *want* to tell me?"

"Yeah," he admitted. "Yeah, you can say that. Yeah. You sure can." Taking a spoonful of soup, he used the hot, strong broth to loosen his constricting throat and then told her,

"You're absolutely right, and I had no intention of doing anything but telling you what's going on. I mean," London downed another two quick spoonfuls then continued, saying,

"if you think the stuff we've gone through before was something, wait until you hear this one."

And hear it, she did. As he finished his soup he went over everything he had told her before the meeting, making sure she remembered everything that had happened earlier, filling in those details he had missed then. Buttering his bread, he accepted a plate full of salad and shells, telling her of his meeting with all the others. He told her everything of Pa'sha's plan . . . everything that had been discussed as well as the final outcome of those discussions. Several times he stopped to savor the shells, some simpler part of his brain fascinated enough by the flavor to interrupt him long enough to make him pay attention to his food. He told her,

"I'm sorry, sweetheart. I'm not trying to stall you—I'm just, well, really impressed. This is good."

"It's hard to offend a woman with comments like that, Mr. London," answered Lisa in a teasing voice, "especially when they're so true. But, go ahead. You were saying . . . ?"

"Well, that was actually about it." Spearing up another bite of shell with some lettuce, the detective said,

"I mean, I have to admit—it's a pretty thorough plan. It takes into consideration everything we know about this beast, doesn't seem to repeat any of the past mistakes we know of, and it looks like it gives us a fighting chance."

"But . . . ?"

"Well, you know what's bothering me. The whole vision thing."

Coming around the table, Lisa took London's hand, pushing his fork gently to the table, guiding him up out of his chair. Leading him out of the dining room and into the living room, she said,

"Come here. It's time to get rid of some of this tension you've got building up."

"Oh?" he asked with a smile. "And what did you have in mind?"

Pushing him down into one corner of their couch, she threw herself along the rest of its length, her feet ending up hanging across his legs. "Easy. I'm going to put all those tight muscles of yours to work."

"Rubbing your feet, huh?"

"Of course."

"That's going to help, eh?"

"Oh yes. It'll be very therapeutic."

"For whom?" he asked, his voice soft and joking. "After all, I'm the one who has all the trauma to deal with."

"You? You're the only one we know of that has a chance of living through tomorrow. Rub, buster. I'm the one with swollen feet from standing around cooking for hours. If I'm going to end up in a coffin, I want my good shoes to fit."

Pushing his knuckles into the side of her left heel, he dug

roughly in an ever-widening circle, the way he knew Lisa liked it, saying,

"Women."

"Oh, yeah," laughed Lisa, one hand over her mouth. "Now there's the clever line of the month."

The detective smiled, moving his hands across the bottom of his lover's left foot, massaging each inch as he went along. Moving upward to her toes, he pulled the cramps from each of them individually, letting the weight of her foot stretch them to their full length as he worked the tension from them all one at a time. Finally, after about fifteen minutes, he switched from massaging to gently punching the bottom and sides of her foot with a steady rhythm. As he did, he asked,

"Sweetheart . . ."

"Ummmm . . . yes?" purred Lisa, not opening her eyes.

"How worried are you about tomorrow?" Still not opening her eyes, the young woman answered,

"I'm worried. I'm worried about dying, about you dying, about whether or not Pa'sha's plan will actually work, and even if it does . . . who's going to die anyway. If I have to think about it then, yes, sure—I'm very worried, Teddy. But if it's true that whatever is going to happen is going to happen and that we have to do things the way they've been laid out for us . . ." Then Lisa paused for a moment, opening her eyes suddenly, asking her next question with a trace of hope borne out of her faith in the detective.

"We do . . . don't we?"

"I guess so," answered London automatically, not knowing what else to say, feeling trapped by his destiny in a way he never had before. He looked at Lisa, seeing his sudden confusion over what fate was doing to them mirrored in her eyes, knowing she was trying to understand. Hoping to explain, he said,

"I just feel like I'm missing something. Like I'm looking at this and not seeing it—not seeing all of it. As if I'm missing the forest for the trees."

"Maybe a good night's sleep will help," offered Lisa.

"Maybe . . ." admitted the detective.

"Then," asked Lisa, her voice growing warm and playful, "why don't we let the food and the dishes wait till morning . . . and slip into the shower—together—and then into bed—"

"Also together?" he asked, teasing her.

"Yeah," she answered, sarcastically, but still smiling. "Together. And we'll make a little magic and maybe that forest will come together for you."

"Sounds great."

"Good," she told him. "Then, there's only one thing you have to do and we'll be all set."

The detective paused for a moment, and then suddenly realizing to what the young woman was referring, he smiled and said in unison with her,

"Rub the other foot."

18

London paced the edge of the island with Morcey at his side, surveying the handiwork of Pa'sha and his men. Clearing the area had been easy. Well-placed bribes had both gotten the park closed early and emptied the island of every person not connected with the detective. Now, pacing their way between the trees, counting off the minutes until the sun set—and the moon rose—London and his partner walked from station to station, checking with each of the crews ... making sure everyone was ready for whatever it was that was coming. As they made their way through the Murder Dog posts, Morcey asked,

"What time is it, boss?"

"Oh, I'd say we've got about an hour. Figure between an hour, hour and a quarter. Hour and a half—tops." The ex-maintenance man's hand twitched unconsciously in the direction of the large Auto-Mag in his shoulder holster. Looking over at the detective, he answered,

"Ain't a lot of time ... is it?"

"No," agreed London. "It sure doesn't feel like very much." As they continued to head for Pa'sha's armored car, situated half-way between the island's sewage treatment plant and the stadium, Morcey said,

"I sure wish we'd had even just a little more time with this."

"More time? Well, not that I wouldn't mind some myself, but why? What were you thinking, Paul?"

"Oh, I was just thinkin' that if Warhelski could have gotten here a week ago, we might have had a chance to take a look for our hairy friend while he wasn't so hairy. I mean, we are detectives ... we might have been able to figure out somethin'—don'tcha think?"

"Maybe," answered London. "But, even if we had been able to pull some clues together, and then known we were absolutely sure ... what would we have done? Try and get the police to lock him up on suspicion of being a werewolf? Execute him without really knowing for sure? Lock him up ourselves? How?

If we did he would simply have torn down wherever we put him in—if Warhelski's estimates of his powers are on the money."

"I see maybe you were givin' this some thought yourself—yes?" asked the ex-maintenance man.

"Oh, I'll admit the thought crossed my mind. But, it doesn't matter much. I figure that's why this thing we're after sent Warhelski his little note for us at the last minute. He knew we'd get it too late to do anything except panic."

"Smart plan."

"What's the matter, Paul?" asked the detective as the pair drew closer to where the others were waiting. "You worried?"

"Ah, okay to say 'yeah'?"

"Sure is, partner," admitted London, his head nodding up and down tensely. "Sure is this time."

"Why, boss?"

"What do you mean, Paul?"

"Why 'this time?' What's so different this time? What're we so worried about?" Before the detective could answer, Morcey continued, saying,

"Yeah, sure, I know. I mean, you had your vision and all but—so what? People been dying for the past year now. Thousands of 'em—hundreds of thousands of 'em. Since when do we get so uptight knowin' someone's gonna die? I mean—isn't someone gonna die every time we turn around?" Then Morcey changed his tone abruptly, telling London,

"Ah, I'm sorry, boss. You must be gettin' tireda hearin' that one by now. I mean, you know nobody thinks anya that's your fault or nothin'." As the two closed in on Pa'sha's massive personnel carrier, the detective reached into himself, looking for the best answer he could find.

"I know," said London. "Don't worry about it. Believe me, I understand. This knowing the future stuff . . . even such a little piece of it . . . it just makes everything seem so—certain. It shatters your hope."

"What does?" came Goward's voice. The professor stepped from around the back of the personnel carrier, pipe in hand, a long billow of smoke rolling from his lips. London looked up at him and said,

"Knowing the future."

"Umm, yes," agreed Goward. "Certain knowledge—something we are absolutely sure about—it is a predicament."

"Yeah," added Morcey. "I'll tell you, boss—next time you get a glimpse into the great unknown . . . keep your eyes closed, will you?"

"But, Paul," said Goward, "we know the future—our possible futures—all the time." As the balding man stared, the professor told him,

"You know that if you point a loaded gun at your head and pull the trigger that bad things will happen to you. You know that if you do not bathe you will stink, and that people will then avoid you. Theodore has told us a possible future. Someone he knows will die tonight. We knew that was possible before he told us. Nothing has really changed except that where we once had the *hope* no one would die . . . we now *know* that somebody will. It isn't pleasant, but then again . . . it doesn't seem to have prevented anyone from coming."

The ex-maintenance man stopped then to think about what Goward had told them while the professor took another deep drag from his pipe. As the professor rolled the smoke around in his mouth, London asked him,

"Tell me one thing . . . I thought you said that the full moon business was just a Hollywood invention."

"I used to think that werewolves themselves were just a Hollywood invention." As the detective stared at him, Goward simply shrugged his shoulders and then added,

"I was wrong."

"Well, that makes it clear."

"Theodore, there isn't much I can say. I'm a scientist, not a prophet. I don't deal in divine knowledge, except that which I can glean from the world's scriptures . . . and I wouldn't put a lot of faith in most of that." The professor took another deep pull on his pipe, then said,

"In all my years of research I've never come across a werewolf, or anything that supported the possibility of one . . . until now, of course. Yes, I'd heard some of the stories of Mr. Warhelski, but one hears stories all the time. Some scriptwriter heard tales of a giant wolfman thing running around in Europe, a man that turned into a monster during the light of the full moon. The week before, he wrote a movie about a man that turned into a bat when he got out of his coffin every night. That week he wrote about a werewolf. He would be as surprised to find out he actually knew something as we are."

"I have told my story for many years," added Warhelski, suddenly. Coming out of the back of the personnel carrier, he looked at London and Morcey, saying,

"It makes a kind of ironic sense. Every time my story has been told, in movies, newspapers, comic books, and pulp novels—and now these days on television—the more people that hear it, the fewer who seem to believe."

"Well, mister," answered the detective, going inside the armored vehicle, "you've got yourself an island full of believers tonight."

"Yes," agreed the one-handed man, watching London disappear out of sight. "Let us hope it is enough."

Inside the carrier, the detective conferred with Pa'sha, asking him,

"So, how's it all hanging together?"

"As they say, little brother . . . so far, so good." Not turning from the massive control board in front of him, his eyes constantly moving from one to another of the seven different video screens build into it, he told London,

"All of the Murder Dogs are in place. I have broken them into five squads comprised of four men each. They are, of course, all armed and ready to go."

"Of course. What're they armed and ready to go with?" asked the detective.

"Flamethrowers, as discussed. Three in each group are carrying the conventional napalm-spitters that most people associate with the term. But one man in each team I have gifted with the Dragon's Breath." London stared at the weaponeer, waiting for an explanation. He was not kept waiting long.

"The look on your face tells me you do not know of it. This is not surprising. The Dragon's Breath is not widely known. But, it is a remarkable invention, a simple shotgun shell that turns any twelve-gauge pump into a flamethrower. Each shell fired releases a thirty-foot-wide ball of chemical fire composed of combustible metals which can travel one hundred yards, burning all in their path. It is one of the most heavenly products yet produced by the much beloved Blammo Ammo Company."

"Blammo Ammo?" asked the detective in a tone which implied he suspected a joke. Understanding, Pa'sha assured him immediately,

"But, yes. I tease you not. This is a most true thing, my little brother."

"Well, whatever. I'll admit that it sounds like it should do the job for us," agreed London, adding after a pause, "if anything can."

"Oh, Theodore, do not worry yourself so much about this

thing." Turning from his view screens, the massive weaponeer stared at the detective, telling him,

"Did we not clean the city of vampires? Did we not destroy the Q'talu? And long before you took us into the monster business—back in the days when we hid behind walls and traded rounds with all sorts of black hearts—did we ever suffer ending pain or mortal wound? Of course not. We are here, hale and full of the sweet, sweet juice of life. It is our way, my little brother. I do not think it will change any time soon."

But then, before London could respond or Pa'sha could speak further, suddenly a quick staccato of beeps swung the weaponeer's attention back to his control board. As the detective watched and both Morcey and Goward crammed their heads in the doorway, Warhelski trying to see past the pair of them, Pa'sha hit the switch that killed the alert signal, grabbing up a command unit at the same time. Jamming the headset on, he cleared the frequency and then demanded,

"Report. Now. What is it?" A voice, which London recognized as belonging to one of the weaponeer's key operatives, came through a panel speaker as well as the earphones of Pa'sha's command unit.

"Someone approaches, my lord."

"Is it our target, Be'juma?"

"No, lord. It be a white man, old but not tired, wrinkled but not bent. He look fine, like he think he belong here. Walk with the purpose of a man belong me lord's tall side. What we do, Daddy-Man?"

Heading out the door, London said,

"I'll handle it, Pa'sha."

"You be careful, Theodore." Turning in the doorway, the detective formed a gun with his hand, squeezing an imaginary round off at the weaponeer, saying,

"Boom boom, big brother."

"All in good time, little Theodore," added Pa'sha, turning back to his control board, trying to call up a video image of the intruder, "all in good time."

Hitting the ground at a trot, the detective called Morcey to follow, telling Goward and Warhelski to return to the safety of the command vehicle. As he and the ex-maintenance man moved across the grass toward the entrance of the park, London stared down over the rolling lawns of the island to the spot where Lisa, Lai Wan, and Jhong were holding their position. He could not see his love, but he had to focus his attention in her direction, just for a moment, to make sure it felt as if she were safe, before heading off in the opposite direction. Within his head, the detective noticed the motion, wondering if it were a new ability he had picked up, or an old one he had finally become aware enough of to notice.

Is this how it works? he wondered. Do we all have these abnormal capacities? Can everyone read the energy in the air . . . and do we then just ignore what we hear coming at us?

One of the voices in his head told him that it just took practice. Another agreed, saying that people are capable of hearing everything that comes at them, they just don't care to listen to much of it—another voice adding that when they do listen, many cannot interpret what they hear. As they moved along, London put the controversy to the back of his head, saying to Morcey,

"You're awfully quiet."

"Ah, I could see you were rollin' around in your head about somethin' so, I figured I'd just wait till you were done talkin' to yourself."

"Am I getting that obvious?" asked the detective.

"Naw—I don't think so. I mean, not to the whole world, or nothin'. Just to us who knows and loves ya." When London did not respond, the balding man asked,

"Jeez, you ain't upset, are ya?"

"No, of course not," answered London, his tone reassuring his partner. "If there's anything I've gotten used to in the past year it's people treating me like I was made out of glass or something."

"Awww, boss," responded Morcey, "I didn't mean it like that, or nothin'."

"I know you didn't," said the detective back, still in the same calming tones. "It's not anybody's fault. I'm just the one the craziness decided to center in on . . . the one fate decided to dub the Destroyer." Lifting his eyes toward the ever darkening sky, the detective muttered,

"Yeah, thanks a lot for that one." Then, turning his attention back to his partner, he asked,

"Do you remember back about four or five months ago, when it seemed like nothing else weird was going to happen? It had only been a few months since the vampires but—I don't know—it seemed like a long time. It seemed to me then that all this stuff was going to pass. That maybe, well . . ." And then London went suddenly quiet for a long beat. For a second, it seemed to the ex-maintenance man that he was going to finish his thought, but he did not, simply repeating in a frustrated voice,

"Yeah. Maybe. Well."

As the pair continued to move briskly across the green, Morcey said softly,

"I know it's this vision thing that's got ya so spooked. Right, boss?" When the detective answered in the affirmative, the balding man continued, saying,

"I, I just wanted ya to know, I mean, I wanted to say, that ah, um, that if it's like, me, you know . . . that it's okay. You understand?" Stopping in his tracks, London turned toward his partner and said,

"No. I don't understand. What? You're saying it's all right if you're the person this thing tears apart? That's supposed to make me feel better—that you're giving this thing your blessing?"

"Jeez—no, boss." Morcey explained, "It's just, I mean, I just wanted you to remember that, like, I got myself into this. Every bit of it. You offered me an out—a year ago, when it all first started. You even pushed me toward it. So I'm sayin' that if this werewolf thing gets me—or some other damn horror movie critter gets me next week—or anything . . . I just want you to know that you're not responsible for me being here. I am. I followed you into this because, like I said—I had to know. And, I guess I'm here tonight because I still have to know." The balding man pointed across the park at the approaching figure they had come to meet. London acknowledged him with a nod. The two started walking again, the ex-maintenance man dropping his voice to a whisper, saying,

"I mean, what was I supposed to do? Go back to makin' sure every floor got enough heat, knowin' that I coulda had a chance to hunt monsters for a livin'? Anyway, I don't know if all that makes you feel better or anythin', but I do have a favor to ask of ya."

"Like what?" asked the detective, unable to think of anything he could refuse the balding man.

"If it is my time, now or later or whatever, I want ya to, like, keep an eye on Lai Wan. Try and make sure she's okay, and all. Cool?" A score of answers raced through London's head, but he passed by fancier sentiments, saying simply,

"It's cool."

And then the pair drew close enough to recognize their intruder. The detective stopped Morcey with a touch of his hand as he shouted out,

"Father Bain. What are you doing here?"

"I've come to see the beast, of course."

As the priest crossed the remaining distance between them, London asked with almost angry impatience,

"And how the hell did you know anything was going on—anything involving a 'beast,' anyway? And how did you know it was going on out here? And, didn't it dawn on you that it might be a little too dangerous here for sight-seeing?"

"Theodore," answered the holy man in a voice as stern as the detective's, "I am not here to take snapshots. I am here to do the Lord God's work. He has led me here. In my head these last two days, I have seen visions of a large, fur-covered monstrosity. Somehow I knew it would involve you ... at this time ... in this place. I began walking this morning. Now, here I am, as are you, in this place." As the priest approached them, Morcey asked,

"You seein' visions, too, Father?"

"All the time, my son."

As Bain reached them, London turned and headed back to his prearranged position, Morcey falling in step with his partner, giving the holy man a shrug of his shoulders. The priest fell in with them, continuing,

"Do you not feel the Lord's presence even now? Do you not think that His hand had something to do with this beast? I do. That is why I am here."

"And," snarled London over his shoulder, tired and frustrated, "just what do you think you're going to do? Sprinkle holy water on this thing? Consign its soul to Heaven with a handful of Hail Marys and the Apostle's Creed?"

"I do not know, Theodore," answered Bain. Although far older than either of the other men, he showed no difficulty in keeping up with them. Coming even with the fast-marching detective, he finished, saying,

"I only know that my God has need of me in this place ... tonight. And that is why I must be here."

London stopped moving forward suddenly, wheeling to answer the priest face-to-face. His left hand came up before his face—one finger extended—shaking. But then, just before he could begin, a blasting howl raged through the dark night air, freezing the blood of all that heard it. It was more than animal, more than any noise simple flesh could make. It was a challenge and a plea rolled together around a terrifying core of pity and hate—a noise of the damned—and more than the damned. Turning toward his partner, Morcey said,

"Boss, I'm hearin' things beyond me comprehension again."

"Me, too," agreed the detective. "Me, too."

And then, the three men began running, mere seconds before the next howl began.

19

"Move!" shouted London, pushing Bain ahead of him, parallel to Morcey. Starting the two other men off in front of him, the detective ordered, "Paul, get him down to the launch site. Have them call the damn chopper in and get him and the girls out of here!"

Then, before either man could answer, another howl shattered the dark air around them. The noise rooted Morcey and Bain to the ground—half through fear, half through fascinated curiosity. Long and deep and mournful—the savage sound of a thing that had known nothing but pain throughout its life—the prolonged, wailing cry danced through the imaginations of all who heard it, painting pictures in their heads of a beast beyond all human reckoning. Slamming his hands against the backs of the pair before him, London screamed,

"Now, goddamn it! Move!!"

And that time the two men managed to find their legs again, running off in the opposite direction from the detective. As London made his way up a nearby hillock, he dragged his personal radio from its place on his belt and shouted into it,

"Pa'sha! Did you hear it? Can you see it?" The weaponeer's calm answer came back to him,

"Yes to both questions, my brother. I heard its most loud noise and I have a fix on its very gigantic presence. The beast is approaching through the confines of the narrows . . . as we knew it must. Our firewagons are already moving forward. Lacey, have you got the sight?"

"Oh, yeah, Daddy-Man. Needle's in the chamber—finger's to the trigger. Bang bang on your mark." His eyes glued to the screen holding the best picture of the approaching horror, the weaponeer continued, saying,

"Take your mark at three after the sonics are in place. Cat—do you be ready?"

"You know it," came the short strawberry blonde's response through the radio. "You just give the word, big man, and I'll fry our puppy's ears off."

"Then consider the word given, sweet child."

In her rough terrain vehicle, the electronics expert hit the master switch she had rigged to set off all of her white sound boxes at one time. Instantly two walls of high-range noise were laid down over the island, allowing the monster only a thin cone of safe ground in which it could travel.

Joining the first of the Murder Dog teams near the edge of the island where the narrows began to recede, London watched as the beast first wandered toward the white noise area. The detective stared unblinking into the darkness, trying to make out some kind of details in the blurred black shape approaching him and the others. He could not tell much. As they continued to watch in silence, Pa'sha's man Lacey, hidden in a tall tree overlooking the approach field, took a deep breath and then fired his rifle, sending a tranquilizer round of Dr. Benson's poison into the monster. As the creature jumped at the unexpected pain, Lacey fired six more times, connecting with all but one of the shots. The beast snarled and thrashed, smashing its massive paws against the then-empty delivery darts hanging from its body. As it began to move forward again—slowly, almost wobbling—Be'juma drew his hand in a line across the creature's path, giving London an idea of where it should hit Cat's beam.

And then, the monster exploded upward away from the ground, falling backward suddenly in an awkward tangle, frantically scrambling across the ground, trying to right itself. Again a raging howl broke from its snout, one filled with sour confusion and anger. Then, suddenly, the detective and his four companions stared in disbelief as the thing moved forward toward them again, purposely moving slowly in the direction of the invisible wall. As the five studied the beast, trying to make out details of its appearance in the masking gloom, Pa'sha's man, Be'juma, told London,

"The daddy-man say you be enemy to some powerful demons, white man." Staring into the detective's eyes, he added,

"That be one hard-looking thing doing the straight walk at us now."

"You getting a little dry in the mouth, buddy?" asked London with sympathy.

"No, but I can understand the asking." Still staring at the thing walking toward them, the hard-faced black man added,

"You think we be man and men enough to kill this demon of yours?" When London's only answer was a shrug of his shoulders, Be'juma answered,

"Ahh, well . . . you be honest, anyway. So, honest man, you think it time we should start a march and give that big bastard the hot welcome he done came for?"

Before the detective could answer, however, the werewolf hit the white noise barrier once more. With a murderous yelp it pushed itself into it, the bristling, thickly furred beast forcing its legs forward one step after another. There was no doubt in the minds of any of the five men at the top of the small rise that the thing approaching them was in pain. Its shoulders shook violently, its head whipping back and forth in animated frenzy. With each step it snapped at the air, as if it could somehow grind the invisible sonics between its shining fangs and kill them.

Finally, though, the beast could move no further forward. A massive shudder tore through its body, followed by another of its monstrous howls. Unable to determine which way to go, deep within the painful wall of sound, the beast began to run in circles, still snapping at the air, running into trees. At that moment, London said,

"Yeah. Let's burn it."

The Murder Dogs all nodded grimly and then moved over the lip of the hill and down toward the monster with a steady tread. At a signal from Be'juma, the outer men on the left cocked their flamethrowers and then fired, the weapons spitting a series of frighteningly long blasts of flaming gasoline and napalm at their target. The fiery arcs hit, coating the already wounded creature in sticky, burning jelly. Finding its legs, the monster ran back the way it came, stumbling blindly, howling in pain every step of the way. From his command center, Pa'sha ordered his second and third teams forward.

As London followed the Murder Dogs, watching the other two squads move in, he suddenly noticed a helicopter rising away from the island. A weight burst within his chest and fell away, joy washing him as he realized that Lisa was safely away from whatever was going to happen. Keeping up with his team, he tried to take in the whole picture of events.

The Murder Dogs continued to move on the creature, cutting it off with either blasts of napalm or balls of chemical fire from the team leaders' shotguns. The detective could not believe the ease with which things were working. Every time the werewolf fell to the ground, trying to extinguish the flames burning into its skin, one of its assailants would blast it anew, relighting its already hideously burned fur and flesh. London could hear Pa-'sha's voice coming through each man's radio, giving them fresh orders, constantly ordering a different man forward to fire upon the monster.

The weaponeer was well aware that each flamethrower contained only five bursts—that with five squads made up of four men each, he had only seventy-five napalm hits to play with, backed up with the less effective but far more numerous Dragon's Breath blasts of each team's shotgunner. Playing his cautious game slowly, Pa'sha continued to orchestrate the attack—slowly, inexorably—moving his grim men continually across the field, herding the monster into the next prepared area.

The thing stumbled blindly—howling, screaming—spittle and blood blowing from its snout with each ragged breath. The poison running through its system, the gasoline and napalm still sticking to it, burning it, filling its nostrils with the smell of its own charring flesh, the monster had given up the attack. Now it merely dragged itself in whatever direction it thought it was being pointed, desperate for some avenue of escape that its hunters might have overlooked. Before it could find one, however, the Murder Dogs suddenly heard their leader's voice in their radios, ordering,

"Pull back—now!"

And, seconds later, the first of the electronic charges were set off. The monster had been driven into the center of the mine field. Now, with the field activated, every step the beast took brought another explosion. Shrapnel tore through it, bits of wire and metal either embedding themselves within the thing or passing all the way through its body. Dozens of the shallowly buried mines were set off at one time, the effect of the multiple detonations practically tearing the beast apart.

As the smoke cleared, Pa'sha swept the area with his cameras, looking for the monster. Spotting it easily, fallen in a broken pile in the center of the field—its only movements the shuddering motions of the dying—the weaponeer called to the helicopter pilot circling the island, commanding,

"Benny—are you ready?"

"We're set as can be. Give up the nod and let's get this clambake over with."

"Give us a moment to mark your target. Watch for a new fire patch and then drag that area."

"You got it, Pa'sha," answered the pilot. "Making my descent in five . . . four . . ."

The weaponeer switched channels immediately, ordering one of his Murder Dogs forward to napalm the werewolf once more.

Instantly his orders were carried out and the creature was bathed in another coating of burning jelly. Moments later, as the screeching monstrosity tried to stand, the helicopter that had been ordered down flew in low over the field, dragging a large binder net inches above the grass. The hook-studded metal net hit the beast with the first pass, tangling the burning creature in its steel wire embrace. A mere second after, the thing found itself being dragged along the ground at high speed, hopelessly ensnared within the heavily weighted binder.

Everyone on the island stared upward at that moment, even the fire fighters, watching as the helicopter began its ascent, waiting for the instant of release. Out in the middle of the field, video camera in hand, Goward continued filming the scene, holding his breath as were all around him, listening to the low hum of the machine in his hand. The helicopter leveled off over the dark, whirling center of the East River, positioning its load directly over Hell Gate. And then ...

"Release!"

With Pa'sha's order, everyone on the island shouted grim hurrahs as they watched the binder fall toward the water. The still-burning creature sank beneath the waves instantly, spinning around the edge of the massive whirlpool for only the briefest of moments before the current and the weighed net dragged it down to the river bottom.

On land, everyone raced for the water's edge. Staring out across the river's surface, into the swirl of Hell Gate, they searched for any sign of the thing, any clue whatsoever that even a piece of the beast might have made it back to the surface. Realizing that it was no time for a party, however, Pa'sha snapped on the open channel, telling everyone,

"Work is not finished, children. You have lived through another night and that is a good thing, but the fires are still burning and we must be collecting ourselves and leaving this place. There is something about fire and bombs that has a strange way of attracting attention, and we cannot pay off every police officer in New York. So, let us be about our business, shall we?"

And, with that, the weaponeer began giving detailed orders, sending men after their cameras, putting them to digging up mines, smothering fires, and disassembling Cat's white sound devices. From around the island, the various vehicles the different teams needed to remove all of their equipment were brought up to the point of Pa'sha's personnel carrier. While the majority of the activity centered around the weaponeer's command center,

London stood at the edge of the river, watching the dark water beyond. As he did, a voice called out,

"Waiting for it to return?" The detective turned to find Father Bain walking up behind him. Cocking his head to one side, London answered,

"Well, let's not call it 'waiting.' All right?"

"Certainly fine by me," answered the priest. Looking out over the river, Bain asked, "Do you think it's dead?"

"I certainly hope so."

"Why don't I feel that answers my question?"

"Because it doesn't. Why didn't you get on the helicopter like I told you to?"

"Because I didn't want to. I came here at the request of Providence. One does not take the directions of the Lord Almighty lightly." His eyes still fixed on the water beyond, the elder priest said,

"I know fair little of what happened here tonight. What that thing was, how it came to be here, how you knew to bring your weapons to greet it. I won't tire you with a thousand questions, but I do wish to pose one. Was it such a thing that it deserved the pain it received tonight?"

"From what I can tell, Father," responded London, "the answer is yes. It was a thing from Hell if there ever was one. It was a werewolf, believe it or not. One that seems to have been around for at least a few hundred years. It killed a lot of people over the centuries, and tonight it came here to kill us. I just hope we made a good job of it."

And then, while the two stood staring out at the river, Professor Goward came up behind them, still filming. Pointing his camera out at the whirlpool, he said,

"So, Theodore, feeling a bit better now that the beast has been dispatched?"

"I suppose," admitted the detective, aware that the sensation of dread that had been plaguing him for the past two days had not yet diminished.

"But . . .?" prompted Goward.

"Well . . . but, I don't know. I guess I'm wondering . . . if that thing is dead, then what was my vision all about? And why can't I shake this feeling in the pit of my stomach?" London turned to address the professor face-to-face, surprised to see Lai Wan approaching with Morcey and Jhong. His brow knotting with concern, suddenly wondering if anyone had actually left on the helicopter, he asked,

"What are you doing here?"

"When Lisa and I were getting on board the helicopter, I was overwhelmed by a feeling . . . a, how can I describe it? A *pulling*, if you will, dragging at me to stay. I told them to leave without me. Something within me, or something outside of me, I cannot say, actually, demanded that I stay here."

"Why?" asked London, a sense of dread creeping up his spine, chilling him, freezing his vertebrae one against another. "What do you mean?"

"I could feel the beast through the ground—the entire time—from even before its first howlings. Its pain, its confusion, its fierce, animal hate . . . all of that came to me, more easily than most. But, there was something beyond its savage nature, deeper beneath its red-hazed instincts to kill everything around it that drew me to stay." As the small band all stared at the psychometrist, she said,

"There was a brain to it, Theodore, a rational human brain, directing the animal, calming it, forcing it to endure its pain, reminding it that it would not die . . . telling it that it *could* not die—reminding it that it would never die until all its crimes were paid for. I watched it, being burned and blown apart, feeling its agony with each hit, feeling it die, over and over, only to rise again and again . . ."

"Wait a minute," interrupted London, tension threatening to crack his voice. "What do you mean, 'feeling it die, over and over'? Did it die, or didn't it?"

Before Lai Wan could answer, Father Bain stepped forward, placing his hand on London's arm. Tugging at the detective gently, he said urgently,

"Theodore, there is something very wrong here. Do you feel it?"

"Yes, it died," answered the psychometrist. "Several times. I felt its heart stop, felt the air run out of its lungs as they were punctured and flattened. There were a hundred spots on it where it had been burned to the bone . . . a hundred more where it had been burned further, but . . ."

"Theodore," urged the elder priest again, "oh, blessed God, I think . . ."

Cutting everyone off with a wave of his hand, the detective suddenly stepped away from the crowd, breaking contact with all the searching eyes, touching hands. Closing his eyes, pulling in on himself, he cleared his mind as quickly as he could, searching for whatever it was that was reaching Lai Wan and Bain. In the background, a small part of his mind heard Morcey's voice, urging all of the others to fall back to the trucks. It heard the psychometrist and the priest leave, heard Goward protest that there was nothing to be afraid of, felt Jhong drawing energy into himself, heard the safety clicking off his partner's Auto-Mag. Then, his eyes snapped open. Turning toward the water, he pointed out toward the nearest edge of the whirlpool, shouting,

"There!"

Following the line of his arm, the others stared out over the water. What they saw was the werewolf, swimming toward them out of the mouth of Hell Gate.

{20}

"Run!" shouted London. "Back to the trucks."

Pushing bodies before him, unaware of identities, he pressed all equally into the retreat. Then, once the stampede away from the shore had been started, he walked back toward the river. Searching for the werewolf, he spotted it again, already halfway to the island.

How, wondered the detective, remembering the explosions, the smell of burning fur and flesh, the agonizing, pain-driven howls. How does anything made of simple flesh and blood live through so much?

A great part of his mind answered that it did not care, shouting at him to join the others in running for the relative safety of the vehicles. The great ape brain, terrified at the smell of the beast coming for it, screamed repeatedly for London to take flight. It took all the detective's mental powers to smother the screeches coming from his primal core and even then they were not silenced, but only muffled for the moment.

In that moment, however, he reviewed in his mind the various menaces he and his friends had faced so far. The flying demons they had met first had been tough, but they had died with a few well-placed explosive rounds. The vampires had been able to heal even gunshot wounds, but it had not taken too many hits to take one of them out, as well. Even the Satan they had faced had had its limits.

But the thing closing on the shore . . . it had been burned—to the bone and beyond—over its entire body. It had been blown apart—more than once. And still it came. It had been poisoned . . . thick doses massive enough to kill hundreds. It had been dropped into a whirlpool with the power to shatter ships of steel and iron like so much tissue paper. And still it came on, swimming in a direct line for London, moving faster with each passing moment.

The detective replayed what Lai Wan had told him . . . that she had felt the thing die. "Several times," she had said. *Several times.*

"Yeah," he said aloud, ignoring the noise of his fellows behind him, concentrating on the approaching monster. "Dead several times and yet here it comes. Well, I guess we're just not killing them like we used to."

The beast was now only a score of yards from the shore. London studied it as it came closer. He stared at its somehow fully regenerated torso, all of the hair on its body intact.

"How?" he whispered again. "How?"

Stunned by the sight of the thing, the detective stepped even closer to the edge of the river. He watched the rhythmic movement of its arms breaking out of and then cutting back into the water—the back of his mind absently noting that the monster swam like a man instead of the beast it resembled.

And then, just as the creature slowed to avoid ramming itself against the shore, London blinked, suddenly certain he had made an important observation. The monster's paw dug into the river's bank, steadying its body in the swirling waters. As the beast struggled its way up out of the river, fighting for any hold that would regain it the freedom of the island, the detective raced over all of the recent comments that had flashed through his brain, trying to determine to which one his instincts were trying to alert him. Before he could make any proper connections between the things he had been thinking and the elimination of the beast drawing closer to him, though, a dark, broken voice called from over the edge of the riverbank, saying,

"So, Mr. London, I commend you."

"Do tell," answered the detective, holding his ground, not sure why. "Any particular reason?"

"You did not run."

"Maybe I'm just stupid."

"If that is so," came the monster's voice again, "then there is at least one trait we share."

London stood stock-still on the abrupt shore, his mind racing, trying to tell him what his deep subconscious had noticed that he could not.

It is the fear, came the rare voice in his mind—the one he heard the least. Instantly he knew what it meant. Despite his external calm, his primal human nature was in numbing rebellion to his actions. Its voice, smothered by his self-control, was still raging beneath the surface of his mind, distracting the part of him trying to make sense of his only clue.

Not the only clue, came the voice again, imploring him to keep thinking. *Not the only one.*

But then, before he could make heads or tails out of what he was thinking, the monster finally managed to clamber up the mud wall of the brink and onto the shore. It stood before London, nearly a foot taller than the detective. Its shoulders stood out as massive as a bull's, the power coming off it like that of a runaway train. As it stood, panting . . . waiting, London ran his eyes over the beast, hard-pressed to believe the evidence they presented him with, even after all of the other bizarre and horrible things he had seen.

He started with its head and worked his way down. The monster's ears were large and pointed, their sharp edges standing straight up. All of it from the ears down was covered with a thick black fur, the hair on its head so uniformly short it appeared close-cropped—everywhere except along the center of its skull. There it grew wild and long, somehow standing up stiffly in a thick, rigid mohawk.

Its face broke from the human as well. It was possessed of a monstrous snout filled with large, wickedly strong-looking, age-yellowed teeth. Above the vicious snout, its eyes shone a deep amber, a dark sickly shade of the color. The creature's tongue lolled out of its head—snake-like—flicking first this way, then that, seemingly of its own volition.

London eyed the crisscross of scars he could see on the beast's chest. Many of them ran together, old wounds healed and opened and then healed and opened again and again—so many times over the detective could not even begin to untangle them. Still staring at the mesh of wounds, he wondered why, if the monster had been burned to the bone and then completely regenerated, the scars could have come back.

We blasted it to bits, thought the detective. We tore it apart—almost atom by atom. How the hell does it regenerate but then come back as its old self . . . teeth still yellowed? Chest still scarred? What the hell is this?

"You appear lost in thought, Detective," snarled the beast in his low, barking voice. "Didn't Warhelski tell you how dangerous that is?" London looked up at the savage thing before him. The beast was a solid mass of muscle—a killing machine beyond the worst of Hollywood's nightmares.

What could kill it? wondered the detective in the few seconds he had remaining to act. Was there anything man had ever invented? Would it take a nuclear warhead? Would that even work? Once things start reanimating after death, itself . . . what power was left that could turn them?

And, to London's mind came the final question—what kind of death had the monster risen from, anyway? It did not move like a thing constructed of reanimated tissue, but as a being still in possession of its soul. Answering the beast's question, the detective said,

"You give a man a lot to think about, friend."

The thing stared at London curiously, its smile suffused with a cruel joy, or so it appeared. The detective dismissed the notion, however, well aware that he could not trust the reading of any human emotion he might think he detected in any of the monster's features save its eyes. As the beast stared back, it suddenly bent one of its knees slightly, bringing its face in close to London's. The detective did not back away. Sensing London did not plan on moving, the creature said,

"So do you . . . friend."

The detective stared into the large, hooded amber eyes of the beast, searching for what it was restraining the monster's hand. It had announced its intention to kill him and all he held dear, it had tracked him as it said it would, and it had certainly been provoked to the point where any violent reaction it could make would certainly seem justified. So . . .

Now . . . now that it has its chance, thought London, *why doesn't it try to kill me? There's nothing left to stop it. Why isn't it doing anything—now?*

And then, the detective's eyes opened larger as he stared into those of the creature before him with a renewed interest. Suddenly he had seen something, or felt something, or had in some way been moved in a new direction. Suddenly everything was beginning to make sense to him. Of course, he thought, of course it's not killing me—it . . .

And then, before another thought could flash through London's mind, something struck the beast before him, something large and fast and explosive. Large chunks of meat and bone flew through the air, pelting the detective and covering the ground around him. London was thrown from his feet by the surprise impact. The monster was hurled away much more violently, heaved all the way back into the river. As the detective struggled to regain his feet, he heard Pa'sha calling,

"Little brother, I have crippled our foe. Run now. I have you covered. Run, Theodore. Run!"

But it was too late. Before the detective could clear his head enough to stand, the beast had returned up and over the bank. The dripping monster came forward low on all fours, its chest steaming, stopping before the spot where London remained sprawled. Catching the front of the detective's jacket, it jerked him upward roughly, dragging his knees across the ground. Pulling its massive arm back, it swung forward suddenly, striking the still dazed London a fierce blow that brought a gushing stream of blood pouring from his face. Dropping the bleeding detective in a jumbled heap, the thing growled,

"And to think that, at least . . . just for a moment . . . I almost *believed* you." Then, turning its back on London, the thing added in a snarl,

"Watch what follows . . . mortal. I'll give you something to believe."

Ignoring the struggling London, the thing raced straight up the center of the island, heading directly into the guns of Pa'sha and his men. As the detective watched through his blurring eyes, hundreds of rounds—simple impacters, tracers, and explosives—tore into the creature, tearing free pieces of its flesh, splashing its blood, and not impeding it in the least. More napalm pumped forward as well, bathing the monster, leaving it a burning humanoid torch, one unstopped by the weapons of man.

The monster tore into the first line of Murder Dogs and shattered the chests of two men with the swipe of one paw. As the beast closed in on its attackers, their shotguns did deadly work as men jammed their weapons up against the creature's body and pulled their triggers—repeatedly—watching fur and meat get blown away from their target until they themselves would join the pools of blood growing on the park's lawn.

The burning monster snapped its jaws on the shoulder of one man, ripping his arm free. Then, as that man's friend blew out the beast's left eye with a well-placed shot, the thing turned on him, snapping its jaws shut on his head. The man was able to struggle for only a second before the thing ripped his skull free from his body with a liquid surge, dragging the man's spine up out of his back.

"Die, beast!"

Pa'sha, who had ducked back into his command center when the beast had approached, now reemerged, two large Auto-Mags in hand. Taking aim, he fired shot after shot, shattering the thing's body with the incredible firepower in his hands. One shot from either of the guns in his hands was enough to cut any man in two. But, the beast did not fall to pieces. In fact, it did not fall at all. Straining against the intensity of the powerful blasts slamming into and through its body, the thing began moving forward against the devastating hail of lead.

Watching from his vantage point far across the bloody, burning fields, finally able to struggle to his feet, London stumbled a few yards forward toward the combatants. But then suddenly his mind finally registered what his eyes were seeing. Knowing the sad outcome of the tableau before him, the detective stopped in his tracks—staring—helpless.

"No," he said, almost to himself alone. "Pa'sha—no."

And then, he watched before him through the darkness and the smoke and the blood in his eyes as the monster reached his friend before the weaponeer could even empty his revolvers. Jamming its paw forward, the beast rammed it into Pa'sha's chest and then jerked it back out again savagely, ripping the weaponeer's living heart out of his body. Showing it to Pa'sha seconds before the life left his eyes, the thing growled,

"Not today."

And then, the giant man crumpled to the ground, falling amid the scattered corpses of so many of his brother warriors. The remaining Murder Dogs swarmed forward toward the weaponeer's killer, guns and blades in hand. London watched their brave battle—watched them lose arms and legs and heads, one after another, dying at the hands of the howling, burning thing in their center. Nothing they did mattered. The thing crushed them each with ease, throwing them about like weightless toys. Nor did it kill them instantly. The beast only hurt them—worse with each attack—looking to see if their bravery could stand in the face of the futility of their battle.

Then, suddenly changing its tactic, the still-burning monster turned and broke away from the circling Murder Dogs. Attracted to Pa'sha's command center, it dug its claws into the side of the massive personnel carrier and began to strain upward. Its attackers continued on—stabbing the creature, shooting it in the back—but it ignored them, concentrating all its efforts on the military vehicle in its grasp. And then, without warning, the gravity of the personnel carrier shifted, allowing the creature to flip the now useless command center as if it were nothing more substantial than a soapbox derby car.

The carrier hit the ground with a stunning crash. The monster ignored it, though, turning its attentions to its attackers. Finally, however, the detective turned away from the spectacle of the carnage, walking toward the park exit. Quite simply, he could watch no longer.

Part of his mind raged, screamed at the death of his friend—*your oldest living friend, you shit. Aren't you going to do anything? Anything?!*

Other voices within his head screamed for revenge as well, but most counseled retreat. Savage thoughts so furious London could not even attach words to their emotion assaulted the detective—gibbering, howling at him to throw himself on the monster that had killed his brother. London ignored all of the debate churning within him, however, simply walking away from everything he had seen, from anything else that might remain to be seen. Before he had crossed much of the park, he was joined by Jhong, who drifted up to his side out of the thickening smoke. The elder warrior told him,

"It has not been a good battle." When London did not acknowledge his presence in any way, Jhong said,

"Your partner is ahead with his woman and the priest. I will guide you to them."

The detective—still dazed, still blinking the blood out of his eyes—allowed the elder warrior to direct his steps. Within minutes the pair had joined Morcey and Bain. The ex-maintenance man said,

"Boss. Jeez, man—boss. Sweet bride of the night—are you okay or what?"

London, his nose and lips still dripping freely, his eyes sore and tearing, the skin beneath them purpling over, did not answer. Morcey could tell that the detective could hear him. But, he was not sure London could understand what he was hearing. Looking at the others, the balding man said,

"I hate to be the one to say it, but I think we'd better give some serious thought to cuttin' our losses and gettin' the hell out of here."

"I agree, my son," responded Bain, his eyes glued to the flaming carnage behind him. "I do not know how this all could have come to pass but . . ."

The priest searched for the words he wanted as the five of them started to move once more, but could not find them. No one blamed him. Then, before the quintet had gone a score of steps, London's knees suddenly buckled, sending the detective sprawling toward the ground. Jhong's panther-like reflexes saved London another hit, catching him in a cradling hold an instant before he could impact with the ground. Then, the elder warrior passed the unconscious detective off to Morcey.

Before the ex-maintenance man could ask what was happening, Jhong turned his back on the others calmly, facing back in the direction from which they had just come. A second later, Lai Wan, Bain, and Morcey knew why. The beast bounded up to them, stopping just short of the empty-handed warrior. Its head cocked at an angle, the thing demanded,

"Give me London, Chinaman."

"I cannot give you a human being," answered Jhong, unconsciously swaying the upper part of his body. "Nor do I think I would wish to do so even if it were possible."

"Do you think you can hurt me, Chinaman?" Without hesitation, Jhong told the creature,

"Certainly. It is within my power to make your life a living hell of never quite healing broken bones. You are a very fast thing. I am faster."

"You are quite sure of yourself."

"I will not hurt you if you stand away and allow us to leave this place."

"That is most kind of you, Chinaman."

Jhong's eyes narrowed as he told the thing, "I am not kind. It should be obvious even to you that soon this island will be filling with firemen and the police. I can hold you at bay until such a time with ease. Then you will have more to kill. Is this what you want?"

The thing eyed Jhong suspiciously, searching the elder warrior's eyes, the way he positioned his body—watching his breath as it made its way in and out of his chest—trying to make up its mind about something. As it did so, Jhong signaled the others to start moving London out of harm's way. As they complied, the thing asked,

"Do you want to fight me, old man?"

"No man seeks combat."

"Are you afraid of me?"

"No," answered Jhong.

"Liar!" snapped the beast. As Morcey and Bain labored to move London further away, struggling to keep themselves between Lai Wan and the beast at the same time, the elder warrior dug his feet into the grass beneath, responding to the monster,

"You are wrong. I am simply not afraid."

"Do you think you can succeed where so many others have failed?" growled the beast. "Do you think you can kill me, Chinaman? Kill *me*?!"

"No—that does not seem possible from any means that I understand. But I did not say I could kill you. Merely that I could keep you here long enough for the police to arrive."

And then, as if on cue, the distant sound of the first sirens could be heard faintly in the background. As the beast and Jhong listened, suddenly Cat's rough terrain vehicle pulled up. The electronics expert kicked open her passenger side door, urging those approaching to get London inside—fast. As they hurried to do so, Cat kept her shotgun trained on the creature, knowing it was useless. As she did, the monster snarled,

"I could kill you all."

"Yes," agreed Jhong, his muscles tensing over, hardening around his bones in layers. "And what would that prove?"

The beast stared at the elder warrior, looking for the meaning behind his words. Its eyes softening for a moment—slightly—it said,

"You speak as if you were talking to just another man. Don't you know what I am?" Not softening his own stance in any way, Jhong answered,

"What you are is up to you. My opinion of you, right or wrong, cannot change the truth your soul holds—no matter what it might be."

And then suddenly, much to everyone's surprise, the monster turned on its heel and ran across the island at an amazing speed, disappearing instantly into the fire-lit shadows and smoke. Throwing her shotgun back into the cab of her vehicle, Cat slid over behind the steering wheel, calling out to Jhong,

"You coming or not?"

Looking at the truck, the elder warrior turned to gaze off in the direction in which the werething had run. His eyes staring into the thickening smoke, finding nothing, he turned back toward Cat and answered,

"Yes, I suppose I should."

A moment later, Jhong was inside along with Lai Wan, Bain, Morcey, and the unconscious London. Cat gunned her motor and sped off into the night, getting them all clear of the park less than a minute before the arrival of the first police cars.

21

The pain in London's head was unbearable. It came in waves so powerful he feared that the energy required in opening his eyes might actually split his skull open. Inside his head, he listened to opinions on what he should do next.

Wake up, came one voice. Wake up and find out where you are. What the hell could be more important than that?

Don't move. The pain is bad enough. Don't move. Listen—try to hear what's going on.

More—reach out . . . feel the currents around you. What's its smell? Its taste? How warm is it? What do you read coming to you on the heat in the air?

Just open your eyes and look around.

Too much pain. Can't you wait a minute? Give this body a little time to heal—will you?

Each of his ancestors advised him in some fashion true to their particular nature. He listened to the chorus absently as he collected his consciousness, trying to pull himself together. Getting his awareness past the red glow of pain playing havoc with his nervous system, he managed a weak blink. The effort made his face bend with pain. Opening his eyes halfway and then closing them again crippled him so intensely he cried aloud.

Spittle burst through the air, flying upward above his head. His intuition telling him he was in a safe place, the detective contemplated not worrying about where he was. Testing other places, bending joints here and there, he found some other minor stiffness and aches, but nothing to match the pain in his face. Again he blinked. Again his eyes crashed shut after the effort, his fear of moving keeping him from screaming out again. Forgetting about looking at anything for the moment, he concentrated on figuring out where he was.

Opening himself to the data traveling through his brain, instantly he knew he was in a warm place, on a bed, under a sheet. It was a quiet . . . still place, antiseptic and soulless—blackened by the sour smell of hopelessness and despair—almost certainly a hospital. Before more than that first split second could pass, however, the detective felt something stir next to him.

"Boss," came Morcey's voice. "Are you awake?"

No, thought London. Not really. Not so you could tell.

"I heard ya give out with a little scream, like, and I thought I saw you blink," said the balding man. "Man, sweet bride of the night, I'd think that would hurt."

What happened to me? wondered the detective. My face. What's happened to my face?

His hand, rising automatically from his side, caught his partner's arm as Morcey passed. The ex-maintenance man broke London's grasp and jumped away from the bed, shouting,

"What?! God?! Ahhhhhh—"

The balding man caught himself after a moment, however, crossing immediately back to the side of London's bed.

"Oh man, boss, Jeezit, Riley—you scared the . . ." The ex-maintenance man cut himself off sharply, his ears going red from the embarrassment of being startled. His split second of nerves passed, however, he caught on to the change in the atmosphere and asked,

"Oh, hey—you're awake. Are you okay, boss? Can you talk? Man, you're awful banged up. But you can use your hand. Can you give me one finger for yes—two fingers for no?"

The detective raised his right hand from the bed, wiggling one finger. Seeing that, Morcey asked,

"Can you hear me clear, boss?" After London wagged his finger again, his partner told him in a whisper,

"I'll try and clue ya in on what's goin' on. We're atta Catholic Church hospital. Father Bain got you in. But there's some big buzz happenin'. No one saw us leave the park, but there's a bunch of . . . Feds, it looks like, givin' the church types a lot of grief." His voice dropping even lower, he added,

"They got two guys on the door, boss. They got two more guys out in the hall—one at each end—and they got two cars outside your window. Don't get paranoid or anything," he added, trying to lighten the situation with a droll note of humor, "but I think they want to get their hands on ya."

Summoning up courage as well as strength, London again lifted his arm from the bed, raising it slowly toward his head. Relieved as he was to feel little pain from the motion, he pressed forward, pointing at his aching face. Catching his meaning, the balding man told the detective,

"That thing broke your nose, boss—bad. Real bad. Your

whole face was mushed in. Lisa told them to fix ya. I backed her.
We could prove we were your partners. We said Lisa was your
common-law wife, flashed a lot of money at 'em and told 'em ta
fix ya up. They put ya back together all right, I guess . . . they
said you'll be okay—for whatever that's worth—but it's, like,
gonna hurt for days—well, actually they said weeks. You were in
surgery for about three hours this morning. Then you were out
for a long time. I mean, for you, it's already tomorrow night."

And then things began to come back to London. Suddenly he
remembered the park—remembered their attempt to stop the
werewolf—remembered when things began going wrong. He
saw the creature swimming arm over arm, clambering up onto
shore, remembered speaking to it, thinking that there was something he just wasn't getting . . .

The detective saw the fateful missile strike again, felt the
monster's rage, its sense of betrayal . . .

Betrayal.

Betrayal? wondered London. Where does a thing like that get
off feeling betrayed by anybody?

His mind told him to analyze his question further, but the detective pushed it aside for the moment, suddenly remembering
more. He saw Pa'sha again—fighting the beast . . . fearless . . .
dying horribly for no good reason. Tears filled London's closed
eyes, running over, forcing him to blink repeatedly. Crying
freely, he found he could not breathe through his nose at all. Before long, he was coughing and sputtering bloody phlegm. The
pain of it all chewed at every inch of his head, leaving him weak
and practically senseless. By the end, however, his body had
managed to block enough of his pain that he could finally open
his eyes. Looking up into his partner's face, he blinked away
tears as he croaked,

"Lisa?"

Morcey could barely understand his words—the detective's
throat was too dry to let him form any completely. As the ex-
maintenance man reached for the apple juice a nurse had left for
London earlier if he were to awaken, he told his partner,

"She's fine. Lai Wan's fine. Jhong and Father Bain, they made
it."

"That's it?" asked London, incredulous. "That's it?"

"No, no," added Morcey. "Ahhh, oh yeah—Cat—she made it,
too. Yeah, I forgot."

London stared outward from his bed in wide-eyed horror. He
could not believe that no one else had survived. The thought that

Pa'sha had died was bad enough for the detective, but to think of all the others that had been there. He croaked out a few more words, indicating his disbelief. As Morcey inserted the straw to the apple juice between London's lips, the balding man told him,

"Naw—most all the Murder Dogs, the truck drivers . . . Be'juma, all of them . . . Jhong conned the monster into not hasslin' a few of us, but everybody else—"

The balding man's voice trailed off for a moment. As London pulled on the straw in his mouth, sucking the relieving juice into his burning throat, he studied his partner's eyes. Looking into the lost depths in the back of them, seeing there how painful, how hideous those deaths had been, he closed his own eyes again and merely listened.

"God, boss—it tore up the trucks and killed almost all the drivers. The fires got out of hand—almost got to the loony bin. But, yeah—Warhelski, he bought it when that thing turned over Pa'sha's cruiser. Doc Goward was in it, too. He's in intensive care . . ."

And suddenly, the sound of Morcey's voice disappeared from the detective's ears. Before London knew what had happened to him, he found himself dressed and out of bed, standing on a long, darkened plane, surrounded by a thick, almost tangible blackness. Sensing a light behind him, though, he spun around sharply, noting that he felt no pain in doing so. When he turned, he found the light to be an intensely bright shaft of yellow-white radiance, coming from some indiscernible spot above him. Before he could wonder about it any further, however, Dr. Goward's voice came to him from the darkness.

"Theodore. Oh, thank God. I was hoping you'd managed to survive." The professor came walking out of the black shadows and joined the detective near the light, looking hale and perfectly fit. "You did survive, didn't you?"

"Well, yes, Zack—of course," answered London, confused for only a second before he realized. "Oh, I get it. We're on the dream plane."

"Yes. Which is apparently the only way I'm going to be seeing people for some time to come. I did a little astral planing over my body—not a very pretty sight." Pulling his pipe and pouch from his jacket pocket, he began stuffing a bowl, telling the detective, "I'm not exactly sure the old body is ever going to wake up—let alone survive."

And then the magnitude of what was happening struck London, threatening to overwhelm him. Staring at Goward's dream plane body, listening to him speak, he tried to understand how a dying man, one likely to never again open his eyes, could summon the energy and will to send himself to the dream plane. Before he could voice a question based on his confusion, the professor volunteered,

"It's quite simple, really. After all, you didn't come here of your own volition—did you?"

"Well, no. Not really. I was talking to Paul and I just sort of disappeared and reappeared here."

"I didn't want to be here, either, when you come right down to it, I suppose," answered Goward. Bringing his lighter up to his pipe, he inhaled deeply, setting the tobacco in its bowl to glowing. Exhaling his first lungful of smoke, he said,

"But I guess there isn't much I can do about it." Taking another long pull on his pipe, the professor exhaled, telling London,

"It's funny how the dream plane works. What it's capable of, what you're capable of once you learn to walk it. For instance— this tobacco is some of the best I've ever had. The smoke is cool and rich and aromatic—everything the television ads used to promise. And yet, it's not real. Is it?"

"I don't know, Zack," admitted the detective. "You're the expert. You tell me."

"It's as real as anything I've ever known. And yet, I know that everything we see when we visit here is created from our own desires. We don't know where we are and we don't know how to get here, yet every time we need to be here, or someone needs us to be here . . . arrival is no problem." Walking off in a path that would take him around the shaft of light, Goward continued to talk even as he disappeared from sight.

"You know, I am frightfully sorry for the problems I caused."

"What're you talking about, Zack?"

"Forcing the issue here, pulling everyone together to fight our furry friend—behind your back, no less. You said we shouldn't do it. You said there was going to be trouble. Now it looks as if I've probably gotten myself killed in the bargain. And not just myself, correct?"

"I'm a big boy. I could have done things differently."

"Nice of you to try to take the blame, but I'm afraid I really mucked the works." The professor came into view on the other side of the light, walking half in shadow, half in the radiant mist. Exhaling another lungful of smoke, he started around the near-blinding illumination again, saying,

"I just had to advance the cause of Zachary Goward, man of letters, seeker of the unknown. I was jealous of you, Theodore. I spent a lifetime looking for answers that fate seemed determined to hand you on a silver platter. When you didn't want to confront the beast, I allowed ambition to blind me. I wanted your center stage, my boy. I should have known better."

"But you were right," said London. "The thing was coming—we had to fight it."

"Now that I'm half dead and wandering in circles, I'm not so sure. You've done a remarkable job of finding the stepping stones so far. For all the good it does me now, I'm no longer convinced that I was all that correct. Something tells me that if your internal rhythm was telling you conflict was not the way to go, then conflict was not the way to go."

The professor's voice stopped as he took another pull on his pipe somewhere off in the darkness. Starting again, he told the detective,

"My ego has done me in—as it does for most in the end, I suppose. My stupidity last night was just a bit more noticeable than most men's. Ego is a terrible thing. Yours put me in the hospital a month ago, but that was nothing. It's mine that's put an end to things."

Coming back into view, instead of making another circle, Goward walked over to the point where the detective had stood since he had entered the dream plane. Taking London's hand, the professor held on to it with a fierce strength, asking,

"Did you know that there was another tree in the Garden of Eden besides the Tree of Knowledge?"

"Ummm—no," answered the detective, somewhat thrown by the abrupt change in the subject. "What kind of trouble did that one cause?"

"None. That was the Tree of Immortal Life, the tree of return to the Garden." The professor's voice paused for a second, then continued, saying,

"Funny, I was just arguing this point the other day." When London made no answer either way, Goward continued again, saying,

"Well, but anyway, if you read the Book of Genesis, it's made abundantly clear that God didn't want man to return. He placed a guardian at the gate to paradise with a flaming sword and charged him to keep man out lest he eat of the Tree of Immortal Life and become as the rest of the heavenly hosts."

And then, the professor released London's hand, stepping back toward the light. Taking another long pull on his pipe, he said,

"It has been a truly unique and distinct pleasure to know you, Theodore. Knowing you has done me a great deal of karmic good, and if I had the time I would explain it, but seeing that I don't seem to have any time to spare . . ." Goward exhaled a long plume of smoke, continuing to talk as he did so.

"Let me just say that like all the stories in the Bible, the one of Eden is a translation of a literal truth. Some thinker caught on to something he couldn't explain in any other way than through the dogmatic tools of his time." Talking faster, the professor began backing away from London, making his way through the darkness toward the column of light behind him.

"My condition, my being here, was caused by my ego. That's what the guardian at the gate with the flaming sword is . . . ego. It's ego that keeps us cut off from the rest of the universe, that drags us down."

London tried to listen to everything Goward was saying, tried to understand it as well . . . to question the meanings and to ask what was happening. Try as he might, he found he could not. But even though he could not explain how he knew what was happening, could not explain how he could be witness to what he was seeing, he still simply accepted it all, trying to at least retain what the professor was telling him. Watching from his vantage point, still not having moved from the moment of his arrival on the dream plane, London stared as Goward took one final backward step, bringing himself into the radiance.

The professor's face took on an expression of, not joy or rapture or even happiness, but of comprehension. Suddenly, the lines in his face disappeared, the sag of age and all its related pains dropping away like thick rain from a steep roof. The pipe dropping from his fingers unnoticed, Goward's face suddenly broke out in a wondrous smile as he said,

"You know, Theodore, it's a lot like the big joke back in the second and third centuries. As people used to say . . . 'Oh, that Yahweh, nice fellow and all—the only problem with Him is He thinks He's God.' "

And then, suddenly, London could *feel* the light. A gigantic, warming presence came into the air around him, a heady, fulfilling, understanding . . . a feeling that smelled of truth—one that filled his veins with music and his eyes with tears. He watched Goward as best he could, losing his exact form in the growing glare coming from the radiance. The light had begun to shimmer more and more intently, the power of it so dazzling the detective was finally forced to close his eyes. After only a moment, however, he sensed that the light had receded to more tolerable levels.

Opening his eyes again, London found himself back in the real world again, in his bed once more, still listening to his partner talk—still alive. As he blinked, again feeling the pain he had earlier, certain then that he was back, in his own physical body in real time, Morcey told him,

"They don't think he's going to make it."

"He didn't," interrupted the detective.

"Huh?" asked the ex-maintenance man. "Whatd'ya mean?"

"Dr. Goward just died." As Morcey stared down at the detective, not sure what to do next, a voice came from behind him, saying,

"That's right. My people just gave me the word over the wire." As London and his partner stared, a man wearing an extremely compact headset came toward them, saying,

"But I find it curious that you know that. Then, really, should I be surprised by anything when it's connected to the ever so righteous Theodore London?"

"And you are . . .?" croaked the detective in his weary voice.

"Michael Roth, Federal Bureau of Investigation. At present here to study you and make sure you stay put for the moment."

"Any particular reason?"

"Oh, quite a few," answered the FBI man. "We've got a number of questions to ask you. We'll be talking about that little party you and your friends had out on Wards Island for starters, then we'll work our way backwards."

"And if I don't want to answer your questions?" asked the detective.

"Then we'll simply charge you, jail you, and take things from there."

"Charge me?" asked London, already knowing the answer. "With what?"

"How about the murder of two million people?"

Well, said a voice in the back of the detective's head, it's about time.

22

London stared at the FBI man with a bit more than passing interest. He was curious over what it was exactly that had led the authorities to him, and why at that particular time. Figuring that he had nothing to lose, he asked. Roth told him.

"Surely you knew the government was studying the site of your confrontation with Q'talu."

"Excuse me?" asked the detective. "You know about Q'talu?" Reading the FBI man's attitude, London stared at him hotly, his eyes narrowing to slits. Controlling his temper, waiting for Roth to confirm verbally that which he had already read in his eyes, the detective asked,

"Are you saying you people knew that thing was coming?"

Roth gave London an overly smug look, showing the detective that the FBI man did not understand the intent of the question as it had been posed to him. Answering in a condescending tone, he told London,

"I'm saying that you're in some fairly big trouble and that you'd better start worrying about what you're going to do about it. If we've nailed down all your little stunts, you've murdered, crippled, maimed, and traumatized well over that two million figure. You're a deranged individual, Mr. London, with a messianic complex the size of the great outdoors. We're here to corral that all in a little bit."

"So glad to hear it," answered the detective, not appreciating much in the FBI man's manner. "But let me ask, just what is it you want from me?"

"What do you think? We've been giving you some rope to play with to see where it would take you, but it's apparently time to pull up a little of the slack in the leash. What you and your clown squad did last night shows that you people are more than just a little bit out of control."

"And," said London, the growl in his voice visibly disturbing Morcey, "you and yours would have been able to handle things so much better."

"What we might or might not have done in the past is irrele-

vant. We're in the here and now and that's the place we're going
to work from. You're going to start by sitting down with our experts and giving them all your information on the dream plane—
how it works, how you manipulate it, the whole ball of wax.
Comprende?"

"And then, you and yours will wisely handle everything that
comes along. Because, like you said, you knew about Q'talu.
You knew that thing was coming. And you've been watching me
ever since then . . . known everything I was going to do . . . were
aware of everything me and mine got involved in. Including last
night—correct?"

Dooming himself to suffer what happened next, Roth sealed
his fate by telling London with a exaggerated sense of self-
satisfaction,

"Your government is always on top of things."

"On top of my ass," responded the detective violently. "I'll
give you more credit than I would have before just for knowing
the thing's name, but I don't think you get what I'm driving at."

"Please," answered the FBI man, his tone sinking into conde-
scension, "the approach of the creature was being monitored. We
knew its ETA just as you did."

"You knew," answered the detective, his voice a cold mix of
anger and despair. Closing his eyes, shaking his head from side
to side, he said,

"You knew it was coming, knew what it was capable of, knew
what it was coming for? And you just sat back and let things
happen the way they did? You let me face that thing and didn't
do anything to intervene. Don't tell me that even our stinking
government is that evil?"

"Mr. London," countered Roth, showing a sudden lack of pa-
tience for or interest in anything but his own agenda, "I think
you might want to get hold of yourself."

"Get hold of myself—I'll get a hold around your stupid neck.
Tell me, Roth—if you brains knew what that thing was . . . knew
it was on its way . . . then where were you? When I was running
for my life, watching people die all around me—including my
best friend—where the fuck were you?"

"I don't think—"

"You shut up!" snarled the detective. Throwing back the sheet
covering him, London swung his feet out over the edge of his
bed. "Do you think this is some kind of game? Do you have any
idea what you're dealing with here?"

As the detective got his balance, the FBI man's hand instinctively went for his weapon. He pulled it free from its holster in a single clean motion, backing far enough away and to the side at the same time to assure himself that neither London nor Morcey could reach him without taking a bullet. Trying to assume command of the situation once more, he braced himself in the standard firing stance and then ordered,

"Freeze it right there, mister. Maybe you don't exactly understand the nature of what's happening here." As the detective took a step toward Roth, the FBI man called out,

"Reynolds, Fergeson. With me."

Instantly the two FBI men who had been covering the room from the hall burst inside, their weapons to the ready. Morcey, standing next to London, not sure as to whether he should be backing up an attempt to rush the FBI men or getting ready to catch the detective if he should fall, asked,

"What's next, boss?"

"Stand clear, Paul," answered London grimly, staring at Roth and his companions. Moving forward slowly, feeling blood begin to drip from somewhere under the bandages on his face, the detective said,

"You morons? You people weren't ready for Q'talu. You don't have the faintest idea of what went on that night." Before anyone could react, London moved his hands upward as if reaching for the ceiling, holding his fingers outward away from himself. As he did, all of the electric lights in the room burst in their sockets, casting everyone into a dull gloom.

"You don't have any idea at all what I've been through . . . what I saved the world from, and what I had to go through to do it." His hands shaking, fingers curling into fists, London stepped forward through the gloom, the low, feral growl of his voice unnerving the three men with the guns at the other end of the room. As the detective moved cautiously, trying to maintain his balance despite the fearsome pain in his head, Roth barked orders at him, saying,

"I'm telling you to stop where you are—*now*, Mr. London. We do not want to harm you, but we will open fire on the count of three if you do not return to your bed immediately."

London stopped for a moment, his arms hanging loosely at his sides. As he stared at the trio of FBI men, his eyes began to shine, reflecting the remaining available light in the room in such a manner that each of the three felt he was looking directly at them. The detective allowed the effect to work on their nerves for a long moment, then he moved his arms again, pointing them at the trio as he shifted his concentration to include their gun hands as well.

Instantly, all three of them experienced an uncontrollable itching in their wrists. Following that, each felt their guns growing suddenly heavier—not slightly heavier, but monstrously heavy. The change came so abruptly that all of the agents were instantaneously dragged to their knees, the man named Fergeson hitting the floor face first. Their weapons had taken on such weight that none of the trio could even work their hands free from their trigger guards. Each of the guns had broken the hospital room's floor, pulling their owners' hands down into the shattered tile. But that was not the worst the detective had in shore for the FBI agents.

Staring down at the trio with contempt, he concentrated on their guns once more, this time raising the temperature of each weapon. The three felt the metal in their hands growing hotter. Not understanding what was happening, reacting only to the growing pain, the agents pulled on their trapped wrists with their free hands, smashed at the floor, pried at their guns, doing anything to escape the blistering agony they could feel in their palms and fingers. Moving forward again on the trio, London looked down on them all with contempt, snarling,

" 'Immediately' is long over, Roth. Why haven't you opened fire yet?"

Ignoring the detective, fighting his way past his pain, the FBI man called into the miniature transmitter built into his lapel, ordering the rest of his men to converge on the room. As London stood by, listening without emotion, Roth told his men in between his painful gasping,

"Move in. Move in. Proceed with . . . extreme caution. I repeat—proceed with extreme caution. But, be ready to . . . wound or kill if necessary. Maximum force . . . is given over to individual discretion."

Then, his orders delivered, the FBI man gave into the searing pain eating at his hand. Throwing back his head, his scream pierced the air of the room, his cries those of a wounded beast. Gone were any thoughts of his approaching agents, the orders he had given them—even his own orders. The only thing resembling a clear conscious thought remaining in Roth's head was the notion of regaining possession of his weapon so he could turn it on the man standing over him.

Pushing everything from his mind except killing Theodore London, he closed his eyes, squeezing them shut against the tears burning their way down his face. Clenching his teeth together, he ground them down one against the other, cutting off his mindless, fear-driven bleating. Then, finally able to ignore the pain in his hand, he worked at raising his weapon—pulled at it, felt the skin tearing from his fingers, his nails burning down into ash—thinking of nothing else. His mind filled with the sight of a bullet screaming across the room, plowing its way into London's forehead, pushing its way out through the back of the detective's skull. He savored the image, sucked at the juice of it, pumped all the satisfaction he could out of the hate in it, using it all to fuel his determination.

None of it did him any good, however. Finally despairing of ever being able to lift his weapon, of escaping London's powers, of being able to do his job or even survive the night—Roth abandoned his ideals of preserving the dignity of the FBI, his mind draining his will of its determination to kill the detective, to kill anyone, to do anything but free his hand. Not caring who heard or what happened to him later, or ever, the agent screamed,

"Enough—please—enough. Stop it! Stop the pain, please! Please—please—please!! Stop it—stop—stop—it—stop it stop it stop it stop it st . . ."

And then he realized that his hand had come free from his weapon and that the pain had stopped abruptly the instant he had left off his ideas of restraining London in any fashion. Kneeling on the floor, his body convulsed by wracking spasms, he pulled his hand up toward his face, trembling to find the power to open his eyes. When he finally did, he stared at his fingers, blinking away the tears blinding him.

"Nothing," he whispered, his voice startled—mixed with equal parts of shame and curiosity. Looking down at his gun, at the floor, he saw that neither of them had been burned, melted, or damaged in any way. As he stared, he felt the fingers of fear again crawling up his back. His nerves jangling, he felt the sweat soaking his suit, tasted the salt of his own tears in his mouth. He knew he had experienced something he could not understand—had known even when it had been happening that what he was caught in was something beyond his comprehension.

Now, even more confused, he pushed himself up from the floor, stunned to find he could use his gun hand to do so. With no pain whatsoever remaining, he started to reach for his gun, then thinking better of the action, left it lying where he had dropped it before. Looking around the room, he noted that Fergeson and Reynolds had done the same. Suddenly remembering his other men, Roth looked to the door, wondering what had prevented them from coming to his aid. Noting the look on the FBI man's face, understanding what was in his head merely from the look in his eyes, London told him,

"I interrupted your communications. They never heard you." Turning toward the pair of Roth's men there in the room with them, the detective explained,

"Sorry you had to share your chief's little lesson here, but I didn't think to stop him before he called you in." Then, almost as an afterthought, he added,

"You can all pick up your guns, you know."

The three hesitated for a moment, then retrieved their weapons. As they began to wonder what London was up to, attacking them as he did, then returning their weapons to them, the detective explained,

"I understand your reaction. Try to understand mine. I lost two good people last night—one of them my oldest friend in the whole world. Then you come in here and tell me the government knew what was going on the whole time—that you've been around since the beginning—letting me take the lumps, letting me watch my friends die . . . one after another." Walking across the room to the clothes closet, the detective began dressing in the suit Morcey had brought in for him as he said,

"Then, on top of that, you announced that I would make up for defending the world time and again while you and yours took notes by becoming some sort of government servant guinea pig. Well, let me tell you, that certainly sounded appealing."

London buttoned his shirt, staring at the three men. Each had reholstered his weapon, all of them sensing the futility of trying the same thing twice. The detective watched the heat coming off their bodies, wondering what they would do next. He himself had no worries. He could leave town, the country, or not, and no one would ever be able to find him again. Not after the night before.

Pa'sha's death, his last words with Goward, both events had loosened the restraints he had placed on himself. He was no longer concerned about unleashing the power of the dream plane. Indeed, he had just proved to himself that it had become such a second nature to him to call upon it that from that point on he would have to watch himself to make sure he did not use it too often, did not get sucked into the God-like feel of it. Goward had warned him of such before, had restated it in the last seconds of his life.

I could have just as easily made it real flames, he thought. Could have just as easily turned them inside out, exploded the blood from their bodies, killed them a thousand times over.

Smiling grimly, the detective told himself,

I'm going to have to get a grip on such antisocial behavior.

Then, he spoke aloud again to the others, telling them,

"Well, anyway, now we've got our little problem to sort out. I've got places to go and people to see. The dead had families I've got to talk to. Look at my face, gentlemen. I've been busted up by a thing from Hell. I'm not in a real good mood. I'm in pain, and I've got a monster to kill. So now, I'm going to propose a new game." Threading his tie, London looked directly into Roth's eyes, then said,

"You and I are going to sit down and have a little talk. We're going to piece together just what the government can and cannot expect from me, and then I'm going to be about my business and you're going to go about yours."

"Yes?" questioned the FBI man, the touch of fear in his voice overshadowed by his returning arrogance. "And just when's this little tête-à-tête going to take place?"

Opening his eyes to their fullest, London stared unblinking into Roth's, telling him,

"Right now."

23

Roth's shoulders, spine, and knees all jumped, his nervous system caught off guard by the abrupt shift in locale. Suddenly, he was no longer in the hospital room, no longer flanked by his men. Looking around, he found himself on an endless red plane streaked with purple dust, unbroken in any direction except by the figure of Theodore London, sitting on a raised pile of the surrounding redness. The FBI man, conscious of his startled pose, composed himself abruptly, straightening his suit, feeling the blood in his cheeks.

"More tricks, Mr. London?"

"Tricks, Roth? After the little demonstration I just put on for you, you've still got so little idea of what's happening around here that you've got to call this"—the detective stretched his arms out, indicating everything around them—"all of *this*, a trick? You must think I'm one hell of a trickster."

"Cut the crap. Just tell me what your demands are."

London listened to the man's words, counted the amount of times he was blinking per minute, watched the steadiness of his fingers break down into nervous fumbling. He could see that Roth was hanging on to his former vision of reality a little too strongly. The detective knew that to push him at that moment might not be easy on the man's sanity. Not caring much what happened to the man who said that he had let the events of the past year just roll off his back, though, the detective told him,

"Let me try to explain something to you. You're pretty much on the edge right now. You're trying to tell yourself that I've flimflammed you somehow—that all of this is just another elaborate illusion ... like the one back in the hospital room where you were kneeling on the floor screaming for your mother."

"Now listen here—"

"Shut up, Roth. Get hold of yourself and stop fighting your senses. I'm going to be straight with you. I looked in your eyes back there and decided that you might have some chance of understanding this. You claim to have been watching me for months. You act as if you know the things that have happened to me over the past year. It seemed to me that if you actually knew there were vampires and werewolves in this world—that if you already believed in the dream plane—that it wouldn't be so crippling an experience for you to go there in person."

The FBI man stared around himself again, taking in the red plane more slowly. Trying to establish some parameters for the place in which he had suddenly found himself, he searched the far ends of what he could see for any signs of anything besides London. In the distance he noted several storms, faraway dots of cloud blasting at the surface with tiny flashes of lightning. Turning back to the detective, he asked,

"We're really on the dream plane?"

"That's the only name I know it by."

"But, how?" asked Roth, his belligerence finally beginning to crumble. "How did you get us here? Is this the way it always looks? Are there other levels to it?" Then, falling to one knee, he dipped his hand into the unsubstantial purple of the dust beneath him, asking,

"Can you shape it any way you want? Can you—can we? Can we actually affect this place?"

Creating another seat for the FBI agent near his own, London answered,

"Pretty much in any way we want to." Crossing over to where the detective was sitting, Roth took the seat London had created for him, posing another question as he did so.

"You keep waving your hands when you do things. Is that necessary? Are you casting spells or something?" Almost laughing, the detective answered,

"No. The gestures are superfluous. I guess it's sort of like a kid saying 'alakazam' as he breaks the electronic eye of an automatic door; or when you move your hands like a conductor when you're listening to classical music. The door will still open, the music will keep playing, whether anyone is gesturing or not. It just involves you more in the process. It's just a way of focusing the will."

Roth could not say anything further, too struck by what the detective had just told him. Somehow, everything ran together in his head, finally forcing him to realize what was happening. He had been watching London for months, was aware of some aspects of the supernatural most people never dreamed could possibly exist. Looking up with the beginnings of understanding in his eyes, he said,

"I'm on the dream plane. We're actually here. It can be done. People can walk the dream plane at will. This is just what everyone wanted to know . . ."

"Ah," said London. "Now, there we go. Excuse me . . . everyone?"

"The think tankers—the organization men behind our surveillance of you and your people—they knew that finding our way onto the dream plane would be a big step forward."

"Toward what?" asked the detective. As his interest grew along with his anger, the storms in the distance began to move forward, rolling across the red plane in the direction of London and the FBI agent.

"Umm, actually, the objectives of the study were classified. No one ever told us why . . . they just gave us our assignments. I mean . . ."

"Oh, please," groaned the detective, rolling his eyes with the hopelessness of it all. "Doesn't anyone ever get tired of offering up that same old chestnut? 'I vus only following orders.' That makes it all right, doesn't it? It wasn't you that caused any of the trouble. None of it was *your* idea. No, of course not. You were only following orders."

"Now wait a minute, London," answered Roth. "You act as if something was going on here. You're insinuating that the United States government had some sort of ulterior motive for what they were doing."

The detective held himself back, forcing himself to remember that Roth truly did seem to be an honorable man. Not cutting him off, but not able to take him seriously, either, London snapped sarcastically,

"I'll try Naive for five hundred, Alex. What kind of idiot are you, Roth? Can you actually not think for yourself or do you just not have the guts to take responsibility for your actions? I'm not insinuating anything. I'm saying point-blank that while my friends and I were dying to protect people, you and the rest of the fat ass government were sitting back watching us through binoculars, waiting for us to unlock the secrets you wanted but didn't have the nerve to go after yourselves. How did it feel, huh, when that bastard who thought he was Satan was tearing us up, when he killed those two priests . . . did you just check it off in your little book? Last night, when Pa'sha died, when men were dying like flies . . . what was going on in your head? Did you ever once think you and your boys should be moving in—did it ever even occur to you that perhaps you should be down there doing your duty?"

"My duty," answered the FBI man, standing up, staring down at London, "was to watch you and yours—period."

"To what end?" snapped the detective, the blood pounding in his forehead. Rising slowly from his own seat, he stepped up close to Roth, jamming his finger repeatedly into the agent's chest, saying,

"Don't you get it? The government didn't care how many people died. If you'd gotten yourself flattened out accidentally in one of our skirmishes you'd have just been replaced the next day by some other smug asshole in a blue blazer who knows how to follow orders. What are they after, Roth? Why the hell does the government want to know how to walk the dream plane? Don't they spy on us enough already without being able to slip into our goddamned dreams?"

"I don't think they had any intention . . ."

"You don't think?" answered London, shouting over the fury of the approaching storm. "I'll grant you that, Roth. I'm certain that you don't think. Tell me, what comes next? Now that you and the other dark suits have moved in and revealed yourselves, what's next? Someone has obviously moved things up from watching the game to participating. So what's the FBI's next move?"

Snow began to whip past the two men. Slamming by on gale force winds which felt almost strong enough to push the pair over, the flakes tore across their skin, stinging wherever they touched. Holding one hand to his eyes to try to clear his vision, Roth answered,

"We were to question you, to find out as much as we could, and then we were to confront the werewolf ourselves." London stared at the FBI man, asking,

"Confront? What the hell does 'confront' mean? Are you saying they wanted you to capture it?"

"Yes," answered Roth, screaming to be heard. "To study it. Too many of the things that you've faced have been able to regenerate themselves. Even you have to admit that that ability is something that would make anyone interested."

"Yeah," answered the detective, stunned as the force of the idea hit him. "I'll just bet it would. And what were their plans for that? A Congress that never dies? Billionaires and movie stars and all the other sucking greedy pigs buying immortality to slop in their troughs like all the other buckets of garbage they take for granted?"

Then, London stopped for a moment, frozen in his tracks. His mind filled with a horrible scenario. An army made up of soldiers with the powers of the werething. Men with guns and bombs who could not be stopped by the same. Battalions of men invading a countryside, unstoppable, unforgiving. And then, his mind saw a greater horror. Remembering that there has never been a weapon created since the beginning of time which, once discovered by one side, has not sooner or later made it to the other—suddenly he saw not one invincible army but two, battling each other to the death, over and over.

His mind filled with the madness of it. All their bullets spent, all their bombs exploded, their uniforms long ripped and burned and shredded away, rolling on the ground, biting great chunks from one another, only to watch each mouthful of flesh regenerate anew. And so they would go—unstoppable—fighting on to the end of time, laying waste to everything else on the planet as they did so. The detective threw his head back at that point, laughing so loud and long he chilled the FBI agent more than the dropping temperature.

From somewhere deep within the storm, thunder echoed across the now snow-covered plane. All around the pair, lightning splattered the ground, sending snow and ice and frozen chunks of red into the sky, filling the air with the smell of burning dirt. Finally, London broke off his bitter laughter. Blood still dripping from his face, his mouth wet with the taste of it, the detective faced Roth once more, saying,

"So, you want to capture the werewolf for the greater glory of Uncle Sam and the United States Congress, do you?"

"Those were my orders."

"Well, why don't you ask him how he feels about it?" And with those words, London closed his eyes, screaming out into the darkness of the great beyond, looking to find Maxim Warhelski's monster wherever it was out in reality and draw it to him.

"How about it?! How about it, wolfman?! What do you think about Mr. Roth's orders?"

As the detective shouted into the storm, another series of thunderclaps erupted in the sky, followed by another, even more tremendous series of spectacular lightning blasts than those previous. And then, without knowing why, both men turned to face the same direction, straining to see through the wind-driven snow and sleet.

As they did, one last incredible lightning blast broke the air. Its flash lit the sky and the land for a thousand miles in every direction, revealing to the pair the form closing on them. The form of the werewolf.

Roth pointed into the snow in the general direction of the approaching monster, shouting,

"You fuck! You crazy shit stupid fuck—you brought that thing *here!*"

"Not really, pal," answered the detective, stepping back from the approach line of the beast, separating himself from the FBI agent. "You're the one who wanted him—alive, that is, I believe. Or at least in one piece." Smiling grimly, the detective added,

"That . . . that's not going to be easy. Better start thinking long and hard on that one."

Then, London narrowed his eyes, searching through the dark night snow for another glimpse of the creature. Catching a short motion in the distance, he shouted to Roth,

"It's only about three miles off. The way that thing travels, you've got maybe—what? Ten minutes? Tops? Better think quick."

"Think what?" screamed the FBI man. Stabbing his finger at London, he shrieked, "Think about what? What's going on? What's happening? What are you doing to me?!"

"Hey, get it together, pal. That thing's coming and it's looking for meat. To answer your questions, I'm not doing anything to you. You did this to yourself. If you didn't want to capture that thing for your Uncle Sam so bad—if you didn't want it in the pit of your soul . . . I couldn't do this. I only allow to happen what you wanted. Any changes now will have to come from you." Backing further away from Roth off into the darkness, the detective continued, shouting,

"I'm giving you a chance to be the big brave hero that brings in the werewolf. You could just wish yourself back to reality and be done with this or you can stay and try and please your superiors. It's up to you—go back home or stay and conjure up whatever you're going to need to stop that thing. Now that you're here, you can do it—any person, any amount of weapons—anything you want at all. You can create it out of thin air now that I've told you it's possible."

"How? How?"

"Finding your way to the dream plane on your own," conceded London, "I'll give you that one—that's tough. But once you're here, miracles are nothing. Anything, anyone you want to help you against that monster—they're yours. You can create a facsimile or bring the real McCoy right here, unless their will is strong enough to defy yours, of course."

The detective took a step backwards, saying,

"So go ahead, dream away—rub the lamp—make a wish. You can have anything you want here. Anything at all." And then, the detective disappeared completely from Roth's line of vision. His voice coming from out of the darkness, he told the FBI man,

"Of course, anyone you bring in here to help you . . . if that thing kills them here—they'll die back there in the outside world just as finally. And bringing them back . . . well, that's one miracle you don't seem to get. So, choose your victims carefully, Roth. Line them up—'cause here comes baby."

And then, the monster's horrific cry split the sky, sounding louder than any of the thunder the FBI man had heard on the dream plane, sounding louder than anything he had every heard in his life. Fear and confusion taking hold of him once again, Roth cried out,

"How can I beat it? I'm all alone. I have no help—no weapons. I don't even have my 9mm."

"Of course you do."

Responding to the detective's fading voice, the FBI agent checked his shoulder holster. He was surprised to find his weapon there where he had replaced it back in London's hospital room. Drawing it quickly, wrapping his fingers around its reassuring presence, he mumbled,

"Very funny. Big deal. As if this is going to be any kind of help against that thing. If I was going stay and take that thing on, I'd need some big guns . . . and backup." Looking off in the direction of the approaching werewolf—his decision made—the FBI man tried to spot the beast, then turned away, shutting his eyes as he thought to himself,

I'd need what? Tanks—batteries of artillery—bombers and jets and attack copters and maybe a thousand regular foot soldiers . . . all of them armed like it was going to be the third world war . . .

"Sir, that thing is getting closer."

Opening his eyes at the startling sound of the strangely familiar voice, Roth found himself confronted with each of his wishes made whole. Surrounding him on the snow-covered field were all the weapons he had dreamed of, suddenly now under his command and ready for war. His attending aide, a four-star general with a face he almost recognized but in the end could not, made no note of the fact that the FBI man seemed stunned almost to the verge of going into shock. Gently prodding his commander, the aide rephrased his comment.

"Very close now, sir. Do you think it might be time to open fire?"

Roth staggered to the edge of the metal plating he suddenly found himself on—the upper deck of a gigantic mobile command center, much like the one he had watched Pa'sha Lowe working out of the night before. Grabbing the edge of the railing, half to keep himself from stumbling over the edge, half to keep him from leaping over, Roth squeezed the bar, fighting at the madness tearing at his brain.

"Oh, please," he begged the air softly. "Oh, God . . . *please*."

He had known that the dream plane was real before he had ever encountered London face-to-face. He had studied it, kept London and his people's unmoving bodies back in reality under surveillance while he knew they were moving around in it. Admitting the deep-buried truth, he had been waiting like a one-year-old at the starting line of the Kentucky Derby for his own chance to walk its boundaries.

But at that moment, seeing the power of the dream plane made solid—realizing what was about to happen—his brain began to boil under the pressure of events. Suddenly it was he and he alone who was in charge—responsible for men and their machines and the lives of each—responsible for everything that happened in the entire world around him . . . his actions, his desires, his needs . . . all to be satisfied instantly, as soon as even his unconscious mind made them known.

Laughing hysterically, spittle flying away from his lips off into the sleet-filled wind, he shouted,

"So I can have anything I want, eh? Anything in the world, in the universe . . . anything I can imagine—I could have had anything my heart had ever desired. Anything!" Looking around himself, taking in the grim stance of his troops, his eyes going up and down the scores of rows of them stretching off into the darkness, he shuddered as he thought,

And I chose this. Again Roth laughed, beyond caring how mad the ring of it would sound to anyone who might happen to hear. Wiping at his tears as they froze to his face, he asked himself, in a frozen voice,

"This? This is what I wanted the most?" Then, abruptly turning away from his troops, he stared out into the darkness, his eyes searching for some sign of the werewolf as he muttered,

"Then this is what I get."

Turning to his aide, he snarled,

"Get some lights going. Get some flares in the air, get some choppers with spots upstairs. Alert the batteries to start shelling the third, second, and first most likely target areas. Then get every other available body ready to follow up." As the general saluted and hurried off to obey Roth's orders, the FBI man screamed,

"Get moving! And forget capturing that motherfucking death machine. Just kill it! Burn its ass. Kill it!!"

Astride his platform, his collar flapping in the growing wind, Roth watched as the plane before him flooded with light. The flying snow hid some of the illumination, the wind weaving it into wretchedly twisted shadows which disappeared layer by layer as more and more power was turned toward the field. Seconds after, the shelling began.

As the FBI man watched, the snow stretching to the horizon disappeared—blasted up into the sky mixed with the scarlet plane's purple dust. Minute after minute passed, each second jammed with the numbing sound of another score of exploding five-hundred-pound shells. They rained out of the sky continually, Roth's hundreds of cannon filling the air with whistling bombs.

His jets, flying above the top of the cannons' firing arc, lay a blazing trail of napalm and rockets, blasting the little solid ground remaining—setting fire to the rest. For a solid half hour they continued their attack unabated, wave after wave of attack planes moving forward through the storm. Hundreds of them crashed down into the blazing target zone, unable to find their way through the driving snow, but their destruction and the deaths of their pilots did nothing to deter Roth.

Whenever he was informed that he had used up all his available fighters and bombers he merely wished for more—ordering them aloft in the screeching laugh which had taken the place of his voice. Finally, however, he was informed that no more planes could be leveled against his foe. When he asked why, his aide informed him,

"The enemy is too close, sir. We'd be hitting our own men if we kept targeting him."

"Too close?" cried the FBI agent, his words more jibbering

than anything else. "How can it be 'close'? *How?!* We've dropped the entire fucking sky on it! How can it keep coming? How?! *Tell me how!*"

"Because," answered his dream plane aide, cold and stiff as any other marionette Roth had ever seen, "he cannot be killed . . . sir."

"Anything that is flesh and blood can be killed," insisted the agent. "Is that fucking thing made up of flesh and blood?"

"Yes, sir," answered the aide.

"Then kill it! Send in the tanks. Send in the men! Send in everything and kill it! Kill its fucking ass and bring me its head."

Giving Roth a salute, the general turned and made his way down the ladder running up the side of the command post, giving orders before he even made it to the ground. Then, he walked away into the storm, barking more commands, all his words and all their answers lost in the noise of the wind. Staring out over the edge of his railing, trying to follow the movement of his tanks and men, the FBI man laughed once more, shaking his fist into the freezing wind at the blasted plane beyond.

"You will go down, you fucking thing! Do you hear me? You will . . . go . . . down!"

The first of the tanks found their target and opened fire as the last word escaped Roth's lips. Even as he spoke it, he saw the body of the werewolf flung a hundred yards by the first explosions, saw pieces of the beast hurled a thousand feet in the air—watched them crash back to the ground, flaming and broken. And yet, still it came on. Regenerating itself anew—time and time again—pulling itself up out of the slushing red muck of the dream plane and advancing once more.

Spying from his perch, the agent watched as the monster tore into his tanks, bending, twisting, crippling their cannon with its bared paws. Howling madly, it ripped loose their treads and shredded its way through their sides with only its claws. It ripped free each tank's machine guns, tore off their hatches, made its way inside, and then killed every man in every tank . . . one at a time . . . one after another. It destroyed them all—the first wave of a hundred, then the next, then the next, and so many more after them that there was no counting up the destruction.

As the last of the tanks surrounded the werewolf, Roth's legions followed, tramping through the ever-deepening snow. They marched forward, the front lines constantly blasting away at their enemy, constantly being torn apart by the seemingly unstoppable killing machine. Lead tore the flesh from its body, splattered its organs. Its claws did the same for its attackers.

Watching from the edge of his platform, half-kneeling, half-hanging over the edge of his railing, the FBI man noted the turn in the battle, his eyes widening with the first light of hope they had seen. As Roth continued to stare, so many bullets struck the monster that parts of it were reduced to mush—so battered, so shredded they could not come together fast enough to regenerate before they were smashed apart again. Seeing this, the FBI man screamed into the storm,

"That's it. That's it! Pour it on! More, more—more! Kill it! Kill it!!"

Roth watched from his vantage point, his wild eyes stretched to their widest with disbelief. Rivers of blood broke their way through the mounting snow, thousands of gallons spilled from the never-ending procession of soldiers making their way up and over the growing hills of their fallen comrades. At the center of the carnage, what was left of the werewolf fought on, clawing, biting, on its back but still lashing out at its foes.

Spurred on by the sight of possible victory, the soldiers fired hundreds of thousands of rounds into the monster. The air thickened with the smell of burnt powder and charcoal. As the never-ending stream of them came on, they marched forward to their deaths uncaring, trigger fingers raw and bleeding. They emptied their weapons and then reloaded and emptied them again—over and over until either their gun barrels melted or they were killed by their monstrous target. But eventually they seemed to finally take their toll.

As the hours wore on, finally there came the moment when the beast fell, unable to slash another victim with its arms cut from its shoulders—unable to stand before its legs were blown away from its body. Following up their one chance, the army rallied, firing more rounds even faster—forcing the creature onto its back, then blowing it to pieces. As the pieces struggled to reform, to somehow drag themselves back to their center, they found that center destroyed. The solders' unrelenting advance finally seemed to take effect as they fired again and again and again—blasting every last ounce of flesh from the monster's bones, then reducing the bones to chips, and then the chips to powder.

"Ah ha! That's it . . . that's done it! We win. It's dead. Did you see that, Mr. Fucking-better-than-everyone Theodore Fucking

London? I did it! I killed it! You couldn't kill it, but I fucking killed it!"

And then, looking over the edge once more, the madness in his eyes finally fading slightly, the FBI man noted that one intact bit of the creature still remained. Staring down at it, he called to his aide,

"Its head! Bring me its head!"

Roth's aide moved forward to carry out his commander's latest order while their troops began to disperse back into the substance of the dream plane from which they had been created. The agent slumped down atop his command post, thoroughly exhausted. Sitting with his back against the railing, he launched himself off into a mad frenzy of crying and laughter, not able to tell when he was stopping one or starting another. He caught hold of himself, however, as he heard his men cheering in the distance.

Turning slightly, enough to see their fading forms disappearing in the still-whirling snow, he savored the sounds of their approval. And then, he noted the focus of their attention. There, walking between their parting rows was the FBI man's aide, carrying the werewolf's severed head above his own. Forcing himself to his feet, the agent brushed himself off, awaiting his victory trophy. His aide struggled his way up the frozen metal ladder of the command post with the beast's massive head clutched in one arm.

"Your spoils, sir," said the aide, holding onto the staggering weight of the head with both hands as he crossed the command post's platformed roof. As he did, Roth focused on the man's face, finally recognizing him. He had thought he might know the aide before, but he had been too distracted, too distanced by his fear to worry about individual faces. At that point, however, he was no longer distracted.

"Dad?" he asked.

"Please, son," answered the aide in the four-star general's uniform, the only real person Roth had pulled onto the dream plane with him, "not in front of the men."

And then, before another word could be spoken, the werewolf's head spun itself around, twisting in the aide's hands. Without a sound it forced its ragged muzzle forward, slashing into the flesh of the aide's abdomen. Blood broke free as the monster's jaws worked, spilling out of the aide as the thing devoured his insides.

Roth moved forward, but it was too late. The werewolf

smashed him away with his newly grown arms, stood over him on his newly grown legs. Growling from deep within his all too substantial chest, he stared down at the FBI man, telling him,
   "Fool."

The agent lay on the platform, gasping for air, feeling the pain of his shattered ribs. He watched as the monster turned its back on him, leapt off the command post roof, and disappeared into the darkness. Then, he looked over at the body of his father and suddenly remembered what London had told him before the battle.

After that, he cried again—longer than any of the other times that day, and with greater reason.

{25}

When it had happened, he did not know. He only knew that something had shifted—that somehow the world had shifted. Sensing a degree of both warmth and light that should not have been there, Roth opened his eyes, suddenly finding himself in what appeared to be London's hospital room. He was on the floor, shaking, unable to control either the nervous spasms running through his body or the mad laughter dribbling up out of his throat. His skin and clothing were dirty, his hair slick with sweat and his chin with spittle. As it began to register within his brain that he was indeed back from the dream plane he slowly regained control of his functions.

Silencing his mad humming, dispelling the shakes vibrating his body, he worked at focusing his eyes on those things around him. Gazing upward, he found his two men staring at him, both of them looking pale and shaken. London sat across the room from him, his arms folded across his chest, a look of bored impatience on his face. Morcey stood next to him, drumming his fingers on the flat surface of the mobile dinner stand next to the detective's bed. Seeing the agent's eyes come open, London asked through the bandages still covering his face,

"Welcome back. Enjoy your visit?"

"You bastard."

"You know," said the detective, "for an FBI man, you've got an awfully foul mouth."

"What happened to you, sir?" asked Fergeson, his voice straining to stay even.

"What—what do you mean? What happened? What's been going on? What?"

"Sir," answered Reynolds, reaching down to help Roth up from the floor, "you've been unconscious for several hours. We thought to move you, but ... ah, Mr. London advised us that such action might not be wise."

"It's never good to mess with people's bodies when they're on the dream plane," interjected the detective. "Never know what they're capable of."

"Yeah, tell me—" And then, as Reynolds's hand began to pull his superior's arm upward, suddenly Roth broke off, giving out with a short yelp of pain. Reynolds released his hold at once, panic shooting across his face. Waving his men off, Roth made his own way slowly to his feet, favoring his left side. He knew he was not broken—that his ribs were not shattered as they had been on the dream plane—but still, the agony running through him was nearly crippling.

"You," said the FBI man, turning on London. "You did it. You did it all. What I . . ."

"Mr. Roth," said London, uncrossing his arms, holding one up as if warning caution, "you and I need to talk—privately. You want to tell the whole world about our conversation afterwards, fine. But before you say anything . . . else, I really do think we should discuss your last few hours."

The agent stared at the detective for a moment, conflicting emotions within him all screaming their own advice. Fear clawed at him—fear of being alone with the man who had sent him to the dream plane, fear that he might send him back, fear that he might not. Curiosity also welled within him, as did a dozen other raging voices, all of their noise blending together, forcing Roth to nod his head.

"Reynolds, Fergeson . . . why don't you two wait out in the hall again?"

The pair turned and walked for the door, not questioning their superior's orders, not looking back. Morcey followed them, knowing both that London would want him to keep an eye on the pair and that the detective would be able to do more with the FBI man if the two of them were undisturbed. As the door closed, London pointed to the chair next to him, offering,

"Why don't you sit down? This could take a little while."

"What did you do to me?" asked Roth. His body achingly stiff from lying on the tile floor for so long, the agent stretched as he staggered across the room, trying to work the pain out of his body. "What was all that?"

"That was the dream plane. That's what your people want—right?" As the FBI man hesitated, London continued,

"Yes—right. Please don't bother to try to lie to me about it—it can't be done."

"That's a little arrogant, isn't it?"

"That's the way it is. I saw it in your eyes. The government wants to find out how to walk the dream plane. You're their mumbo-jumbo whiz kid. They put you in charge of watching us because you're their top boy when it comes to anything that smacks of the supernatural—correct?" When Roth merely nodded, the detective said,

"Thank you. Keep telling the truth and maybe we'll get somewhere here. Now, why don't you tell me what happened in there? I see you survived the werewolf. That's something, anyway. I wondered if you would."

"But you called it. You brought it down on us. And then you left me there."

"Almost right, but not quite," answered London. "You're the one that wanted that thing—at that moment, anyway. You could have forced it out of your dream—all you had to do was not want it there anymore. You could have gotten rid of it immediately, just like you could have simply come back like I told you . . . right?" Again the FBI man nodded, too drained, too frightened to attempt to deceive London. As Roth then just stared at him, unbelieving, London told him,

"There are two ways to take someone else to the dream plane—by following a desire of your own, or by following their desire. I took us there to see what you wanted. You wanted to confront the werewolf. I took you there . . . I gave you what you wanted. Now, why don't you tell me why you wanted to confront that thing and what happened when you did."

"It . . . it was horrible. It was the worst nightmare I ever had." Slowly, bit by bit, the agent managed to relate his story to London, telling him everything that had happened to him on the dream plane as best he could remember it. The detective made no comments other than to quietly encourage the shaken Roth to go on—to reach for every bit of detail he could, no matter how disturbing or painful. Finally, after nearly half an hour, the agent reached the end of his story. As he told London about the slaughter of the general who looked like his father, he became aware of an uncomfortable shift in the detective's expression. Curious to the point of concern, he asked,

"What is it?"

"The general who looked like your father . . . I take it your father isn't a general?" Roth shook his head. "Was he ever in any branch of the military?" Again the agent shook his head. "At any rank?"

"No," answered the FBI man. He found himself somewhat shaken by the tone in London's voice, and yet he could not figure out why. Wanting to know, however, he continued, saying,

"He was never in the service . . . he was never a cop. My dad was a factory worker—he never even wore a uniform . . . of any kind. Why? What is this?"

Going cold inside, wishing he did not have to take things any further, the detective said,

"Is your father still alive?"

"Yes. My mother died a few years back. Dad's not in the best health, but he's still alive. Why?" And then, London's words from when they first reached the dream plane returned to him. The horror of their meaning suddenly burning into him, Roth grabbed the detective's shoulders, demanding,

"Why?!"

"Maybe," answered London, for once not able to meet another man's eyes, "maybe you should check."

The FBI man sat back, stunned—filled with a sudden flash of dreaded understanding. Like a man condemned, he pulled his still-aching body up out of his chair and limped the short distance to the phone by the detective's bed. Sitting on the mattress, he quickly got an outside line and then dialed the retirement home where his father had lived since his last heart attack.

A woman at the other end picked up after the second ring. She was bright and cheerful, pleased to hear from the agent, happy to tell him that she had indeed seen his father that day and that the old gentleman had seemed in the best spirits he had been in in weeks. When Roth expressed his concern, asking her to please check on him, her cheerfulness came down several notches. She had soured because of his request, but she had picked up the urgent note of concern in his voice. Asking him to hold, she told him she would be right back. He told her that that would be fine and then settled in to wait. He did not have to wait long.

London watched as the FBI man received the news the detective knew he would. The agent got himself off the phone as quickly as he could, stunned and broken and filled with sorrow. Recradling the receiver, he turned to stare at London, his eyes filling with tears. He wanted to hate the detective, wanted to blame him for what had happened, but somehow he found he could not.

"Why?" he asked. "Why can't I hate you? My father's dead. Why isn't it your fault?"

London stared at the FBI man—knowing what he was in for, wondering how he would take it. The agent had started shaking again—almost as hard as when he had first returned from the dream plane. Knowledge was crawling around in his subconscious, demanding entrance to the upper deck.

"Well," started London, "my guess was that you were ready to hound me to whatever lengths it took to get the secret of reaching the dream plane for the government. I could have gotten away from you, but then you would have just hounded my friends. You know you would have. And if in the end, after you had finished ruining our lives for the greater glory of the state, and you still didn't have what you wanted, you would have just kept looking. And sooner or later you'd have found someone willing to give up the secret. And you wouldn't have gotten it like this. No—you'd have had them locked away somewhere in some room with doctors and drugs and people insane enough to ask for access to all sorts of things that maybe no one should be allowed to have."

The detective took a long, summing up breath, giving himself a second to look the FBI agent over again as he had before he had taken him into the dream plane. Seeing in the man the same things he had earlier, he decided to go ahead and tell him,

"I looked at you earlier, and I decided you were a man who could take responsibility for his actions. I think you know all this, and you know that sooner or later everything I just said would have happened. I think you knew deep down that if the government was searching for the dream plane it was best that you or someone like you was there when they did. You set yourself as the yardstick—if you couldn't handle whatever the dream plane turned out to be, then you'd be the judge of who got it and who didn't." London nodded as he talked, unconsciously agreeing with his own words. Suddenly he noted Roth shaking his head in much the same manner. Pushing, he told him,

"Trust me when I say that I could hide from you."

"Yes. Guess that would be pretty easy for you," answered the agent absently, now only half-listening to the detective, half-lost in thought. Appealing to that half, London kept going, telling him,

"I could keep my network hidden from you, too . . . take the whole thing underground. But that would force me into a position I don't want to occupy. I'm not the Shadow. I don't want to don a cloak and cloud men's minds and remind people that the weeds of crime bear bitter fruit. I just want to lead my fucking life—okay? You mess with this stuff and people die. People keep coming to me and dragging me into their shit. Sometimes not too many people die. Sometimes a lot of people die. But Jesus goddamn it to hell and back—I'm telling you—every time one of these things gets started, somebody's going to die."

London looked away and then back, fixing Roth with his stare. The FBI man seemed somewhat dazed. Not caring if the agent was hearing him or not, the detective told him,

"Over the last year ... this year of note-taking for you, remember? How many people dead? How many of my friends—all of them, gone? Almost everyone in my life these days ... I didn't know before a year ago. Why? Because all of my friends from before that, they're all dead. Just like my family."

"I'm sorry," said Roth in a distracted voice. As he stared through London, looking at the wall behind the detective or something unknown beyond it, he suddenly came into focus, asking,

"Why? Tell me why?"

"Why what?"

"Why my dad?"

The detective stared at Roth, seeing the pain in his eyes. He knew the man understood, knew that he would not have to make up his own mind over what to do—that the FBI agent was enough of a man to shoot straight with him. London was willing to play by those rules. He had to. They were all the dice had to offer. Not knowing what to say to the agent's question, however, the detective told him,

"I don't want to play armchair psychiatrist with you. Maybe your father was too strict with you or something ... I don't know. All I can tell you is that for some reason your subconscious grabbed him—his soul, and dragged him there just as I did to you. You wanted him there in a subordinate role for some reason. To watch your victory, just to push him around ... I don't know. You're the only one that *knows*. And, I'm not pushing you to tell me what or why. I'm just saying that you're the only one that can answer that question."

London let the agent think for a moment longer, and then—mostly out of pity—he told him,

"The reason you can't summon up a good hate for me is that from what I've been able to tell, a person can't affect the dream plane unless they're ready to take responsibility for their actions. Good or bad—it doesn't make any difference. A person can go there with the worst of intentions and perform any miracle you might name. I know ... I've met a few who did just that. But even the ones that created nightmares never tried to blame anyone else for what they did."

London watched Roth grieving for his father, for his crime. The detective looked at the grief of the man, watched him unravel slowly as he absorbed the totality of his crime. To be able to manipulate the dream plane, Roth had to be a man of convictions—whatever his morality, there were beliefs within him to motivate it.

But living up to the responsibility of murder—it was not a light thing. London had killed nearly two million people during his first encounter with those who could manipulate the dream plane. But he had finally been able to pull himself back from his crime because he had been in the right. How, he wondered, was Roth going to feel about what he had done when the power of miracles had been placed in his hands? As if reading the detective's mind, the FBI man pulled himself up, and suddenly said,

"I killed my father."

London said nothing, allowing Roth the floor. The man's voice trembled, cracking with bitterness as he cursed himself for his inability to handle godhood.

"I did it. I didn't know what I was doing—but I did it. I wanted it done—and I don't even know why. My chance for anything, to be anything, do anything, have anything—I chose to be the worst caricature of a government employee . . . unthinking, bombing and shooting to the end." Laughing with tears in his eyes, he took London's hand in his own, saying,

"I get the power of God, and what do I do—kill my father, lose the prize, blow the job." And then, suddenly, Roth straightened visibly—just a tiny bit—pulling some inner strength to the fore. His voice changing, he let go of the detective's hand and said,

"Doesn't play well with other children."

As London stared, waiting for the explanation Roth's tone made inevitable, the FBI man said,

"That's what they used to put on my report card. Doesn't play well with other children. Dad was a big believer in not doing things one's own way but the way that was best for the group. Always. Every single time. There was a bit of the socialist to Dad. He cured me of—shamed me out of—whatever—that problem. My father just didn't get the fact I didn't want to be like 'other children.' "

Then, the FBI man stood up, suddenly projecting an air which said that he was changing the subject. Giving him the right, London stood up as well, waiting for the agent to say his piece. He did not have to wait long.

"Something just hit me," said Roth with an almost electric start. "I did everything I could to stop the werewolf. Everything.

I fought and fought and fought. So did your friends and all their people. And nothing stopped it . . . either time. Except you. And your Oriental friend. You both stopped it."

"We did?" asked London, not remembering having stopped the monster at any point. "And how'd we do that?"

"You stopped it with words."

And suddenly a thought passed through London's head, one so horribly simple he wondered why it had not occurred to him before.

London went up the stairs of his brownstone cursing life, tired of it—weary of where it continued to take him. He stood in front of his door—*his* door . . . *he* owned it—wondering if after the next time he went out, he would ever see it again. He stared at the handle of the sturdy carved oak door, touched it. The detective marveled at the sheathing web of silver covering its cold black iron, wondering why no one had ever stripped it away to sell in one of the city's three hundred and twenty-eight thousand pawnshops.

He stared up at the windows, admiring the radiance of their thick heavy-lead panes, wondering why they had never been broken. Never. It made no rational sense to him.

"Why?" he said aloud, backing down several steps to look his home over. "Why *this* place? Why did it survive when everywhere else around is such a nightmare?"

It was waiting for you? asked a voice from the back of his brain.

Maybe, he answered. Maybe. Why not? It makes as much sense as anything else. Why else would the different stone carvings that dotted the top of its fourth floor have never fallen, or been stolen, or shot at? Why have none of them ever been brought down by bricks or rocks or any of the other missiles at hand that could be propelled by hate or boredom or one of the thousand other natural fuels the city provides free on every corner? Why was every other part of it so perfect—the crack-free wainscotting? The even, heavy wood stairs, the solid roof, the large, circular skylight?

Sure, he thought, it was waiting for me. Why not, indeed? This good guy stuff ought to be worth something.

Then, another voice asked him just how dangerous the detective felt life could become when one fell too far into such a self-centered view of the universe. Once everything and everyone becomes just more of your playthings, it asked, what then? Certain are you that you've become so important?

"No," he said aloud, talking to the wind, emphasizing his

point, making it solid with sound. "No, goddamn it. But sometimes the answer can be positive, you know. If I'm supposed to believe that every time I turn around fate's going to shove some beast from Hell onto my dinner plate, it can put a goddamn steak there once in a while, too—all right?"

There was no answer forthcoming—nor did London need one. He boiled inside, not knowing whether to laugh or cry, seeing sense and futility in both actions. Stepping back down a few more paces, he stared up at his house, wondering if indeed it were possible that fate might have brought him to it as it had to so much grieving discovery of both his self and the things around it. Unable to blink, he drank the place in, thinking,

Why? And how—*how* did I find this place? What led me here? And if life had it in mind to give me such a palace . . . why did it have to wait until now?

Having no answers, he bent his head and went back up the stairs, through the front door, and up to his main living area. He found Lisa inside, asleep on the couch. She had been at the hospital when he had been operated on, had waited there without leaving while he had been unconscious, through his trip to the dream plane and back, and his first talk with Roth. After the FBI man had realized the extent of the power the dimension of the will could allow one to exert, he had made it clear to London that he would not be watching the detective any longer.

But he had also said that the two of them had a lot to talk about . . . immediately. After that he had sent Fergeson and Reynolds to dismiss all of the other members of their agency from the hospital. Once that was accomplished, the pair were to begin dismantling all of their other observation operations as well. The two, from their own run-in with London, and just the little they had seen of their superior's encounter with the detective, were all too happy to comply . . . if for no other reason than it allowed them to leave the hospital.

While Roth had briefed his men, London had sent Morcey down to take Lisa home. He was to let her know that everything was all right, and then go home himself and get some rest. The detective would let his partner know the outcome of his meeting with the ˜BI agent in the morning.

Lisa, however, was a different matter.

"Sweetheart . . ."

Her he would have to tell right then.

"Hey, wake up."

He stared down at her, watching her first waking motions. He studied the way she stretched her hand out over her head, the beginning, half-fist, half-cramp set to her fingers. He watched as her left brain started up the motor functions of life, moving her lips, stumbling for speech, blinking her eyes, trying to focus on the familiar. He smiled as her right brain spotted him in the information coming in, waking her up to the fact. Her smile matched his, then passed it. Her stretching arm curled down automatically around his neck, pulling him toward her.

"Hi, big guy."

"Hi, yourself," he said, glad to be with her . . . wondering for how long.

"I missed you."

"I missed you, too, sweetheart."

"Yeah?" she asked, her voice dark and husky from the sleep still dragging at her. "A guy that really missed me would have kissed me by now."

"Would that be a big guy?" he asked in a kidding voice. "Or would that be just any guy?" Lisa punched him in the side of the neck—a stinging rocking blow that both reddened the detective's ear and set it to ringing. He had known it was coming, could feel the air moving in front of her hand—knew exactly how hard it would hit.

"And what was that for?" he asked, not knowing if he was more stunned that he had allowed her to hit him or that she had done it in the first place. She told him,

"For scaring the ever-loving crap out of me—that's why."

"I'll try to behave in the future," he told her. She made to answer, but before she could, the detective moved his mouth against hers, kissing her the way they both wanted him to. He leaned into her heavily though still on bended knee next to their sofa. She pulled him down, both her hands behind his head, the nails of one digging sharp circles at the base of his neck. His head pulled up from the sharpness of the pain, just enough to allow him to shift his lips.

Kissing her along the side of her jaw, he moved back and down, lingering on her neck just below her ear. Lisa clutched at the detective's shoulders, tearing at his shirt, her legs moving back and forth, rubbing against each other. Losing himself in the heat of their passion, London circled around to the front of his love's neck, spreading kisses across her shirt.

Her eyes closed, Lisa relaxed into the couch, only one of her hands touching the detective's head, gently moving it down and along, knotting his hair around her fingers. But then, she tensed suddenly, her hand pulling at London, breaking the spell of the moment. As the detective looked up, Lisa said,

"You didn't tell me what happened." Her eyes going wide, propped open by fear of the future, she asked,

"What is the government going to do? My God—I was just so glad to see you, I forgot. What's going to happen? What are they going to do? Tell me."

He did. He gave her the entire story, from waking up in the hospital to finding Morcey and the FBI watching over him, to Roth's encounter with the werewolf on the dream plane and all that happened to him because of it. Of course, Morcey had already told her parts of the story, but she wanted to hear it from London—all of it in order, with his interpretations. She was relieved to hear that Roth had turned out to be an honorable man. Not trusting his dishonorable masters, however, she asked,

"But what happens next? Okay—so Roth understands things now. Great. But how does showing him anything stop the government from wanting to turn the dream plane into their next super weapon? From wanting to turn *you* into one?"

"Roth is dismantling the units who have had us all under observation. He and his people took a lot of footage of last night. He plans to show them what the werewolf was capable of, emphasizing the fact that I didn't do anything throughout the night except get my face pushed in. He's pretty sure they're not going to be very interested in me."

"Why not? What about bringing to justice the murderer of two million people? There's a lot of good press for the current administration in solving that one."

"They're going to solve it."

"What?" asked Lisa. She could tell from London's tone that he did not mean that the FBI agent was going to turn the detective in, but she had no idea what he meant past that, either. Before she could get overly concerned, he told her,

"The missile I used in Elizabeth was Pa'sha's. They'd already been able to make that connection on their own. Roth and I talked with Mama Joan. She's leaving the country, going back to Jamaica for a while." The detective grew quiet for a moment, then continued, telling his love,

"It was funny. I would have thought she would have blamed me, but she didn't. Not this time. She told me that Pa'sha had told her that I didn't want to fight the werewolf. He'd told her that he had to do it. 'What he be take on hisself be his business,' she said. Roth suggested Pa'sha take the blame for the explosion in New Jersey. I told her. She thought it was a good idea. 'My boy,' she said, 'he be want protect his brother. I got let him to do what he think best.' "

Still sitting on the floor, London stared over the top of the couch, looking at the framed sketch that hung over his mantelpiece. It was an imaginative city scene from ancient Rhodes, one showing its famed Colossus still standing, arm stretched out over the harbor, pointing off toward the horizon. Pa'sha had loved the simply rendered pen and ink piece, claiming that it made him feel connected to the past.

Now, big brother, thought the detective, you are the past. Enjoy it, my friend. You may have gotten the better part of the deal.

"Is it Pa'sha?" asked Lisa, not able to think of any other reason for the sad look on London's face.

"Yes," he answered. "Mostly. Some is just this whole ugly thing. He's going to go down in the history books as some sort of terrorist. His people will take another black eye, more hate gets thrown in the wrong direction, more stupidity gets unleashed, more misunderstandings . . ."

"And what should you do?" asked Lisa tenderly. As his eyes met hers, he fell into their fine blue softness, not interrupting as she continued, asking,

"What? Go to the government and tell them about the dream plane—show them how to get there? Would you trust them with that secret? Would you trust any government on the face of the planet with that power? Would you?"

"No," he told her, his voice filled with sorrow. "Not really. But, I mean—there has to be someone, somewhere that can do this and not get full of himself . . . not screw it up. I'm not that special."

"Oh, Teddy," answered Lisa, sliding across the couch to be able to put her arms around her lover. Hugging him close to her, her head pressed hard against his, she whispered, "Oh God, don't you know how special you are? All this time, all these things . . . I mean, it's no picnic being the girlfriend of an avenging archangel, but darling—for God's sake—*special*? You're in a class all your own. Can't you tell?"

"Maybe," answered London, hugging the woman in his arms as fiercely as she was him, "I just don't want to."

"Too late for that," she answered. Releasing some of the pressure on the detective, she told him,

"Do you think if you weren't the only one there is to do these things that I'd let you go chasing around the world after this werewolf?" When London simply stared, Lisa told him,

"Yes, I know you're going after it. I could tell as soon as I woke up." When he continued to stare, she said, "Am I right?"

"Yes," he admitted. "You're right."

"Want to tell me why?"

"Sure."

Untangling their hug, the detective got up off the floor and joined his love on the couch. Pulling a sheaf of papers from his inside jacket pocket, he said,

"I promised Roth that if he could throw the government off our trail that I would take care of our hairy friend. He gave me a number of interesting bits of information to help that along. A lot of it we already had—either from Zack or Warhelski—but he did have these." Unfolding a heavily marked-up relief map of the world, London said,

"This shows the attacks Warhelski had charted—ones he was absolutely certain were his monster's. Look at this . . . first, his village in Poland, Srem . . . if you take that as a starting point, and follow it to the next known attack, here in Hrinova, it makes a nice little arc. Now, a couple of years later we're in Hajduhadhaz, then in Karaganda, then Afghanistan . . ."

As the detective talked, his point became obvious—the beast they had battled the night before had for years worked its way across the face of Europe and then Asia. Pointing to various stars drawn in over different points which did not fall on the arc, London said,

"These all show places where the monster announced it would be."

"You mean like here in New York?"

"Yeah, right," answered the detective sourly. "Exactly. Which makes it look as if whenever it isn't out picking a fight, that it has someplace it's trying to get to . . . somewhere in upper India, lower China, maybe."

"Do you have any idea where?"

"I stopped by Lai Wan's on the way home. Paul had her waiting for me. She laid hands on the map and came up with the name A'alshirie. Didn't mean anything to her—wasn't in her world atlas, either. I'm just going to fly to Jiggitai, the last place the thing hit, and see what I can find out from there."

Unfolding a sheet of notepaper, he added,

"This was something else interesting that Roth's people had. Warhelski's sword, the one that the thing twisted up into a ball, the FBI's seen it before—run tests on it. They even got a print off it, left in his dad's blood. The water in the blood had evaporated decades ago, of course, but that left print traces invisible to the eye. They were able to get it with a laser scan. They were never sure if it was the monster's or not until after our run-in with it. They have all the prints they need now, though, and they were able to prove a match. It's also a match to one other they had on file."

Lisa caught a note in the detective's voice, letting her know that something was up. Waiting quietly, motionless in her corner of the couch, she sat in tense anticipation as London pulled a photograph out of his bundle of papers. It showed the remains of an archway set in a stone wall constructed of massive bricks. The arch was topped by the bas-relief of two lions, one of them headless. Pointing through the arch, as if indicating the walled-in field beyond, the detective said,

"This is a copy of the great sarsen ring of Stonehenge, but it's in Mycenae, not in England. Anyway, a sword that was taken from this place was found to have a print that matches both Warhelski's and those taken from the battle zone."

"And the importance of all this?" asked Lisa, giving the detective his cue.

"Warhelski thought he had proof that this werewolf thing is at least a few hundred years old. The sword that was recovered in Mycenae . . . it was bronze. The experts say it went into the ground in the High Bronze Age. That's the second millennium . . . B.C."

"That's a long time ago," said Lisa.

"Yeah," agreed London. "It seems our pal's been around more like three thousand years instead of three hundred."

27

London thought of Lisa for the ten thousandth time since leaving New York. His musings centering on her seemingly endless strength, he wondered again how she had been able to deal with the life they had led ever since their first meeting. The night before, they had talked for a long time after he had shown her the photograph of the Mycenaean Gateway. They had talked about all the hell fate had put them through since their lives had crossed, about the rare good times, and those savage things that had come along to destroy every peaceful moment.

The two had also spent a moment discussing the possibility of dinner, but neither moved toward the kitchen. They knew each other too well, could read each other's souls the way ordinary people interpret street signs. Neither could hide anything from the other . . . neither wanted to. Seeing the same desire in each other's eyes, they simply rose from the couch and headed for their bedroom. Later, as the detective had earlier studied the outside of his building, wondering if he would ever see it again, Lisa had wondered about how cruel fate was to bring her to her lover's home, to then turn and send him away from her for only God knew how long.

So far, thought the detective, the vision of Lisa's chestnut curls and soft blue eyes moving from the center stage of his mind, it's been what, six weeks or so, and I'm still not standing in the A'alshirie town square.

Actually, he suddenly realized, it had been longer. He had already spent nearly two months getting as far as he had. Two days of it in jets, one in a twin-engine job, one more in a single prop job. The next five by rail and truck and jeep. Then the journey had gotten difficult. The detective had spent the following nineteen days on mule back, and the twenty-nine after that on foot.

He had brought plenty of money, but money had been able to help him only as far as the mule he had purchased in the last real town he had seen. After that, he had found fewer and fewer people who seemed to have a need for cash. They had no place where they could spend it—no needs to fulfill which they did not fulfill themselves—nothing to spend it on. For nearly the last week, he had found no one who ever understood what any of the currencies he had hidden in his various pockets were. Some of them had never even seen paper before, let alone money.

"I'm tellin' ya, boss," Morcey had told the detective when he had driven him to JFK International for the first of his jet flights, "you oughtta be lettin' me go with ya."

"I'm the one that has to do this, Paul. As much as you like monster hunting, I think this one is mine."

"Awww, but you're always hoggin' the good stuff up at the end. I didn't get ta go with ya to Chicago, or stay with ya in Elizabeth, and I was all laid up when you went after the vampires ... I mean, I don't know ... it just ain't fair."

"Life's like that, pal," London had answered sympathetically. "I just get the idea that I'm the man for the job this time."

"And, no offense or nuthin', but why is that?" Speaking honestly, as always, the detective offered,

"Something ... what to call it? Fate? I don't know ... but something seems determined to drop this in my lap. Remember, that thing chose us, not the other way around. I get my vision that keeps me from fighting—but then, as Roth pointed out, *not* fighting seems to be what keeps people alive with this thing. First for me, then Jhong."

"Then, hey," Morcey had asked while turning off the beltway's exit for the airport, "if you two have got the secret of this thing down, why aren't you taking Mr. Oriental Philosophy with you?"

"Jhong seems to be gone," answered London. "I even asked Lai if she had heard from him. Apparently after he got all of us out safely, he disappeared. Big surprise, really—right?"

"Not like him to skip out on a good brawl," said the ex-maintenance man. "What's with that guy, anyway? He always sorta spooks me out."

"Jhong plays by his own rules," answered the detective, wishing somewhat that the elder martial artist were going with him. "We didn't call him, remember? He showed up to tell us that trouble was coming."

"And how did he know that?" asked Morcey, turning onto the road that would take them to the terminal London needed.

"Don't worry about things so much," responded the detective. "Jhong's into the follow-your-senses end of this stuff a lot more than either of us. Let's just hope that if he's hit the road again that it's because his end of things is done. From what you've told me, we wouldn't have gotten off Wards Island if he hadn't bluffed that thing down."

"Hey," answered the balding man, "I'm alive. I'm not complaining."

"Neither am I, pal," agreed London. "Neither am I. What I am saying though, is . . . seriously, I need you here. I need you to watch over Lisa—keep her mind off me being gone. I mean, who knows how long that's going to be? And, back in the real world, I need you to help her run the store. We may have a pile of money in the bank, but we still have a business to run. I mean, let's face it, this *is* going to take a while. I've still got to find the thing, remember?"

And you're not doing a very good job, are you?

"Hey," London muttered aloud into the biting cold, telling the voice in the back of his mind, "I can do without a cheerleading squad, all right?"

Whatever you say, answered the voice.

The detective did not respond. Arguing with the various whisperings that filtered through his brain rarely produced anything positive. The voice was right; he had been searching for nearly two months and had not found his objective yet. Of course, he could assert, from what he had heard so far, it was not supposed to be an easy place to find.

A'alshirie, the name Lai Wan had given him, appeared on no maps. The team's subsequent search for the place had proved only that no airline, no travel agent—that no one in New York City—had ever heard of the place. Finally London had simply decided that no matter how much more Jhong was 'into the follow-your-senses end' of what they did, that he was going to have to do a little of it himself and simply have faith he would be able to track the werewolf down because he believed he could.

It had proved to be the right approach. Once he had been forced by the terrain to abandon mechanical transport, he found himself in a new land, one that knew more about the world and life than what could be read in encyclopedias and maps. The people in every village he had found along his way all seemed to know of the place he was seeking. Indeed, they knew it not as a country or town, but as a specific mountain. However, they also knew that there was no way for any man to reach it.

"You can see the peak of A'alshirie, but you cannot touch it," one old man told him. Sitting over bowls of rice porridge flavored with scallions and garlic, the ancient mountaineer had advised him to turn back, saying,

"Many have tried to reach her, but none we know of have, young man. Ever. There are those that tell a story of a bridge hidden beneath the snow that can carry a man from the mountain closest over to A'alshirie, but the idea is merely illusion. That story is a myth."

"So are a lot of things," the detective had replied with a smile, undeterred. "But, you know, it's been my experience that that fact doesn't seem to stop them from existing."

The villagers around the old man had not understood London, of course, but sensing his earnest need to get from the one side to the other, they had told him what little they did know. He had thanked them all as best he could with open smiles and honest warmth, the only coin of value in a land which did not know from cash and real estate. Indeed, if he had not been able to open himself to them, to show them his intentions clearly simply by allowing them to look into his unblinking eyes, they would have run him off—no matter how much gold he might have offered.

He had traveled six weeks on like fare, bothering those he came into contact with only to assure himself that he was still pointed toward the mountain everyone believed was a myth but knew the direction of nonetheless. Plain dough buns fried in burning sesame oil and bowls of tea had been extended from one field hut to the next, and the detective had crossed sixty leagues on their honest hospitality.

Toward sundown, three days earlier, he had come across a solitary hut in the middle of an extended plain. The only trees he had seen that day stood next to the timeless home, one which could have been built the year or the century before. There London met an old woman who told him that from the best anyone knew, there really was a bridge of some sort between the two mountains. But, she was forced to add, there was also no known way to tell where it was located.

"No way known to me, anyway," she told him. "But I'll tell you this. People have come and they have gone back and forth to A'alshirie—I've seen it. Not many and not often, but . . ." She pointed a single finger upward, holding it close to her head in a knowing way, saying,

"How many more than one does it take to prove that there *is* a way? How to know where that way is, though . . ."

And then, at that point, the woman had simply spread her hands and given the detective a shrug and a smile. London thanked her for that much, telling her that if a way was there, he would find it. That night he had slept under the thatched lean-to next to the woman's home, his back to the wall of her chimney. Then, the next morning, he had set out to fight his way up the mountain the locals called Thumb to the Sky, the last barrier between A'alshirie and himself.

And then, the worst of his trip began. Relaxing within his head, he allowed those of his ancestors who knew something about making their way up snow-covered mountains to take over, guiding his limbs as he thought about exactly what he was going to do when he finally found the monster he had been tracking. Rationally, he knew that not battling the thing was somehow the key to winning out over it and yet . . .

He stumbled within his mind thinking, *and yet* . . . reminding himself again and again that the beast had killed Pa'sha—a crime he could not let go unanswered. The weaponeer had been more than a friend, more than a brother to replace those he had lost— Pa'sha had been a part of him, the part of him that laughed at the world. He had been the calm that understood his duty, that patiently waited for each storm and rode it out, laughing at those who ran when the first drops started to fall.

Pa'sha's death had affected him—seriously, deeply. He would have never subjected Roth to the dream plane before that—never. He would have found some other way, gone on the run, taken everyone underground if he had had to. But, waking in a world without his "big brother" had left him cold—cold and angry and unforgiving.

Throughout the rigorous climb, he had thought much on the subject. He had not had much else to do. With his ancestors tending to the ascent he had slept, watched the scenery, or brooded, waiting for the moment when he would finally reach the top. Then, after three days, he began to sense an excitement in his head. Instantly he knew he was closing on some point where finally he would be able to make it over the mountain he was climbing and begin to descend toward . . . what?

That's the question, isn't it? he thought. So I get over this mountain and then what do I do? Everyone agrees that old A'alshirie is unclimbable. A few old people tell me there's a bridge of some sort under the snow that's piled up between Thumb to the Sky here and werewolfville. But no one's supposedly ever found it except those who know where it is.

"Oh yeah," he said aloud, steam bursting from his mouth, "this sounds great."

And then, the moment of discovery finally came. One hand after another reached upward until finally the detective pulled himself up and over the edge of an extended ridge connecting the Thumb to the mountain next to it. When he did, he finally received his first unobstructed view of A'alshirie. It was far away and twice as forbidding as Thumb. His ancestors shuddered within him, letting him know that none of them had ever made it to the top of anything like that.

It was a daunting needle of rock and ice, looking to be a mile distant and as hard to climb as a tower of molten rock or broken glass. Far below him, in the canyon formed by the two peaks, London could see absolutely no clue as to how anyone could cross from one mountain to the next. The valley between them was clogged with snow, one long, unbroken sheet of it.

London stared out over the never-ending blanket, looking for any slightest hint as to where the bridge he needed might be. None offered themselves to him. There was nothing to be seen—which meant the detective would have to rely on senses other than sight to find his way across.

28

The lone, dark speck advanced downward slowly against the never-ending white overhanging the mountain. Moving in toward the rock face, a closer view showed the speck to be London and the surrounding white to be a vast abundance of frost-hardened snow. Up close, one could see that the oppressive, ages-old blanket was one deep enough to have obliterated all signs of life in every direction—all except, of course, for the detective moving downward over its crust.

In a few spots to either side of London the ragged top branches of trees showed through the packed icy surface of the snow. He had considered heading for one or the other of them to use as an anchor, hoping to lower himself down the mountainside, but they were feeble things his ancestors told him— useless—not worth his consideration.

But the problem the detective now faced was that he had no other options, either. He had reached the sea of frozen snow which lay between his position on the Thumb to the Sky and the distant A'alshirie. He knew he could not simply walk across it, that its seeming hardness was far too deceptive to trust. He knew that even if he abandoned the massive pack he had brought with him so far he would still, sooner or later, hit a patch of snow softer than the others, and that he would sink, slowly, down through its surface until he either froze to death or smothered.

"Swell," he whispered, listening to the word hang in the frozen air around him. "So now what do we do?"

How to choose? he wondered. Where was the bridge he had heard the rumors about? He had hoped for some kind of clue— had thought that something—*something*—would make itself apparent. A bit of snow jutting from the crust, a wave or a shape or a shadow of some kind under the snow that might reveal the hidden bridge . . . anything—anything at all. But he had found nothing. The snow was unbroken between the two mountains, unmarred, singular in its color and appearance in every way the detective's usual five daily senses could register.

Deciding that he was getting nowhere fast, London asked himself why he had gone up and come down the Thumb in the way he had. True, he told himself, his ancestors had done the actual climbing, but he had picked the way.

"Why?" he asked aloud. "What was so special about this way over the ten thousand others I could have taken? Did I bring myself here for a reason, or did I just allow myself to be led here?"

It was an important question. If the detective had unconsciously followed some inner voice that had led him to the bridge that was supposedly under the snow, then he would be all right. But, if he had not, if he had just gone up and down and was where he was now with no purpose at all, he would sink and freeze and die, and no one would even know where to look for his bones.

That's the problem with this philosophy crap, he thought. Goddamned force of will shit. Sounds great sitting around the dinner table, but . . .

Then, he stopped himself, seeing no need to give in to self-doubt. He was either in the right place or he was not, and nothing he could think of was going to let him know which it was until he simply pushed off from the "security" of his hold on the cliff wall and tried to cross the snowfall before him to the next mountain beyond. Clinging securely to the ice-covered stone of the mountain side, London steadied himself for his first move forward. It would be a dangerous moment, letting go of his only obvious handhold for the one his senses might have led him to, the one that might be under the blanket of frozen sleet before him . . . *might*.

The detective's eyes glanced one last time through the reflecting sunlight as he decided to take a rest and build his strength before attempting his crossing. While he did, he stared at the snow through his smoked goggles, looking for some spot of white that appeared in some way more solid than the rest—solid enough to hold his weight, perhaps for an hour or more as he stood on it and judged where he should step next. As he clung to the side of the Thumb, he regulated his breathing, relaxing, sending his inner senses outward to feel their way through the snow.

As best he could tell, he had found what he had been searching for. Deep inside himself, he knew he had come to the foot of the bridge he was looking for—*knew* he knew where the right spot was. But, he hesitated, saying aloud,

"Man, it's one thing to know you're right and something else to prove it."

Trained for years, by both others and himself, to always have proof of his convictions before he acted, it was something else to risk his life with no physical proof he would survive. Then, deciding it was time to look for some, he relinquished control of his conscious actions and let go his hold on the rock wall behind him—one hand at a time.

Cautiously, his left foot—large snow pad slowing its sink into the soft crust—broke down through the surface. Second after second passed—his heel disappearing—then his toe, then his ankle. As his foot sank deeper, his right arm came to the point where it was stretched to its limit, right hand to the point where it had to be released before he could go any further. With faith in his instincts, he said,

"Oh, well, nothing ventured . . ."

And then London let go his gloved fingers, forcing himself to go limp as his decent picked up speed. Making himself breathe, he watched as his boot fell completely beneath the snow line. Moment after moment, the cold white crust continued to rise—far past his ankle, deeper, up his calf, over his knee, ham, thigh . . . and then . . . he stopped. His boot had hit something solid, hard—*flat*.

Centering his weight on it, he said a short prayer of thanks within his head as he made ready to move his other foot forward. He would have to plow his way through the snow with his body—slow, exhausting work, but, he thought wryly, certainly better than dying.

Working his way forward, he watched as his feet made their way automatically through the snow—each step slow and measured, searching for the correct next bit of footing—wherever it might be. His mind stayed relaxed, buried behind the ancestors to whom he again delegated authority over his body. They worked carefully, searching out the bridge one step at a time. In some places it was broken away, in others, curved to one side or the other. London relinquished all control, letting those better equipped to make the crossing than himself get all of them across. The detective instead again busied himself with wondering what he would do once he got to the other side.

Somewhere ahead of him was some place called A'alshirie. What it was, where it was, London did not know. Why the werewolf had gone there, he did not know either. Back in the United States, the detective had debated what forms of protection to take with him. Arms and modern air travel, even for licensed investigators, are not easily mixed. In the end, the detective had packed only two weapons—securely secreted in his check-in luggage, his .38 pistol, Betty, and his handmade knife, Veronica.

Mental fingers reached out to touch them as they came to mind, feeling Betty's reassuring presence under his arm, Veronica's at his side. They had seen him through quite a number of rough times. London was fairly sure they could see him through what was ahead.

As the detective plowed through the snow between the two mountains, sometimes only ankle-deep, sometimes up to his waist, sometimes even higher, he wondered how long it would take him to reach the other side. He estimated the distance he had covered at roughly a quarter of a mile. That had taken him over an hour. His best guess was that he still had almost an entire mile left to go. As the others in his head kept up the pace, he let his mind wander through his body, checking out his other systems.

By nature not a heavy man, he had eaten all he could before he had left and while he traveled—whenever possible—even asking for extra meals on all his flights. By the time he had set out to cross the border from Nepal into the Chinese mountains, he had put on an extra thirteen pounds. Now, he found that almost all of that had been burned away.

He had been eating during his climb, dried meats, vegetable pastes, other minimum taste/maximum benefit foods. Despite his best efforts to maintain himself, however, his internal investigation found his white blood cell count to be down and fatigue poisons flowing through his system at dangerous levels. Giving over full motor control to his ancestors, the detective closed his mind off, allowing himself a nap. If anything was going to bother him, he reasoned, it could probably wait until he got to A'alshirie . . . *if we get to A'alshirie* . . . came one of the voices in his mind.

"Right," he whispered back, willing his consciousness to sleep. *"If."*

London's ancestors woke him while they were still a score of yards out from the next mountain. When he asked why they had brought him up to consciousness early, they directed his attention to the figure of a man seated on a stone bench in front of a small fire. Wondering if he was a guard or someone sent specifically to meet his coming, the detective shouted in English,

"Hello. You waiting for me?"

The man's head turned at the sound of London's voice. He stood, his garb marking him as a monk. He seemed pleased that the detective had seen him, but he did not answer London's question. Using those modern languages available to him through his ancestors, the detective asked the question again, first in the French of the 1800s, then in the German of the 1600s. After that he tried an even earlier version of Portuguese, which finally got him a response.

"Hello. Yes. If I understand you correctly, yes. I was sent to meet you."

"Who sent you? Why did they send you?" asked the detective, wary by nature, but sensing no hostility from the man at the fire.

"Teacher Toun," came his answer. The young monk continued, saying, "He knew someone was coming across the bridge ... knew you would be tired and hungry—cold. I was sent to build a fire and cook a meal. I am Tai. I will be your guide to A'alshirie."

Pushing his way through the last of the snow, London reached the edge of the mountain. Tai extended his arm, offering the detective a hand up. London took it, as well as the hospitality extended by Teacher Toun. The fire's coals were the remains of hard teak, a good, solid long-burning wood. The meal was a thick broth, heavy in vegetable fiber. The two ate in silence, taking each other's measure. Nothing the detective learned from his search of the monk gave him any reason to not trust the young man. Deciding to see what he could find out, London asked,

"So, you're going to take me to A'alshirie?" When Tai agreed with his statement, the detective asked,

"Well then, would you mind telling me just what this A'alshirie is?"

"No," came his answer. "Of course not. A'alshirie is a Buddhist retreat, one purposely hidden as far from the normal routine of man as possible. It was first built many years ago. Some say hundreds, some say thousands. No one, not even Teacher Toun knows for sure."

"So, it's some kind of holy place?"

"You could say that, I suppose," answered Tai. "Those who first built it meant it only to be a hard place to find as a protection for those who wanted to live out their lives in peace, trying to gain enlightenment. Any others who might want to reach it would have to be strong in their resolve."

London let go his desire to ask any more questions for the moment, deciding to wait until the time seemed more convenient. At the end of the meal, Tai cleaned his small travel pot with snow. Then, after establishing that the detective was ready to leave as well, the young monk put out the small fire, storing those coals still usable in a carry pouch hanging from his belt. As the two of them started off, London felt the moment was right and began his questioning anew.

"It's pretty hard to get to A'alshirie, isn't it?"

"Yes," agreed Tai. "It is quite difficult."

"And you said that it was kept that way on purpose?"

"Yes. If nothing else, the Chinese Communists have no use for faith—I think not ours, or anyone else's. They have destroyed many temples in Tibet. Some feel it is only a matter of time before they come to our mountains."

"So," asked London, "you don't care much for strangers in A'alshirie?"

"Oh no," said the young monk with strong disagreement. "A'alshirie was built as a sanctuary for those with no place else to turn. Those who need to find us"—the young man smiled, spreading his hands as silver steam escaped his lips—"the Buddha will make sure they do."

"Then," asked the detective, "why did Teacher Toun send you to help me?"

"Because," the young monk answered without hesitation, "you did not come here to find A'alshirie . . . you came here to find the wolf."

Not expecting such a direct answer, London stopped in his tracks. He stared at Tai's back, watching the young monk forge his way forward along the snowy path for a long moment. Then, finally, London started moving again, thinking to himself,

Well, when you're right, you're right.

After that, the pair marched through the mountain passes in silence, both waiting for their first sight of A'alshirie, both for very different reasons.

29

Several hours later, the detective and his young guide arrived at the entrance to a hollow depression between the mountains. The lower they descended the warmer it got, until finally London was forced to shed the majority of his outer garments. The pair entered a massive cut-stone complex, one obviously built and rebuilt a number of times over the centuries. London stared at the staggering array of trees and shrubs, the vast vegetable gardens and forests, shaking his head that such a place could still be hidden away from the world. Everywhere he looked, statues and carvings and paintings graced the buildings, or were hidden amongst the vegetation. The corners of all the roofs were mounted with standing figures, sometimes animal, sometimes human.

Tai took the detective through the cut-stone streets of A'alshirie, walking slowly to allow him the time to soak in all he was seeing. Finally, however, he brought London to Teacher Toun, who greeted him with the same smile and open arms the younger monk had back at the bridge. When the detective marveled over the unusually temperate climate between the mountains, the older man explained in practiced, formal English,

"The ground in A'alshirie is underlaid with heat. Our lakes are naturally warm. We are also blessed with hot mineral baths, geysers . . ."

"Yeah. We have a place where I come from called Yellowstone. Same kind of thing."

"Would you like to rest?" asked Toun. "Or would you prefer to see our guest immediately?"

"Your guest? And that would be . . . ?"

"The wereman, to be certain," answered the elder. "Yes. We have been expecting you for some time now. So has he. He is waiting for you in the morning temple."

"Now wait a minute," said London in raised tones, struggling to understand. "You build this place to keep people out, yet you let this murderer in. I come to get him, and you send out a welcoming party. Call me suspicious, but some of this doesn't strike me as quite kosher. What kind of sanctuary is this? What gives here, anyway?"

Understanding the detective's confusion, the elder sat down under a large willow. Making motions for London to join him, the monk waited for the detective to position himself comfortably on the ground, then answered his questions.

"I know it must be hard for you to comprehend. You are a man of violence—of sharp moods and very quick decisions. And please—understand—I am not judging you in this. This merely is what is. A'alshirie was built for all peoples. Those who need to find it always do. Those wishing to come here for some other purpose, their bones fill the snow between the mountains."

"Yeah, all right, fine," said London, not satisfied. His anger rising slightly, he added,

"Maybe even your 'guest' needed to find this place and the Buddha guided him here. But what about me? I didn't *need* to find A'alshirie, or your guest for that matter. So how come everyone's so eager to put the two of us together?"

The old man stared at the detective. Wondering how the man before him could make such a—to him—clearly false statement, the elder monk opened his hooded eyes fully, letting London see him clearly as he answered.

"Sir, the wereman needed to reach A'alshirie, but not as a sanctuary. He needed to find a place from where he could not run. He has run for so long . . . too long. He has been waiting here for someone to arrive . . . to put him out of his misery."

" 'To put him out of his misery'?" repeated the detective, wondering where he was being led. "Correct me if I'm wrong, but aren't you guys supposed to be against that kind of thinking?"

"There are many stages in a man's life. Every person travels the same path, but each according to their own nature," responded Teacher Toun. "Our guest's nature is, unfortunately for him, one of constant chaos." The elder stared off into space for a moment, then turned and said,

"Most people go through three or four levels only of existence in their lifetime. Then they stop. They tire of change, or they learn one lesson or another so harshly they are afraid to try any others. Sadly, with most people it cannot be helped." Looking into London's eyes, Teacher Toun said,

"It was many years before I understood that no one can be taught anything about life. Each must experience it all—every bit of it—for themselves. Thus, how long they stay on any one path—whether child or thief or beggar, merchant, farmer, killer, builder—a moment or twenty years—it is all up to them."

The old man looked off toward the setting sun, his expression first sad, then happy. Watching him, the detective somehow suddenly knew the old man was staring in the direction of the morning temple. Looking back, the elder confirmed London's feeling by saying,

"We have tried to comfort him as best we can. He has conquered much, but the blood of his past weighs on him. He needs help we cannot give him." The elder spread his hands wide, using them to gesture as he said,

"It is not our part in life to challenge. No, he needs you, Mr. London. He needs the kind of release only a man such as yourself can give him."

"And what would that be, Teacher Toun?"

"Only you will know that," said the elder, rising up from his cross-legged position. "When it comes, you will know."

"And so will he. Right?" asked the detective.

"Of course," answered Teacher Toun, his smile wide and beautiful. "Of course."

London stared at the outside of the morning temple for a long time. It was a building of white walls and red trim, stark and peaceful and beautiful in its simplicity. The elder Toun had instructed Tai to bring the detective clean clothing. London had been led to the monk's hot baths where he steamed himself, cleaning away the months of field and mountain. The clothing Tai brought was silk—a set of black robes decorated in bright orange and yellow trim with matching slippers. He put them on gratefully, noting that none of the monks seemed dismayed when the detective strapped on Betty and Veronica. As far as they were concerned, both London and their guest had found their way to A'alshirie on their own. To the monks that meant fate had destined them to meet and that whatever happened at that meeting was up to them.

Moving forward, the detective put himself at the entrance to the morning temple, wondering what came next. Should he approach with a weapon drawn?

What would be the point? he wondered. What good could any weapon do? He had seen bullets and poison and fire used against the monster. Patting his .38 in its place of concealment beneath his robes, he said aloud,

"I don't know, Betty. Maybe not this time."

But, despite his lack of an answer, he still needed to know. Was the werewolf ready to fight or was he tired of slaughter? And, even if he was tired of all the slaughter, could he help himself? If he truly did not want to do what he did, then why did he keep doing it? Did he have his own little voices inside— murderous little voices that only spoke up when it was time to kill?

The sun is *setting*—came one of the voices in London's head, one with an ancient Germanic sound to it, one which even long before the events of the previous two months had had no trouble at all believing in werewolves. London weighed what he knew with what he felt, thinking to himself,

Then again—why come all the way to A'alshirie to start a fight? You come to a place like this to heal, or die. Not to cause more trouble. Disrupting a holy place—no matter who thinks it's holy—just brings more grief than it's worth. You don't do that until you just don't care anymore. It's only when you don't care that you graduate to true evil.

So, answered the voice, *all you have to do is decide just how much this thing cares. Then you'll know how evil it is.*

Yeah, thought London. That's it in a nutshell.

Stepping into the morning temple, the detective discovered three separate entrances to whatever lay beyond. He chose the path to the right for no particular reason. After walking through only a few rooms, he came to one with a long pool inlaid in its center. The room was half lit by four massive candles molded of black and golden wax—one on a stand in each corner—and half by the rapidly fading sunlight still edging its way in through the windows.

The room's walls and ceiling were constructed of an expertly cut shining white marble. The stone was veined with dark black mineral deposits, the resulting effect vaguely that of a savage lightning storm. Potted tropical plants stood on both sides of the pool at regular intervals, their deep green colors reflected in the still water.

And then, as the detective moved further into the room, suddenly he saw a figure at its opposite end. The form, humanoid in shape, sat cross-legged at the head of the pool, staring into its waters. Its bulk marked it as male. Despite the shadows created by the giant candles and the rapidly disappearing sunlight, London could not mistake its form.

Most of its body was wrapped in robes similar to those the detective was wearing, but its head remained exposed, the sight of it assuring the detective that he had found his prey. He saw the same large and pointed ears, their sharp edges still standing straight up. The monster's thick black fur bristled, alerting London that the thing knew he was approaching. The detective stared at its face for a moment, at the monstrous snout and its large, wickedly strong-looking teeth.

All right, hotshot, he asked himself, now what? Go on, big man. Avenge your pal. Take that thing on.

Above the monstrous snout, the beast's eyes shone their deep yellow, the same dark sickly shade London remembered. Its tongue lolled out of its head, not flickering this time, but moving from side to side in canine fashion. As London forced himself to take a step forward, the horror he approached turned its head slightly and said,

"You're not Warhelski."

"Yeah, and you're not Lon Chaney, Jr. So what?"

The beast did not stir from its pose of perfect meditation. Its snout sniffing at the air, it said,

"Oil. Powder. Gunman, are you?" When London said nothing, the creature at the end of the pool sniffed at the air again, his gaze not turning from the water as he said,

"I do not smell very much steel. Small gun. Very few bullets. Not very effective. Where is Warhelski? He would not make these kinds of mistakes."

"Warhelski couldn't make it," answered London, wondering why the thing did not recognize him.

"Even Warhelski fears me now," said the beast, his tone sad and faraway. "Even Warhelski."

"He's not afraid of you," answered the detective. Trying to force the issue, he shouted, "He's dead. Remember?"

"Dead?" The creature said the word almost without comprehension. For the first time it turned its eyes from the water, staring at London. Looking up, confused, it asked again,

"Dead?"

"Yeah, dead," said the detective. "You murdered his family eighty years ago. Him you only killed two months ago. That's why I'm here."

"You are Warhelski's avenger?" asked the monster in a cold, faraway voice.

"Yeah," answered London. "His and a few others." The detective tried to get a hold of himself—*you can't fight it,* several voices shouted at him from within. *Fighting this brute will not allow you to prevail. Can you fight that? Can you?*

But Pa'sha, he thought. Pa'sha and Zack and Warhelski and all the others. If I'm not supposed to kill it, what am I supposed to do? What the hell am I here for?

And then, another thought hit the detective. It was not yet quite sundown. If the beast changed by the phases of the moon, why had it already taken on its werewolf form? London had not been so foolish as to forget to count the days. He knew fate had delivered him to his prey on the first day of the new full moon. But, there was no moon in the sky yet. How had the thing transformed?

"So, you are an avenger, now, Mr. London," whispered the beast matter-of-factly, finally coming out of his seeming fog, remembering the detective as a person. "And you have come to exterminate me. Tell me, how will you be doing that, exactly?"

"I don't know. Teacher Toun says we'll have to cross that bridge when we come to it."

"You could kill me."

"I don't know," answered the detective seriously. "You seem pretty unkillable to me."

"You could try."

And then, the sun's last rays slipped beneath the horizon. As London watched, the monster suddenly shivered, his body wracked by thrashing spasms. As the detective froze, not knowing what to do, he saw the first rays of the new moon filter through the window. As the beast turned toward them, they splashed fully across his yellow eyes, deepening their color, filling them with a jaundiced fire. Noting London's confusion, the creature threw back its head and snarled,

"I understand. You thought it took the moon to turn me into . . . into this. No. The moon does not make me into a monster. I did that to myself—a long time ago. The moon only makes the monster kill."

And, with those words, the beast began to rise.

30

For some reason, London's eyes went to the ragged crisscross of scars that covered the beast's chest. Thinking of the last time he had seen them, he silenced the angry voices within his head as he said,

"Come on, pal. Calm down. You don't need any new scars."

The creature began to reply, when suddenly it doubled down in obvious pain, falling back to the floor. Meditation forgotten, its clawed hands ripped their way free from the folds of its robes, catching the floor a split second before its snout smashed against the white marble beneath it. A deep scream bellowed out of the beast and rolled across the pool—one so great it rippled the water as it echoed from the room. Forcing its body back into an erect position, the beast snarled through clenched fangs,

"As you may have noticed . . . you didn't pick a very good day . . . to get here."

"Blame my travel agent, pal."

Before the thing could answer, it doubled over again, howling in pain. Its balled fist raised up and then came down against the marble flooring, the violent slam of the hit splitting the night air beyond.

"Leave me. Leave this place," screamed the monster, looking up from the floor. "Get out while you still can."

"Not what I was sent to do, pal."

"You don't understand," snapped the beast, ragged lines of saliva matting the fur of its snout. "I've tried. But it can't be stopped. The blood calls and there's nothing I can do! I've tried. I've *tried*!"

London stood his ground, watching as the creature worked to contain the rage growing within it. The detective's hands ached to arm themselves—gun, knife, club—whatever. He could smell the thing's growing desires—felt the blood within him screaming to embrace them himself. His leg muscles tensed automatically, ready to charge the thing, spasms building as part of him wondered why he was not charging it already. The beast's fist slammed against the floor again, splintering the two-inch thick slab anew. Walnut-sized chunks flew into the pool, shattering the water's surface.

Oh, great, thought London, looking at the yard-long cracks in the marble, watching the beast's chest rise and fall with more obvious frenzy with every passing second.

Yeah, guys, good thinking, he spat at the voices in his head calling for combat, let's just run right over and duke it out with the furry psycho, huh?

And, almost in answer to the detective's mental question, the beast hissed, "Get out, damn you. Get out of here!"

"Sorry, pal," answered London, leaning back against the stone wall. The fingers of his left hand clearing a passage through his robes to Betty, he answered,

"Not in the cards. My contract says I'm supposed to put an end to your little problem."

"There *is* no end to it!" the monster bellowed, its fist slamming against the marble one last time. Marshaling its will, it began pulling itself upward again. Halfway up from its doubled-over position, it turned its head suddenly to stare at London. The detective watched as its fearful eyes suddenly darkened over, the cloudy yellow of them filled with a burning scarlet.

"This is what I am," it said, its words falling out of it in a tumbling blur. Frozen in its painful crouch, it screamed,

"I've lived with it for so many centuries I cannot remember them all. This is the way it has been for me since the beginning of time. There is no end to it, there is no way to part from it. This is all there is!"

"Yeah, it's always so easy to just give up and blame something else."

"Give up?" snarled the monster, almost in disbelief. "Give up? Give up what? Hope?!"

Turning full around, the creature stared at London, shouting at him,

"There is no cure, there is no hope. There is only the moon and the pain and the killing that never stops!! Now, go—you stupid fool. Run—*Go!* Run—*Now!!*"

And then, before London could react, the beast's back went straight as it finally managed to force itself erect. Tearing its robes away from its body, it revealed the near seven-feet-tall frame the detective remembered—its legs bent by canine design. Claws clacking against the stone floor, it steadied itself, back bent, paws ready. The greedy pain that had driven the beast for thousands of years pushed it forward, all its senses driving it for blood—eyes ready to see some, tongue lashing, nostrils flaring, ears listening for the sound of it beating within a still whole heart, every inch of skin tingling, waiting for the sloppy feel of blood matting its fur.

"Is this all you are?" demanded London, his voice strong, held in place by a brain that had seen plenty of monsters in its time, just as fearsome as the one before it. "Did you come all the way to A'alshirie just to follow the same, stupid pattern? For God's sake—for your *own* sake, you stupid son of a bitch—*fight it!*"

"I can't . . . can't. Couldn't then. Can't now."

As the beast's legs began to move it forward around the pool, closing the distance between it and London no matter how hard it struggled to resist, the detective shouted,

"Never? There's never been a full moon that didn't see blood? Never a month in how many decades that hasn't known the same tired ritual? Never?! You've *never* been man enough to stop yourself—not *once*?!"

The creature skidded its foot to a halt. Its claws dug thin scratches across the floor, chips of marble popping up and into the pool, drifting down through its clean waters. As the thing forced itself to stop, its body shook with anger, screaming for blood. The din of its scarlet demand pounded in the beast's ears, almost deafening it. Paws stretched out before it, the monster begged London,

"Kill me. Stop it all. Kill me . . . please."

"Don't give in," responded the detective. "You came here to put the past behind you."

"The past?" snarled the beast, its voice barking more deeply with every passing word. "What do you know of the past?"

"Only what you tell me," answered London. "You said you couldn't stop it 'then.' When? When couldn't you stop it?"

But rather than answer, before the detective could react, the monster launched itself toward him with unbelievable speed. The two collided, the beast knocking London off his feet, sending him sprawling backwards. The detective hit the floor hard, painfully, sliding into one of the potted plants with enough force to overturn it and send it splashing into the pool. London tried to move, but it was no use. Before he could even determine exactly where he had fallen, the thing was on him again, its left leg crashing into his side.

The thing's claws tore into the detective's side even as the force of its blow lifted him from the floor. London sailed through the air, watching thin streams of blood falling away behind him.

Then, the detective crashed against the marble once more, landing hard, the air bursting from his lungs. His back aching, side screaming with pain, London tried to see what was happening, but before his head had even begun to move the werewolf was on him—again. It dragged the detective upward, holding him in one hand, its claws digging into his already injured side. Not bothering to struggle, knowing he could not do anything, London wet his throat as best he could, trying to speak. His body wracked with pain, nerve ends screaming from the pressure of the monster's grasp, London gasped,

"When? When couldn't you stop it?"

And then, suddenly, the monster's and the man's eyes locked. Instantly their wills surged up in opposition—the force of each's soul pouring out to test the other. Immediately, the beast flung London aside, bouncing him painfully off the nearest wall. Howling in madness, it struck out against the closest wall, cracking it. Again and again it slammed its fists against the marble slabs until finally it stopped, sinking to its knees, begging in its monstrous howl,

"Help me."

"Help yourself," answered the gasping detective. "Tell me what the hell is going on. What . . ." London choked, gagging on a thick wad of bile and mucus stuck in his throat. Heaving it out onto the broken marble floor, he continued through his coughing,

"What did you . . . mean—couldn't stop it before? Before what? When?"

Dragging himself to his knees, his head spinning from the force of the last blow the creature had dealt him, the detective felt blood running down his face. He knew his nose had been broken open again. Ignoring the pain, he steadied his hands, trying to clear the voices in his head. Anxiety raced through his brain, prompting him to take the werewolf to the dream plane where he could deal with it. He was not Roth, his ancestors reminded him. He was stronger, wiser, had more power than the FBI man. He could destroy the thing.

But London silenced them with a thought, one past simple revenge. There was a key to solving the problem at hand—a solution that involved him simply standing his ground. Clearing his throat, making sure he still had voice left, he told the beast,

"You don't need my help. You've stopped this before—haven't you?" The beast nodded its massive head, but the detective noticed, it also continued on toward him. As it approached, he said,

"Then stop it again. You're the one who has to do it." Playing a hunch, he added, "You didn't do it that one time before, and you've been paying for it ever since. Do it this time. Stop the cycle. Do it!"

And then, to the detective's amazement, the monster stopped in its tracks—unsure—hesitant. Following his advantage, London continued, talking rapidly while the thing still had itself under control.

"You've just never believed it could last. You let this curse—whatever it is—become your excuse. Just easier to give in to it than to keep it at bay." The detective held his side tightly against the throbbing pain, his eyes still not quite focusing. Sucking in a deep breath, fighting the urge to cry out as his lungs expanded against his bruised ribs, he closed his eyes for a moment, then said,

"You knew, deep inside, that if you ever admitted you could control it, that it would become your responsibility to do so—that you'd have to stay in control of it forever."

Dragging himself painfully over to where the creature stood, he grabbed the beast's fur in his hands, dragging himself up its sides, shaking as he shouted,

"And all of it because of whoever it was you killed way back whenever. Who—who was it?" asked the detective. Shaking the monster as best he could, he screamed in its face, demanding,

"Who did you kill? What started all this goddamned madness? Who was it?!"

"It was my brother," admitted the beast.

And then London reached his feet, high enough to look into the monster's eyes. As he watched the madness flee them, replaced by the horror of their master's memory, the beast said,

"My crops were failing . . . his flocks were strong. He worked hard. Not me. When the harvest season came . . . I, I demanded a share of his efforts. He said . . . no to me. Turned me away. Said his family had to eat. Called me lazy."

"And you killed him."

"Yes," answered the beast. "Before I knew it, there in the light of the new moon, I picked up a branch and shattered his head. Then I had his wife, and then I killed her, her and the children both. After that, I went to his corrals . . . slaughtered his animals . . . filled my belly . . . then slept in the middle of his dead family, gorged and drunk."

Suddenly filled with knowledge, London released his hold on the monster. Sliding down the front of its furry body, the detective settled himself into as painless a position as possible as the thing finished telling its tale, one to which London already knew the ending.

"After that," it said, its barking voice filled with tears, "in the middle of the night . . . God cursed me with the mark of the beast. I was the first man to know greed and envy—I was *the first man* to strike down his own brother!"

The beast threw itself away from the detective then, falling to its knees, finally saying the words it had never been able to mouth, howling to the heavens,

"Abel—my brother—forgive me!"

And then, no sooner were the words out of its mouth, when Teacher Toun suddenly appeared in the morning temple. Taking no great note of the condition of either the room or the two combatants before him, he said,

"Ah, gentlemen . . . it seems that you have come to your moment."

"Yeah?" asked the detective. "And just what the hell would that be?"

"Check and mate, Mr. London." Looking at the werewolf, the elder asked, "You are not going to kill Mr. London, are you?"

The beast sat sobbing on the floor, howling in despair, ignoring the elder monk. Not distressed, Toun said,

"No, I thought not. The spell is over, Mr. London. You have won."

"Won?" asked the detective. "What the hell did I win?"

"Your revenge. You have shown our poor Cain the error of his ways. You have forced his acceptance of his crimes, and thus his repentance."

"You knew," said London, staggered. His breath still coming in blowing gasps, he repeated, "You knew."

"That he was Cain, cursed from the beginning of time? Yes, we knew. But there was nothing we could do for him. Would confronting us have stopped him? Would killing us have turned his fury? We were merely more victims. It is hard to teach mercy when you are weak and your opponent is strong."

And then the detective finally had it all. Even with his knowledge of how to manipulate the power of the dream plane, he would not have been able to beat the monster. It was suddenly obvious to London that that had been the source of the werewolf's powers, as well as its curse. For thousands of years, Cain had lived apart, a creature of guilt, coming to men in search of forgiveness, not knowing how to ask for it.

Suddenly the detective could see how it had happened—guilt had driven Cain to use the dream plane to curse himself. He had seen what he had done the next morning and forced himself along a path of pain instead of redemption. So convinced had Cain been of his evil that from that point on he had used his ability to manipulate the dream plane to reinforce his view of himself.

How many others had been given the same clues? wondered the detective. How many others had been approached by the beast, as had he and Jhong, and had neither shown fear, nor attacked the monster? How many thousands, maybe millions, had died by not having the strength to show the beast the pity it needed to stop itself?

"Sadly," answered Teacher Toun, once again responding as if reading the detective's mind, "we shall never know."

And then the monster turned to stare into London's eyes, curious to see if what he had heard in the detective's voice before had really been there. Knowing what the creature wanted, London told it,

"Yeah, I thought about it, but something told me that the only thing that I could do was to give you your chance—you know, to prove you could resist. If I'd fought with you while you were still trying to convince yourself that none of what you've done is your fault—that it was all the fault of your curse—well, we know what's happened to all those who've tried that before."

Teacher Toun smiled, resting his hands on the beast and London's backs as all three of them started walking for the outside.

"This is good," said the old monk. "I think maybe you have both learned much."

"Can I, I mean, is it possible now," asked Cain, his voice more human—less of a bark, "for me to . . . die?"

"I would think so," answered the elder. "Now that your conscious mind knows—admits to what it has done—your defenses will not be so automatic. To call upon your restorative abilities now would take a sustained, conscious effort."

When they reached the outer courtyard of the morning temple, the trio found it had started to snow, a light dusting of powder just beginning to settle on the ground. The temperature was still warm, and from the monk's lack of concern the detective felt sure it was a common occurrence. Once again, hearing his unasked question, the teacher assured him,

"It will all melt soon. But the contrast of it always strikes me so."

As the three of them looked out over the fields of A'alshirie, glistening in the moonlight as the light flakes continued to fall, the beast stood with tears in his eyes, saying,

"It's so beautiful."

"Yeah," agreed London, summoning the strength to hold his fingers steady. Sliding his hand into his robe, he withdrew it a moment later, Betty tight in his grasp. Purposely looking away from the detective, Cain whispered,

"Thank you for coming, Mr. London. Tell those that I have . . . tell them that I, I . . . oh, please . . ."

"Don't worry. I'll tell them."

And then the detective raised his arm and pulled the trigger of his .38 three times, sending a trio of lead slugs tearing through the beast's head, shattering its brain, coating everything nearby in blood. London watched as the other side of the monster's head exploded outward . . . watched as its arms jerked wildly out from its sides for the moment . . . watched as its gigantic body toppled over sideways. The werewolf's shattered head smashed against the ground, its lifeless eyes unmindful of the flakes falling into them. Unperturbed, Teacher Toun turned to London and said,

"It is for the best. You have acted very well in this. This cursed life is at last over. Some day soon he will be given the chance to begin again. When that day comes, I am most certain his long burden will finally be removed from his soul."

"Yeah, that's swell," answered London.

Then, tired and limping with pain, the detective left the teacher's side, heading back to the monks' bathhouse where he could soak his bruises and try to forget the new blood on his hands and face and clothes, and on all the snow around.

Exciting New Mysteries Every Month

BERKLEY PRIME CRIME

__**FINAL VIEWING** by Leo Axler
0-425-14244-2/$4.50
Undertaker Bill Hawley's experience with death has enhanced his skills as an amateur detective. So when a blind man is found dead with an exotic dancer, Bill knows the death certificate isn't telling the whole story.

__**A TASTE FOR MURDER** by Claudia Bishop
0-425-14350-3/$4.50 *(Available in September)*
Sarah and Meg Quilliam are sleuthing sisters who run upstate New York's Hemlock Falls Inn. Besides bestowing gracious hospitality and delicious meals, both find time to dabble in detection.

__**WITCHES' BANE** by Susan Wittig Albert
0-425-14406-2/$4.50 *(Available in October)*
"A delightful cast of unusual characters...engaging."–Booklist
Herbalist China Bayles must leave her plants to investigate when Halloween hijinks take a gruesome turn in Pecan Springs, Texas.
    Also by Susan Wittig Albert, available now:
__ **THYME OF DEATH** 0-425-14098-9/$4.50

__**CURTAINS FOR THE CARDINAL**
by Elizabeth Eyre 0-425-14126-8/$4.50 *(Available in October)*
"Sigismondo and Benno are captivating originals."–Chicago Tribune
A raging prince has murdered his own son. Now Renaissance sleuth Sigismondo must shield Princess Minerva from a heartless killer.
    Also by Elizabeth Eyre, available now:
__ **DEATH OF THE DUCHESS** 0-425-13902-6/$4.50

Payable in U.S. funds. No cash orders accepted. Postage & handling: $1.75 for one book, 75¢ for each additional. Maximum postage $5.50. Prices, postage and handling charges may change without notice. Visa, Amex, MasterCard call 1-800-788-6262, ext. 1, refer to ad # 505

Or, check above books Bill my: ☐ Visa ☐ MasterCard ☐ Amex	
and send this order form to:	(expires)
The Berkley Publishing Group	Card#_____
390 Murray Hill Pkwy., Dept. B	($15 minimum)
East Rutherford, NJ 07073	Signature_____
Please allow 6 weeks for delivery.	Or enclosed is my: ☐ check ☐ money order
Name_____	Book Total $_____
Address_____	Postage & Handling $_____
City_____	Applicable Sales Tax $_____ (NY, NJ, PA, CA, GST Can.)
State/ZIP_____	Total Amount Due $_____